From Bad to Cursed

AVERY KANE

KISSINGSHARK PUBLICATIONS

Copyright © 2022 by Avery Kane

All rights reserved.

No part of this book may be reproduced in any form or by any electronic or mechanical means, including information storage and retrieval systems, without written permission from the author, except for the use of brief quotations in a book review.

❀ Created with Vellum

Prologue

My mother is dying.

That was the only thing I could think, sitting next to her bed as a hospice nurse checked her vitals. Over and over again, the loop played in my head.

She's dying. This could be her last breath. Look how frail she is. How could this happen?

Harriet Shaw—Harry to those who knew and loved her—would be gone by the time the sun rose. That was inevitable. And as much as I didn't want to say goodbye to my mother, deep down, I recognized that her last breath would be a relief.

The cancer had come on quickly, the only sign being a yellowing of her eyes. I'd thought it was a trick of the light at first—we owned a witchcraft store in downtown Salem, and we purposely kept the lighting dramatic because the tourists liked it—but out in the sun, it had been more obvious. I told her to check with her general practitioner. She said she would, then didn't.

The second hint that something wasn't right was pain in her lower back. When I asked, she told me not to worry about it. She was old—her words, not mine—and, of course, back pain was part of the natural aging process.

The third and fourth symptoms appeared in the bathroom, and I wasn't privy to them. She didn't mention them until after the next symptom decimated her. By then, it was too late.

The final symptom had been two teeth falling out in as many days. Apparently, pancreatic cancer could cause that. When she went in to see the family doctor, he immediately sent her to the hospital. Within twenty-four hours, we had a diagnosis, and it wasn't good.

My mother wasn't one to dwell on her problems. She didn't cry out for attention or wax poetic about the state of the medical field. She didn't even shed a tear. She did, however, start imparting wisdom to me at every turn.

They'd given her three to six months to live. She made it four. The cancer ravaged her like a wildfire. The end came faster than I'd anticipated, which didn't make it any less brutal. She'd gone into hospice six days before, and since then, I hadn't left her side. The pain she felt was immense. The drugs they gave her made her incoherent most of the time. That didn't stop me from talking to her whenever she opened her eyes.

Those instances were coming fewer and further between, however.

"I never told you about men, Rowan," she said in a raspy voice as Aunt Mindy moved to stand behind my chair. She rested a hand on my shoulder, an act of love, and smiled at her sister.

Sometimes, I thought everything was going to be harder on my aunt than me. They'd spent their entire lives together, joined at the hip. Both of them had raised me. At the end, the three of us were together in our small Salem house, and the walls felt as if they were closing in.

"You've told me about men," I countered with a smile.

I refused to fall apart in front of her. Sure, I sometimes closed myself in my room to shed as many tears as possible. I refused to do it in front of her, though. My mother was the type who would put on a brave face for my benefit. I didn't want that. This was about her, not me.

"I've told you the basics," Mom replied. Her eyes were closed, a serene smile on her face. "I haven't told you the important stuff, though."

When I darted my eyes to Aunt Mindy, she seemed as baffled as I. She held out her hands and shrugged, as if to say, *"You know as much as I do."*

"Okay." I was twenty-seven and had talked to my mother about sex more times than I could count. Sure, the conversations were always embarrassing, but I wasn't going to stop her if she had something important to say. "Lay it on me."

"I just have five things to tell you."

"Just five?" I grinned despite the pain zipping through my abdomen. "I guess I can take five lessons to heart."

"The first is that size *does* matter."

My heart stuttered. *Did she just say what I think she said?* "Um..."

"You heard me." Despite her frail voice, Mom was firm. "The only people who believe size doesn't matter are men. A crayon is not the same thing as a good-sized zucchini. Never settle for the crayon."

"I've never been much of a colorer," I replied as I rubbed my forehead wearily.

Aunt Mindy's amusement was obvious as she ducked her head and hid her chuckle in a throw pillow.

"The second thing is that foreplay is necessary." Mom seemed to be in her own little world. "Men will tell you that foreplay isn't important, but the only reason they believe that is because they're selfish. Insist on foreplay."

"I ... guess I can do that." I was hating the conversation with a fiery passion but couldn't stop it.

"We're talking tongue, fingers, and toys. It's all necessary. There's a catalog hidden in the bottom drawer of my dresser if you need help with the toys. Or, better yet, ask your aunt. She's a connoisseur."

I slapped a hand to my forehead and refused to make eye contact with my aunt.

"The third thing is about dinner," Mom continued. Her voice was becoming weaker by the moment.

When I glanced at the nurse, she shot me a small nod. It was happening. Right then. She would be gone in a few minutes.

I swallowed hard. "What about dinner?" I asked as I fought to keep my voice from cracking.

"Men today don't want to pay for dinner. That's their job, so don't let them weasel out of it. Coffee is not dinner. Paying for half the meal is not how it works. Women have to give birth to children. That means men pay for food."

"Men pay for food," I parroted back. "Got it."

"Some people say you can't order the most expensive thing on the menu if you don't want to put out, but that's hogwash. If you have to sort through the crayons, then you should get lobster at every meal."

My heart gave a little heave at her earnestness. "I'll always order the lobster," I promised.

"The fourth thing is about the way men present themselves. I'm not a clothes snob—you know that—but presentation is still important. If they're going to wear flannel, make sure it's clean. No ripped jeans. And, for the love of all that's holy, if there are pit stains on the undershirt, then run away. I mean ... you can't date a man with pit stains."

"That wouldn't be on top of my to-do list," I agreed readily.

"Underwear is important too," she continued, perhaps unable to even hear me anymore. Her voice was so frail that it was almost nonexistent. "Boxers are preferable. If you do date a man who wears briefs—wears them, doesn't embrace being brief as a life goal—then make sure he doesn't wear those white ones. Any guy who wears the white ones usually has brown spots in the butt. You do not want to marry skid mark guy."

I was well and truly at a loss. "I would think that goes without saying," I said as I squeezed her hand.

Her fingers had gone cold. As much as I'd convinced myself death would be better at that point—the pain she constantly struggled with was too much for one person to bear—I wasn't ready to say goodbye.

Memories of my childhood flashed in front of my eyes as I clasped my hands around hers. I remembered dressing up like a witch and "cursing" people on the sidewalk during the run-up to Halloween. I remembered drinking hot chocolate when we hunkered down for a nor'easter. I remembered eating stuffed lobster for Christmas every year. She was the star of every memory. She'd been larger than life before cancer knocked her down a peg or two.

Oh, geez, what am I going to do without her? She was the center of my world, for better or worse. My father had taken off when I was a kid. I barely remembered him. He'd decided that being a husband and father was too much responsibility. Last I'd heard, he was living in Texas and working on a farm. He sent letters every seven years or so. He didn't even bother calling. He was not a factor in my life.

It was always Mom and Aunt Mindy. They'd started the store when I was eight, built it up until it was one of the premier stops for tourists, all while teaching me about customer service and balancing the books. It was expected that I would take over the store one day since I was the only heir.

Aunt Mindy had never married, but she'd been like a second mother to me.

At least I would still have her.

"There's a fifth thing," Mom rasped. She'd slowed considerably in just the last five minutes.

I nodded and squeezed my eyes shut. *Just hold it together a few more minutes,* I ordered myself. *When she's gone—and it won't be long—you can fall apart. You can crawl into bed and stay there for days. Just hold it together for her now. Don't let the last thing she hears be your heart breaking.*

"What's the fifth thing?" I asked. Surprisingly, my voice was even. I sounded strong. I didn't feel it, but I sounded it. Right then, that was the thing that mattered most.

"You have to end the family curse."

I stilled. "What, now?" I couldn't possibly have heard her right.

"The curse," Mom insisted. "You have to end it."

"I ... don't think I know what you're talking about." I flicked my eyes to Aunt Mindy, but she looked more agitated than amused. "I didn't realize there was a family curse."

"Yes." Mom moved her head ever so subtly and licked her lips. "There's definitely a family curse. We Shaw women are doomed to never find true love as long as the curse remains."

I rubbed my cheek, confused. "Um..."

"It's an old family tale," Aunt Mindy explained. "Our mother supposedly ticked off a voodoo queen, and she cursed us so we would never know true love."

"That sounds ... very weird."

Aunt Mindy held out her hands. "Mama Betty was a bit of a loon. She went through six husbands."

I'd heard the stories. "She also thought she was Marie Antoinette reincarnated, there at the end, if I remember correctly."

"Yeah. She reacted poorly to any guillotine jokes."

"Because there are so many of those in everyday conversation." I made a clucking sound with my tongue, then refocused on my mother. "Whatever the curse is, you don't have to worry about it. I don't believe in curses. I'll be fine."

"I didn't believe in curses, either," Mom said. "I thought it was rubbish. Look what happened to me."

"I don't understand."

"I married your father. He wasn't even a crayon. He was a swizzle straw."

"Oh geez." I cringed. "Can we not go there?"

"We don't have a choice. This is it." She sounded so matter-of-fact that my heart squeezed. "You have to find the woman who cursed us, or maybe find another voodoo queen and get her to lift the curse. I was never clear on that. You have to do it. Otherwise, all the women in our family will be doomed for eternity."

She'd clearly lost her mind, which wasn't much of a surprise. She was on a truckload of morphine.

"I'll end the curse," I promised. Of course I didn't believe in curses, but right then, the only thing she needed was for me to tell her what she wanted to hear.

"You don't believe," Mom said, sighing. "I know. I can tell."

"I believe," I insisted. "I'm going to end the curse."

Aunt Mindy shot me a sympathetic look and moved to sit on the side of Mom's bed. She rested a hand on Mom's chest, as if monitoring the beat of her heart, and closed her eyes. A single tear leaked down her cheek, almost breaking me.

"You'll figure it out soon enough," Mom said. "The curse will pass on to you now. Just be careful, and don't fall for skid mark man when you're coming to grips with what's happening."

"Mom, I can guarantee I'm never going to fall for skid

mark man," I reassured her. "That is the one thing you don't have to worry about."

"Good." Mom let out a rasping sigh as she said, "Michel."

I waited for her to continue. When she didn't, I squeezed her hand. It was icy cold. Death was imminent. "I don't know what you're trying to say, Mom," I prodded. "I just ... don't understand."

"Michel," she repeated. "The curse. It's Michel."

"Is that a first name? Is it a last name?"

She didn't answer. Instead, she pulled in one more raspy breath. "Mommy loves you." She barely eked the words out before her chest stopped rising and falling.

That's when I broke. "I love you too." I buried my face in the blankets covering her, pushing all thoughts of a ridiculous curse out of my head. "I'll make you proud, Mom. I swear it. I just... Go with peace. It's okay to let go. I'll be okay. I'll always be okay."

"She will, Harry," Mindy said, her face splotchy and red as tears dripped from her jawline. "I'll be with her every step of the way. I'll take care of our girl until I see you again. You have my word."

I wondered if Mom heard us. I had no idea. I wanted to believe that, at the very least, she felt our love as she slipped away.

"She's gone," Aunt Mindy said after a few seconds, her eyes darting toward the nurse. "Right? She's gone."

The nurse nodded. "She's no longer in pain. You can let go now."

The suggestion rankled. I would never let go. I would live my life in a manner that made her proud. That was the only option I had.

I, Rowan Shaw, was officially on my own. I could only hope I would turn out to be half the woman my mother had been.

One

ONE YEAR LATER

"So, you moved to New Orleans because you're cursed?" Antoinette "Toni" Charles studied me with the sort of concentration I reserved for deciding if the full-fat latte was worth the extra walking I would have to do later in the day to burn off the calories.

I nodded as I ran my hands over my new work shirt. When I decided I had to move to the Big Easy and follow through on my promise to my mother, I hadn't given much thought to what I would do to make a living. Once I arrived in New Orleans, I realized my meager savings would only get me so far. That meant getting a job, and I landed on Hex Appeal, which just so happened to be owned by Toni's mother, a famous voodoo queen in the city's French Quarter.

"A real curse or one you made up in your head?" Toni was the matter-of-fact sort and liked to have all the information when she formed an opinion.

I'd learned that over the course of three interviews, all of which were ten times more serious than the interviews I'd conducted while lining up help at the Salem store when looking for a temporary replacement to help Aunt Mindy during my absence. She couldn't handle everything herself while I was off on my adventure, which meant bringing in several part-time workers. She hadn't been thrilled but understood my determination to clear up my little inconvenience.

"I don't know." I offered a shrug. I'd decided to treat the whole thing like a joke because I was the only one who believed the curse was real. "I guess it could go either way."

"Oh, come on," Toni groused. "I need way more than that."

I didn't blame her. If some random woman from another state had shown up at the Salem store and said she was cursed, I would've thought she was crazy too. "I just had a string of bad luck," I said, choosing my words carefully. "It was so bad, I decided I needed a break."

"Yeah, but you live in Salem." Toni folded her arms across her chest. She was thirty and flirty—something she told me on a regular basis—and had one of those faces I was convinced belonged on a runway rather than behind a counter.

"What about it?" For lack of anything better to do—I certainly wasn't in the mood to make eye contact—I reorganized the new tarot card display by the register.

"Salem is supposed to be magical."

For some reason, that struck me as funny, and I burst out laughing. "And New Orleans isn't?"

"Of course it's magical. It's just ... different." Toni wrinkled her ski-slope nose. "I mean ... it's Salem. It's famous."

"I hate to break it to you, but New Orleans is famous too."

"I guess." Toni let loose a heavy sigh, clearly unconvinced. "It's probably one of those things where you become jaded by your hometown."

I could see that. "Probably." I went back to organizing. I hadn't worked for anyone other than my mother and aunt for, well, ever. I'd never worked for anybody else and had no idea what to expect.

"We need to go back to the curse," Toni insisted.

I hated that she was so fixated on that. "It's not a big deal." I offered a one-shoulder shrug. "Like I said, I ran into a string of bad luck and decided a change of scenery was imperative."

"Yeah, I'm not going to just let it go." Toni was firm. "What sort of bad luck are we talking? I once knew a woman who yanked out a chunk of hair from a tourist because she was convinced it was a weave and got the sort of lice that leaves you bald as payback. Is it that sort of bad luck?"

I frowned. "I don't think that's a thing," I said finally.

"Oh, it totally is." Toni lowered her voice to a conspiratorial whisper. "There are these lice nobody wants to talk about, and they eat your scalp so hair don't grow no more. If you're not careful, they'll burrow in through your ears and eat your brain."

I blinked rapidly several times. "I'm not a scientist, but I'm almost positive that's not a thing."

"It is in the Quarter." Toni winked to tell me the story very likely wasn't true. "What sort of bad luck did you have?"

"It was all of the male variety."

"Like what?"

I scowled at the tarot cards. "I really don't want to talk about it."

"We're best friends," Toni insisted. "You have to talk about man trouble with your best friend."

I didn't know how to respond. "We've known each other for a week and a half and spent a grand total of six hours together," I said finally.

"So?"

"So ... um..."

"We're best friends," Toni reiterated. "I have the gift." She tapped one side of her head. "I know we're going to be friends forever. I could tell that the second we met ... even though you wear man boots, which is something I didn't think I'd ever be able to tolerate."

Instinctively, I glanced down at my feet. Like a moron, I'd worn Uggs to New Orleans when I moved. I hadn't thought ahead to proper NOLA footwear, which had been a mistake. Not only was the weather too hot for Uggs, but there was no getting vomit out of sheepskin after unfortunate projectile incidents. I found that out the hard way after wearing them on Bourbon Street.

"They're not man boots," I said automatically. "They're normal in Boston, where we get snow."

"Yeah, snow sounds great in theory," Toni said. "In practice, though?" She let loose a little shudder. "Nothing is worth wearing man boots. Trust me. You have a cute figure. You need to show it off."

I frowned as I glanced down, wondering if my figure was cute and if that was even a compliment. I had questions.

"I'm not just saying that because I like women," Toni continued, clearly oblivious to my internal monologue. "I think you should know that since we're best friends. The peen doesn't do it for me. I think it's completely aggressive and unnecessary. That doesn't mean I'll hit on you, though, so wipe that thought straight from your mind. That's not how I roll."

My frown grew more pronounced. "You know I'm from the East Coast, right?" I prodded finally.

"I am familiar with U.S. geography."

"The East Coast is really liberal," I said. "We don't give people crap for stuff like that. We're open and welcoming to everybody in Boston. Well, except for Yankees fans. We hate them. Everybody else can totally hang out, though. It's a live-and-let-live society."

"So is NOLA," Toni said. "Nobody cares that I'm a

lesbian here in the city. I guess my mother does. She's convinced I just haven't met the right man yet. That's a whole other thing." She tossed a dismissive wave. "The problem is that, once you get out of the city, the politics shift a bit."

I cocked my head, considering. "I guess I didn't think about that. It makes sense, though."

"The South is not a stereotype," Toni warned. "Unfortunately for all of us, if the stereotype decides to make an appearance, it's usually covered in beer and Mardi Gras beads and urinating in public on Bourbon Street."

I had to bite my lip to keep from laughing. "That's quite the picture you're painting."

"Bourbon Street is nothing if not entertaining," Toni explained. "Locals don't hang out there. Only tourists do. Sometimes we play a game where we try to guess who will face-plant in the gutter, but in general, we treat Bourbon Street as if it's another country."

"That's how we feel about Essex Street in Salem," I mused. "We have to work there—that's where the tourists go, and they have the money—but when it comes time to have dinner and hang out, we avoid the tourist areas like the plague."

"I'm betting it's like that in any town that relies on tourism," Toni said. "We know we need the money, but it often feels as if the tourists are trampling on our town when they get here. A lot of them show respect, but too many of them treat the streets like a garbage can and the people like throwaways. I don't like it."

"Yeah, the business owners in Salem are stuck," I said. "We can't survive without tourists, but we also can't enjoy our own city most of the time because the tourists are catered to, and we're shuffled to the side."

"It blows." Toni looked momentarily serious, but her eyes were sly when they slid back to me. "Let's go back to this curse. I want to hear about the run of bad luck that sent Rowan Shaw fleeing from a town as cool as Salem."

"You really don't."

"But I do."

Ugh. I pushed out a sigh that was half a groan and briefly pressed my eyes shut. She wasn't going to let that go.

I decided to give it to her with both barrels. "Do you really want to know?"

"I asked, didn't I?"

"Fine, but it's not pretty."

I rested my elbows on the counter and reminded myself that she'd asked. She would regret it by the time I was done. The tale was just that pathetic.

"It started with a guy named Ian," I said.

"Oh, never trust a guy who only has three letters in his name," Toni intoned. "Ted. Dan. Axl. Leo. They're all psychos. That was your first mistake."

Finding her impossible not to like, I let loose a laugh. "Apparently, I didn't realize that. I do now."

"That's something."

"Anyway, Ian came into the store not long after my mother died." Looking back on the memory was difficult. "He was charming, had a smile at the ready, and asked me out. I wasn't looking for a date—I was still in mourning—but he was persistent and came into the store five times in the same day. Finally, because I'm a sap, I relented.

"He took me to one of my favorite restaurants," I continued. "Ledger. We ordered nice meals, had a few cocktails, and then he said he had to go to the bathroom."

"Uh-oh." Toni was already cringing.

"It took me a full thirty minutes to accept that he wasn't coming back," I confirmed. "I was so convinced it was some sort of mistake—we'd had a magical conversation over dinner, after all, something that felt like it was leading to a true connection—that I even sent one of the male servers into the bathroom to look for him."

Toni made a face. "Not there?"

"Nope. I got stuck with a three-hundred-dollar dinner bill. The next day, I happened to be walking past the wand store, and guess who I saw inside ... pestering another sales clerk for dinner? This time at Turner's Seafood."

"Another expensive restaurant?"

I shrugged. "Expensive enough."

"That dude was clearly evil," Toni noted. "You can't assume you're cursed if it's just one evil guy."

"I'm not done." Then I did smile. It was either that or cry. "Then there was Sven. He was one of the new guides for the ghost tour company. He said he came all the way from Sweden. He had an accent and everything. Sadly, I later found out he based his accent on *The Girl with the Dragon Tattoo* ... and he was wanted for sleeping with women in various states and emptying their bank accounts before moving on. Thankfully, I didn't give him any money. I just lucked out when the cops finally caught up to him."

"He sounds like a dick," Toni acknowledged. "Still, two guys."

"I'm not done." The smile I shot her was feral. "Then there was Anthony. He was from New Jersey."

"You can stop there," Toni said softly. "I've met plenty of Anthonys from New Jersey. I already know how this story is going to go."

"Then there was Bancroft. He wore nice suits. Said he lived in Boston but was looking for a home away from the hubbub. He liked Salem. Apparently, he also had a wife he'd left in the hub and kids he'd left in the bub. He emptied the family bank accounts before fleeing."

"All this in a year?" Toni was incredulous.

"I'm not done." I was resigned to telling her about all of

them. "I was determined to prove that I wasn't cursed, so I kept going out on date after date. It didn't go well."

"Yeah, I'm guessing not." Toni rubbed her chin and waited.

"Mike was eighty grand in debt because he liked to bet on the ponies. Terrence was wanted by the health department because he was openly trying to spread herpes as some form of a game. Before you ask, I stopped sleeping with them after Sven, thankfully. I was just down to dating at this point.

"Cole had a thing about fire," I continued. "He was always carrying this Zippo lighter and flicking it. Turns out he flicked it at his ex-girlfriend's house in New York before moving to Boston. Then there was Ricky, or was it Grant? Hmm. I can't remember. No bother, though. Ricky had a foot fetish and worked at a tanning salon. He set up cameras in the booths and put the footage of women undressing online. Grant married his first cousin when she was eighteen, knocked her up and took her Chevy, and then divorced her and was on the run from his family."

"Wow." Toni's eyes were as wide as saucers. "You've had quite the run there."

"I'm not done."

"Oh, come on!" Toni threw her hands in the air. "Now you're just messing with me."

"There are only two more." I offered her a sweet smile. "Griffin liked wearing women's underwear. Before you judge me, I don't care what sort of kink you have. I didn't care about his fetish ... until he stole all my underwear. I literally didn't have a single pair left when he ran.

"Finally, that brings us to Brody," I continued, exhaling heavily. "Brody decided he wanted to be that guy on that reality show, the one where the guy has, like, four wives."

"*Sister Wives?*"

I snapped my fingers. "That's the one. He already had

three wives, and they all lived on the same floor in the same apartment building. On our third date, he took me to meet them. He didn't bother telling me about his plan until I was already there ... and they were measuring my hips to see if I would be able to push out a baby naturally."

Toni's mouth dropped open. "Girl, you have to be making this up."

"Oh, if only."

"That is just the absolute worst." She shook her head, clearly dumbfounded. "Now you know why I date women. You still get the drama, but you don't get anybody trying to marry a fourth wife."

"If I rolled that way, I would totally go for it." I meant it. "To be fair, something tells me I would have bad luck with women too."

"That is just ... un-freaking believable."

"I'm kind of numb to it now." Sadly, that was true. "Now you know why I needed a change of scenery, though."

"Yeah." She bobbed her head. "I totally get it. The thing is there are nutty men everywhere. I mean ... *everywhere*. You can't go picking up men here without someone overseeing your choices. You obviously have a bad picker."

"That could be it," I agreed. "Or it could be that I'm cursed."

"See, I want to tell you that's in your head, but those stories..." Toni trailed off. "How about, just as a precaution, you run any dates you plan on having here through me? I'll help you pick a good one to break your bad streak."

I didn't have the heart to tell her that I had no intention of dating. No, I was there for a specific person. I was going to find whoever had cast the curse on my grandmother—or at least find a descendent—and nip my little curse in the bud. That was my one and only concern. "I'll definitely let you have a crack at judging anybody I meet."

"It couldn't possibly hurt."

Because I was desperate to change the subject, I decided to turn the conversation back to her. "So, your mother really won't accept that you're a lesbian?"

"Oh, my mother is fierce." Toni let loose a low cackle. "Like ... she could be a lion, she's so fierce. She likes to think she's worldly too. I came out when I was fourteen, told her I liked girls and that boys were stupid, and she just nodded. I think she thought I was trying to mess with her. As I got older, though, she got more worried. She started actively setting me up with various dudes from the neighborhood."

"Oh, yeah? How did that go?"

"I told you the peen is way too aggressive, right? Well, that should serve as your answer. She's convinced, if she just finds the right guy to introduce me to, that I'll change my mind. We're having a thing right now because I refuse to go on any more of her blind dates."

"Do you have a girlfriend?"

"No, and it would help things if I did. My mother would never mention setting me up with a man in front of someone else. Good manners and all that. Unfortunately, while I don't have the same bad luck as you, I am a little too picky. I haven't had a girlfriend in two years at this point."

"You're still young."

"Yeah, but I'm feeling that pull. You know—hearing the voice."

I was confused. "What voice?"

"The one that tells me to mate for life. You know the voice, right?"

Honestly, I didn't. I'd never heard that voice. "Right now, I'm just trying to embrace the voice that points me toward a man who isn't wanted in five states for passing bad checks. That would be a definite step up for me."

"Which one was that?" Toni demanded.

"Oh, didn't I tell you about Mark? He also liked to unzip his pants on the bus and 'wink' at women over the age of eighty ... if you know what I mean."

"Wink?" After a moment, revulsion fluttered over Toni's features. "What did I tell you about the peen? Nothing good comes of playing with it."

I held out a fist to bump knuckles with her. "You're preaching to the choir. Trust me."

Two

I understood retail. If anything, I might've understood the ins and outs of owning a store better than Toni, who'd taken over the day-to-day operations of Hex Appeal from her mother only four months before. The voodoo thing threw me, however.

"So, you sell actual hexes?" I pointed at what looked to be hand-sewn sachets on a display table, encased in plastic bags and available for $9.99.

"We sell dreams," Toni replied as she stared at her phone screen. She didn't look happy about whatever she was reading. "Unbelievable," she muttered under her breath at one point.

I went back to looking at the hex bags. "Can you really promise fame and fortune for ten bucks?" I asked after a beat.

"What do you think?" That felt like a trick question.

"I think that you can get neither without putting in the work. Actually, I believe that you can't get anything without putting in the work, but I'm considered a pessimist in Salem circles."

Toni lowered her phone and put her full focus on me. "I can see why you would be considered a pessimist," she said finally. "As for putting in the work, I happen to agree. Sure, there are a few people who luck out here and there, but hoping for luck isn't a successful business plan in my book.

"Like, I lucked into being Madam Cleo's daughter," she continued. "That means I get to run a store even though I haven't earned it. Eventually, though, I want to own a different type of shop."

"Really?" I turned to face her. "What kind of shop do you want to run?"

"Magic books and lattes."

"Oh, yeah?" I smiled. "We have a book section in the Salem store. We serve lattes too. It's fun."

"Do you miss it? Salem, I mean. You seem to miss it."

The question was harder to answer than it should've been. "I miss my mom."

Toni made a sympathetic clucking sound with her tongue. "It sounds as if you two were tight."

"We were. As for Salem, I don't know." I held out my hands. "Once she was gone, the city lost a lot of magic for me. I'm hoping, after I spend some time here, that when I go back, the magic will return. It's a crapshoot, though."

"Yeah, I can see that. New Orleans is my favorite city in the world. It's always been magical to me. I swear I see things others don't. I can't imagine ever leaving."

"Have you traveled anywhere?"

"A few places. Although recognizing New Orleans as my home doesn't mean I'm opposed to travel. There are a lot of places I want to visit."

"Like where?"

"London. Stonehenge. I've always desperately wanted to go to Greece."

"What's in Greece?"

"The sort of history we can only dream of in this country.

I mean... New Orleans is ancient by the United States' standards. It's not Greece, though."

"I can see that." I went back to looking at the hexes. "What's in the bags?"

"Herbs. Dried flowers. Madam Cleo adds a bit of magic."

I pointed at one labeled Smite Your Enemies and arched an eyebrow. "They're not dangerous, are they?"

"No, but that one will totally give you the trots if you're not careful. You're supposed to pour it in somebody's coffee or tea. Then, a few hours later, they're forced to either sit on the toilet for twenty-four hours or constantly run there if they don't want to have an accident."

That sounded horrific.

"Aren't you afraid of being sued?" I asked.

Toni gave a lackadaisical shrug as the bell over the door jingled to signify somebody was entering the store. "Not really. The main ingredient is those gummy bears you can get online that give you explosive diarrhea. My mother grinds them up and makes them into a powder. It works too. I used it on a few girls in high school when they made fun of me for being a lesbian."

"Ah, Lana and Lacey," a man said from the other side of the display case I couldn't see through. "I remember when you hexed them. The other girls in school complained about the smell from the bathroom for three days. Good times."

Toni shared a low chuckle as the man approached the counter. "Hello, Jasper. It's been a long time."

Once he moved a few feet, I could get a better look at him. He was tall—at least two inches over six feet—and he boasted a full head of black hair that offset a set of ridiculously blue eyes. His shoulders were broad, his waist trim, and he had one of those mischievous smiles that belonged in a romantic comedy movie.

"I saw you two weeks ago at Luther's crawfish boil," he

replied. "That doesn't mean I didn't miss you or anything, though."

"Oh, right." Toni wrinkled her nose. "Now that you mention it, I did see you there. You brought some teenager and had your hand up her shirt the entire night."

"You wound me," Jasper countered, although he didn't look particularly bothered by Toni's negative attitude. "I don't date in the kiddie pool. All my dates are twenty or older, and you know it."

"She was wearing a cheerleading uniform," Toni insisted.

"Oh, don't be absurd." Jasper shook his head. "She just likes plaid skirts."

"Uh-huh." Toni didn't look convinced. "What was her name? Muffy? Twinkie?"

"Bambi."

"Is that supposed to be better?"

Jasper offered a shrug. "I have no idea. The only reason I remember her name is because Joe and Lenny were at the boil, and they kept making Thumper jokes."

"You would find that funny." Toni shook her head. Despite her words, a small smile appeared at the corners of her lips. "You know, you should really thank your parents for all that charm oozing out of your pores. If anybody else had your reputation, I wouldn't let them through the front door, let alone welcome them into my store."

"Oh, you love me, and you know it." Jasper leaned forward and pressed a surprise kiss dead center on Toni's forehead. "Just like I love you."

"Oh, geez." Toni gave a choked laugh. "You are the worst."

"I'm awesome, and you know it." As if realizing for the first time that they weren't the only two present, Jasper slid his eyes to me. His smile was instantaneous. "Who is your friend?"

"Nobody you need to worry about," Toni replied. "Why

are you here? If you want more love potions, I'm not selling them to you. I'm surprised that thing in your pants hasn't fallen off, given how often you use it. I'm not encouraging that behavior."

"Oh, whatever." Jasper rolled his eyes. "Is she your girlfriend?" His tone took on a teasing lilt, but he didn't appear to be throwing judgment around. Instead, he strolled over to me and extended his hand. "Since she's not going to be polite and introduce us, I guess it's on me. Jasper Bentley."

I took his hand and shook it because that was the polite thing to do, but I felt out of my element. Toni and Jasper obviously had history. I didn't want to insert myself in the situation and stick my foot in my mouth, something I was prone to do. "Rowan Shaw."

"It's nice to meet you." Jasper's smile was blinding as he released my hand. "How long have you and Toni been a thing? While we're at it, why didn't you bring her to the boil, Toni? I would've loved to interrogate her there."

"Rowan isn't my girlfriend," Toni replied. "She's a new employee. She doesn't play for my team."

"Really?" The way Jasper looked me up and down the second time made me distinctly uncomfortable. "Isn't that interesting?"

"No, it's not." Toni jabbed a finger in his face. "Don't even think of doing ... whatever it is you do to get women to drop their panties for you. I've yet to figure out what that is because I find you unbelievably repulsive. She's on the no-touch list."

"There's a no-touch list?" Jasper's laugh was warm. "Is it like the no-fly list? Wait, I don't want to know the answer to that. How come I haven't seen this list?"

"Because it's up here." Toni tapped the side of her head. "All you need to know is that she's on it."

"Did you know you were on a list?" Jasper asked me.

"I didn't know I was on her no-touch list, but I've created one for myself, so it's okay that they overlap," I replied.

"How many people are on your list?"

"I only worry about myself."

"And her luck with men already sucks," Toni added. "You're a disaster in human form, so there's no way she's taking a chance on you." Toni shaded her mouth with her right hand so that only I could see her lips. "Girlfriend, he's supposedly hung like an infant. Like ... we're talking pacifier territory here. He's not even worth a good roll in the hay."

"Ugh." Jasper mock clutched at his heart. "I'm definitely wounded now."

"That doesn't mean it's not true." Toni's expression was grave when it landed on me. "Let me give you the rundown on Jasper here. We went to high school together. We were in a bunch of classes and had to study with one another occasionally. Even back then, he was known for fancying himself as the poor man's George Clooney."

"George Clooney has nothing on me," Jasper drawled as he leaned against the counter, appearing unbothered by Toni's assessment.

"He thinks he's every straight woman's dream," Toni continued. "Sadly, because he played football and looked good in those little pants they wear, girls fell for him left and right. Once he ran through all the female hearts at our school, he started branching out to other schools. It was disgusting."

"This is about that cheerleader, isn't it?" Jasper prodded. "You're still mad she went for me instead of you."

"Calliope was better than you," Toni growled. "You went out with her twice and broke her heart."

"Which primed her for you."

"She's not gay." Toni looked legitimately mad. "Stop talking about her. She's still better than you to this day."

"You're better than me too." Jasper leaned in and batted

his eyelashes at her. "If I thought you had a chance, I would've left her for you to romance. She didn't go for the boobs, though. She was all about the butt. My butt."

"You are a butt," Toni muttered. Even though she looked morose, she couldn't stop herself from smiling at our guest. "I really hate you sometimes," she complained.

"You love me." Jasper didn't appear to be suffering from an ego bruise despite Toni's words. "We would've been the power couple of Benjamin Franklin High School if you would've just ignored your inner urges and allowed me to show you the power of my tongue under the bleachers."

"You make me want to punch you in the nuts," Toni complained, shaking her head. When her eyes landed on me, they held a warning. "No matter what he says, don't fall for it. I know you've got your own thing going on, but he's a man whore. Given your track record, you don't need to add him to the mix."

I found the notion of adding anybody to the mix funny. "Oh, I don't think he would make the cut for me," I teased. "He doesn't look like he's heading to prison anytime soon."

Toni snorted, seemingly genuinely amused. "He's worse than those guys you told me about."

That wasn't possible.

"I told you about the herpes guy, right?" I said in challenge.

Jasper made a horrified face. "What, now?"

"She doesn't have herpes," Toni said with a dismissive hand wave. "Supposedly, a guy she went out to dinner with was trying to spread herpes to as many people as possible. She dodged a bullet."

"Well, that's good." Jasper looked genuinely relieved. "I feel bad for people with herpes. It's one of the ones you can't get rid of. I'm still freaked out at the prospect of somebody spreading it intentionally."

"Says the man whore," Toni muttered. "Seriously, don't even look at her."

"She's cute," Jasper complained. "How can I not look at her?"

To my surprise, my cheeks flooded with warmth. I'd been thinking myself immune to the male species at that point. Given the curse, I had no reason to even consider taking one on. That one seemed particularly dangerous. I was in look-but-don't-touch mode.

"Fine. Look at her all you want." Toni was having none of it. "Stay away from her, though. She's a woman with substance. She's trying to get some perspective, which is why she moved here. She doesn't need you making a mess of things."

Toni was serious when she fixed her eyes on me. "Just so you know, no matter how good-looking he is, I wasn't lying about him being a man whore. He refuses to date a woman for more than a month. Like ... ever. He might be good in bed—at least, that's what I've heard from those who are fans of the aggressive peen—but he's left a trail of broken hearts in his wake."

"You're exaggerating," Jasper protested.

"Cindy Biltmore?" Toni challenged.

"What about her?" Jasper's face was blank. "I heard she was happily married."

"She's been married six times, and she's not even thirty yet. She has four kids, and her boobs hang to her belly button. She blames it all on you."

"That doesn't mean it's my fault." Jasper was adamant. "It sounds to me as if she's made poor decisions since I last saw her." He made a face. "That boob thing sounds unfortunate too. Hers were nice if I remember correctly."

Toni turned to me. "Jasper took her to the junior prom. His month with her ended at midnight. So he went to the dance with her and left with Sally Carruthers. Cindy was never the same again. She still curses Jasper's name when it's brought up in her presence."

"If I remember correctly, she was banned from being near scissors senior year," Jasper noted, his eyes vacant as he looked back at his colorful past. "That incident in art class really ruined things for her."

"Yeah, the art teacher was her third husband," Toni said. "He was on disability, and she thought that made him a catch."

Jasper cocked his head, seemingly thinking, then shook it. "I still maintain that's not my fault. She obviously has terrible taste in men."

"She does," Toni readily agreed. "It all started with you."

"Whatever." Jasper tapped his fingers on the counter. "What were we talking about, again?"

"How you're not going to hit on my new worker." Toni was firm. "I don't care if you think she's pretty."

"She's uber hot." Jasper winked at me, a gesture that caused weird fluttery things to happen in my stomach.

I was brutal when I clubbed those internal butterflies to death.

"She's off the market," Toni said. "She's on a man hiatus. When it's time to break her fast, I'll be finding an appropriate guy for her to go out with ... and it won't be you."

"See, I think you're selling me short," Jasper complained. "She could be the one."

"The one to what?" I asked dumbly.

"The one to have me changing my ways," Jasper replied. "I mean... I think we look good together." He sidled closer to study our reflections in the mirror behind the counter. "All that dark hair we share. Those blue eyes. We would have beautiful babies."

Rather than consider the offer, I made a face. "Yeah, I

think I'm going to agree with Toni on this one. You might be the king of the Quarter. I'm staying away from men for the foreseeable future, though."

"Oh, see, I got another one ready for you, Toni," Jasper teased, his eyes twinkling. "She might end up playing for your team after all."

"Leave her alone," Toni growled. "Seriously, just ... leave her alone. You're not her type. You're definitely not my type. That means your dating options are limited in this store."

"I guess it's good I didn't come here to pick up a date, then." Jasper tapped the end of Toni's nose. "I need more of those hex bags for the tours. We're out."

"The ones that you pretend to find in the walls to wow the tourists?" Toni asked.

Jasper nodded. "We bought a hundred of them a couple months ago, but apparently, we've gone through the whole box. The tourists gasp when we stumble across them during the voodoo tours. It increases tips."

"I think I've got about twenty of them in the back," Toni replied. "I can call Mom and have her make some more. Will twenty get you through the rest of the week?"

Jasper nodded, suddenly all business. "That should be fine. How is your mom, by the way?" His smile was back. "I miss seeing her in here."

"You just miss working your charms on her," Toni fired back.

"She did always get me," Jasper agreed. "She said I was going to do great things with my life, experience great love. She's been spot on so far."

"Oh, whatever." Toni made a groaning noise. "Mom is fine. She basically stops in when she feels like it and is halfway to retirement. I'll grab those hex bags from the back. Rowan, can you ring up twenty of the hex bags? We give the Bentleys a deal because they buy in bulk. They're only seven bucks each for them."

"Sure." I moved behind the counter as Toni disappeared into the storage room and rang up the tab. "Here you go." I handed the slip to Jasper.

"I'm really not as bad as she says," he offered out of nowhere as he dug in his pocket for his wallet.

"Excuse me?" I was confused.

"Toni. She just likes to give me a hard time. I'm not as bad as she says, though. I'm not a man whore. I just like a variety of women. I'm up-front about that from the start."

"Good for you." I honestly didn't know what else to say.

"I just don't want you to get the wrong impression of me."

"I don't have an impression of you either way," I replied. "Like Toni said, I'm off men. You would be wasting your charms if you spent them on me."

"That's kind of a bummer."

Is it? "Something tells me you'll be okay."

He offered another playful wink. "Something tells me you're exactly right."

Three

I wasn't tired after my shift. I was used to working long days in Salem. Toni invited me out with her friends—and it didn't feel forced—but I politely declined all the same.

"I still have some unpacking to do," I lied. I hadn't brought very many items to New Orleans because I was hoping my relocation would be a short one. I didn't say that to Toni, of course—I wanted the job, after all—and I felt guilty. I didn't expect her to stop in for a visit at the apartment I had rented, though, so I wasn't too worried about being pegged as a filthy liar.

"Well, you're only going to be able to use that excuse for another three days," Toni warned. "That's going to be my limit. Then you're going out with us whether you like it or not."

I couldn't suppress the laughter that bubbled up. "So, basically, you're saying you're going to force me to party."

"It's New Orleans. You have no choice but to party."

"Good to know."

I set out to walk the route back to my apartment. The

voodoo store was located on Governor Nicholas Street, only half a block off Bourbon. One of the first things I'd heard upon arriving in the city was to avoid Bourbon Street like the plague. That made sense—at least for the people giving me the advice—but when walking home after dark, I preferred a well-lit route. It didn't hurt that, because of the drunks who took over the street to the point of overflowing, about five police officers were stationed on every block, which made for a safe walk home.

I'd rented a unit in The Annex, which was located on Iberville Street, and I had a good fifteen-minute walk to get home. That wasn't bad because I got to do a lot of people watching, one of my favorite things. I couldn't help but marvel at how different the people were in New Orleans, compared to Salem. That didn't make it any less fun, and it was a learning experience I quite enjoyed.

"Hey," someone called out.

I opted to ignore them even though I couldn't be certain the call was pointed at me.

"Hey!" That time, the voice was more insistent and closer.

I squared my shoulders, preparing myself for the drunken sexual harassment that was sure to come. When it didn't, I slid my eyes to the right and found a familiar face.

"Oh, hey." I pressed my lips together and took in Jasper's smiling countenance.

He was standing with a group of people, including a blonde who seemed to be giving him some severe side-eye, and he had some sort of cocktail clutched in his hand.

"Were you going to walk on by without saying anything?" he asked after a beat. "I'm hurt."

"I didn't see you there." That was the truth.

"That's probably because you were too busy avoiding eye contact." Jasper didn't bother checking the road before stepping off the curb and heading in my direction. "Rowan, right?"

I nodded. "You remembered. I'm impressed."

"It's an interesting name. You don't hear it often." He stopped in front of me, his grin widening. "I like interesting names."

"It's actually one of the most common names where I come from," I replied. "You can't cross the street without running into a Rowan up north."

"And where is that, exactly? I can't remember what Toni told me between bouts of busting my balls. If she did tell me, the information flew right out of my head." Jasper's smile was friendly, and he never moved his eyes away from my face, even when people skated around him.

"Salem."

"Massachusetts?"

"Yup."

"So, you're a witch." His grin widened. "I happen to love women in pointy hats. Have I mentioned that?"

Hiding my eye roll wasn't an option. "That's a very stereotypical thing to say. I don't deal in stereotypes."

"But you don't deny you're a witch."

"My family runs a witch store in Salem. You never deny you're a witch up there."

"Hmm." Jasper's expression was hard to read. "Where are you going?" he asked after a beat. "If you're looking for somebody to hang out with, I have some friends." He gestured toward the group across the way. None of them—well, other than the blonde—were looking in our direction.

"Oh, that's not necessary." I shook my head. "I'm just heading home. I don't think I'm up for a drink tonight. I'm tired." I wasn't, really, but I didn't want to infringe on his party. Nothing was worse than including an outsider who didn't get all the jokes.

"Oh, come on." Jasper made a petulant whining sound. "I'm a fun guy. Ask anybody."

"Toni?"

"Oh, Toni loves me." Jasper didn't seem bothered by what I was inferring. "We were good friends in high school, no matter what she led you to believe. We're still good friends. She just doesn't appreciate my dating habits."

"You mean your man-whore ways."

"See, that sounds like an insult. I'm a popular guy."

"It's because you're fun, right?"

"Totally." His grin widened, and he glanced around. "Are you out here alone?" he asked after several seconds.

"I'm walking home. This is Bourbon Street. Isn't there a saying about never being alone when you're on Bourbon Street?"

"Not that I'm aware of. If you want to be alone on Bourbon Street, visit before nine o'clock tomorrow morning. This city sleeps until eleven and makes no apologies for it."

That made me laugh. "Good to know."

"Yeah." He blew out a sigh, seeming oddly reluctant to let me pass. "Where do you live?"

"The Annex. I did a six-month rental."

"Oh, that's a nice place." He bobbed his head. "They have this great rooftop lounge thing with a pool."

"I haven't been up there yet, but I read about it online when I was doing research for a place to stay. I plan to check it out eventually."

"How long have you been in town?"

"About a week."

"And you haven't checked out the rooftop lounge? That's sacrilegious." He eyed me with fresh interest. "I'll walk you home," he volunteered out of nowhere.

I was caught off guard. "Oh, that's not necessary. It's only a few blocks."

"Yes, but it's dark, and you're a newcomer in a strange land." He grinned again. "I could use a break from the noise."

"But ... um..." I licked my lips and gestured toward the blonde. "I think your friend is going to be upset if you take off with another woman."

"Savannah?" Jasper snorted. "Don't worry about her. She's got a bad attitude. She doesn't like outsiders."

"And you do?"

"I like everybody." He inclined his head toward the street. "Come on. I'll give you the five-cent tour on the way."

"Is there even anything of interest in this area?"

"This is New Orleans. There's something of interest everywhere."

Because I believed him, I merely shrugged. "You don't have to. I'm perfectly fine getting home on my own."

"I want to." He was insistent. "Come on." He lightly placed a hand on my back and prodded me to cross the street. As we drew even with his friends, he snapped his fingers to get their attention. "I'm going to walk Rowan home. I'll catch up with you guys later."

"Sure, man." A dark-haired guy bobbed his head and went back to talking to the others.

Nobody in the group appeared upset about him splitting off. Well, one person seemed upset. The woman he'd identified as Savannah glared as we continued walking. Nobody else seemed to care.

"Do you want me to come with you?" she called out.

"I'm good." Jasper waved at her but kept his eyes on me. "I'll catch up with you guys later."

"You don't even know where we're going," Savannah groused.

"I believe that's why we have phones." Jasper didn't spare her a glance. "Come on, Rowan. I'll show you all the places to avoid."

Once we were off Bourbon Street, the noise diminished greatly, which allowed feelings of discomfort to creep in. I was one of those people who couldn't tolerate silences—even if they were relatively comfortable—so I scrambled to fill it.

"What is it you do?" I asked out of the blue.

"I'm a tour guide."

I frowned. That wasn't what I'd been expecting. "Seriously?"

"Yup. My family owns one of the tour companies. We do multiple tours a day."

"Huh."

He chuckled. "You don't sound impressed."

"It's not that," I replied hurriedly. "I'm familiar with tours. Salem is full of them. I was going to say that I didn't see you as a tour guide. That's not true, though. It actually makes sense that you're a tour guide, given how much you love to talk."

"Oh, see, that didn't sound complimentary," he chided, wagging a finger. "Some people like a good conversationalist. I'm guessing you're not one of those people."

Am I? I hesitated and considered the statement. "I like talking," I said finally. "I just happen to believe that you should have something to say when you open your mouth."

"I always have something to say."

"Yeah, you're like my mother that way." My heart panged as my thoughts drifted to her.

"Does your mother live in Salem?" Jasper pointed toward a building as we passed. "That's the Bombay Club. You go through the tunnel. The drinks there are amazing, and it's quiet, if you're into that sort of thing. Like ... you can take a book in there and read it while having a cocktail. I'm betting that's your sort of thing."

I bristled. "I think you're saying I'm boring."

"Not even a little." He shook his head. "I happen to love

reading a good book over a blackout bramble. People think I'm weird because of it, but I don't care."

That wasn't something I'd expected him to admit. "What's a blackout bramble?" I asked when I couldn't think of anything else to say.

"Just the best drink ever. I'll take you to get one when you're feeling up to imbibing. You didn't answer the question, though. Does your mother live in Salem?" He talked quickly, like he was in a race and if he didn't get all the words out, he would lose them forever.

My eyebrows moved toward one another. "My mother is dead."

"I'm sorry." He looked appropriately contrite as he slid his eyes toward me. "I didn't know. Was it recent?"

"About a year ago." I swallowed away a fresh set of tears. Why talking about her death was still so hard for me, I couldn't say.

"And she owned a magic store?"

"Yeah, with her sister." I managed to smile. "Aunt Mindy is back running the store. I still have her."

"What about your father?"

"He took off when I was a kid."

"I'm doubly sorry."

"It is what it is." I offered a shrug. "I have only one vague memory of him. It doesn't feel like a loss because I never knew him."

"I don't believe that." Jasper sipped his drink. "Just because you don't know what you're missing, that doesn't mean you're not missing it. I have a great father. He taught us all about running the best tours at a young age. He's larger than life. I can't imagine not having him in my life."

"You're lucky."

"And you're alone," Jasper mused out of nowhere. "Is that

why you moved to New Orleans? This is the sort of city you're never alone in."

"Salem is that sort of city too," I assured him. "Also, I'm not alone. I have Aunt Mindy. She's great. She was like a second mother to me when I was growing up. After my father left, she moved in. We all lived together."

"Yeah, but ... that's still only one person." Jasper looked pained. "I can't imagine having only one relative. I'm from a big family."

"Oh, yeah? How many brothers and sisters do you have?" I had no interest in getting to know him, so asking him personal questions seemed like a waste of time, but I was nothing if not polite.

"I have only one of each," he replied. "I have sixteen cousins, though, and we were all raised in the city together. They're kind of like siblings."

"Sixteen?" I tried to imagine that and came up empty. "Wow. I don't have any cousins—at least that I know of. I guess it's possible I have some on my father's side, but I was never around them or anything."

"That makes me sad. Some of my best stories start with 'I was really drunk and with my cousin Brian, and we decided to head to Jackson Square.'"

I chuckled. "Like Jackson Square, do you?"

"I love everything about this city." He was firm. "What about you? Do you think you'll stay here, or is this just a stopover as you decide what you want to do with your life?"

That was a fair question.

I didn't have an answer. "I don't know yet."

"Well, you're young. You have time to decide what you want."

"What about you?" I took a moment to study his strong profile. "Are you here forever, or is this just the start of your adventure?"

"Oh, I'm never leaving this city." Jasper was adamant as he shook his dark head. "There's no place better than New Orleans."

"Have you been anywhere else?"

"A few places. And before you assume I'm afraid to travel, that's not it at all. I love traveling. I just always want to come back here. This is my home, and it always will be. Some places take up residence in your heart and never let go. That's New Orleans to me."

"Huh." I rubbed my cheek, absorbing the words. "It's nice that you feel you belong here," I said finally. "There's nothing better than knowing where you belong."

He went silent after I spoke, and when I risked a glance at him, I found him studying me with dark eyes.

"What?" I asked defensively.

"Nothing." He shook his head.

It didn't feel like nothing.

Suddenly, I wanted nothing more than to say goodbye to him. "We're almost to The Annex."

"It's not nothing," he countered after a beat.

I was confused. "What's not nothing?"

"Just a second ago, I said it was nothing. That's not true. I just didn't want to make you feel uncomfortable."

"Okay." I dragged out the lone word.

"Do you not know where you belong?" he asked in a low voice.

The question shouldn't have surprised me, yet it did.

"I don't ... know." I held out my hands. "I thought I did. A year ago, when saying goodbye to my mother, I was sad but thought I knew how my life was going to play out. Now, I'm not so sure."

"How did you think things would go?" He looked genuinely interested.

"I thought I would work in the store with my aunt until

she retired, take over day-to-day operations so she could do the stuff she wanted to do, meet a nice man, have a kid or two, and then die." I was trying to be funny, but my attempt fell flat.

"So, you wanted the American dream," Jasper mused.

"I wouldn't say that."

"If that's not the American dream, what is?"

"I ... don't..." I trailed off, considering. He had a point, loath though I was to admit it. "I don't think there's anything wrong with wanting what other people want," I said as I straightened. "I've always wanted to be a mother and wife."

"I didn't say there was anything wrong with that," Jasper countered. "My mother is a mother and wife, and she happens to be one of my favorite people in the world. My sister is neither, and she gets on my last nerve. One day, though, she'll be a mother and wife because that's what she wants too. I'm not opposed to the American dream."

"But it's not what you want," I surmised.

He held his hands palms out and offered a rueful smile. "It's not that I don't want that. I just don't think that far ahead. New Orleans is the type of city where you can pick a different dream for every day of the week."

"I'm guessing that means you pick a different woman for every one of those dreams," I said.

He choked on a laugh. "I like that you say whatever comes to your mind. As for your take on the situation, you're not wrong. I like women. I love them. They're like ice cream. I can never settle on one flavor. There's nothing wrong with that. It's not as if I'm not up-front about who I am."

"You seem pretty open about it," I agreed as The Annex popped into view. "Does your friend Savannah know you want to sample other flavors?"

"Savannah is ... a transitory friend."

I arched an eyebrow. "Is that code for a one-night stand?"

"Oh, I never do one-night stands." He fervently shook his head. "There's no joy to be found in a one-night stand."

"No? I would've thought one-night stands were right up your alley."

"I can see that, but no. See, people are always nervous the first night. That means they can't relax. I tend to go for one-week stands. They're more my speed. That way, you can get the nerves out of the way and really enjoy one another."

"One-week stands, huh? Wow." I laughed because that was the only thing I could do. "I guess, as long as both sides know what to expect, there's nothing wrong with it. You're consenting adults."

"But you don't approve," Jasper surmised.

"Oh, I don't judge." That, I meant with every fiber of my being. "I'm all for people living however they want as long as they don't hurt others."

"So, what's the problem?"

"I didn't say there was a problem."

"You act as if there's a problem."

"See, I think that's your perception. Other people have told you it's a problem, and you've internalized it to the point where you assume everybody is judging you. I don't want to be judged, and in return, I don't judge others."

"No?"

"No."

He rubbed his chin as we slowed our pace. The sidewalk for my building was directly across the road. "You're an interesting woman," he said after what seemed like a long stretch of staring.

"Thank you. I'm not going to be a one-week stand, though, so you can get that out of your head right now."

He laughed again. "You're assuming I have ulterior motives. Maybe I'm just being a nice guy."

"Well, thank you for being a nice guy." I gave his arm a

hearty slap. "I appreciate it. I can take care of myself, though. You don't have to tear yourself away from this week's stand to worry about me. I've got everything under control."

"You know, people who say they have everything under control are usually the ones who have nothing under control."

"Well, that's not me. I'm good to go."

"If you say so."

"I *know* so. Anyway, thanks again for the escort. You should get back to your friends. It's NOLA, right? You don't want to miss out on the party."

"Funnily enough, I was just thinking the same thing about you."

I feigned patience despite my growing agitation. "Have a good rest of your night." I wanted him to go. No, I *needed* him to go. He was starting to make me feel uncomfortable. "Party it up. Have a good time."

"That's the plan."

"I'm sure I'll see you again."

Jasper's lips spread in a soft smile. "Oh, I guarantee you will."

Four

I headed straight upstairs to my unit. I'd settled at The Annex because furnished units were available. I thought that would mean I would be forced to grapple with the sort of furniture most people ignored at garage sales, but I was wrong. Everything in the apartment was not only clean but also pretty and comfortable.

I threw myself on the couch, reached for the television remote, then thought about Jasper.

He was annoying on a level I wouldn't have thought possible. He had a way about him that set my teeth on edge. Someone being that good-looking should've been against the law when I was on a man fast. Sure, Toni had warned me about him—I wasn't a one-night stand or even a one-week stand—but he was one of those appetizers someone couldn't help but sample even though it was clearly full of empty carbs and fats. It would be a fleeting thing but worth it in the moment.

Given my luck, however, he would give me food poisoning. Because of that, I wouldn't even bother. I didn't need any added distractions.

I started flipping through the television channels, frowning at the offerings. *When did reality television take over everything?* I couldn't help but feel I'd been forced to learn about the Kardashians against my will, and I was more than a little bitter about it.

I flipped for another two minutes before turning off the television. Before Jasper walked me home, I'd had no interest in learning about my neighbors. I still didn't, yet the look of consternation on his face when I let slip that I was basically a recluse had stuck with me. Why did I care that a guy who was clearly uncomfortable being alone with his thoughts believed I was antisocial and maybe a little pathetic? I didn't care. Not even a little. Even as I thought that, I pushed myself to a standing position.

It was probably time I get to know the neighbors, not because of Jasper but because I was going to be living there for at least six months. Having a friend or two—no more because that wasn't necessary—couldn't possibly hurt.

I grabbed the keycard to my unit and slipped it in my back pocket before heading to the elevators. I knew regular parties were held on the roof—I'd heard them when walking around the building in an effort to settle down at night—but I'd yet to see the setup for myself. That was about to change.

I didn't know what to expect when I exited the building onto the roof. In my head, I pictured ten or fifteen people, all young hipsters, drinking White Claw and smoking e-cigarettes. What I found was at least forty people, a bartender, and a pretty pool with people splashing about.

"Huh." I stared at the scene for what felt like forever though the real time was probably only sixty seconds.

"Are you lost?" a man asked from behind me.

I jolted at the voice's proximity, and when I turned, I found an amused man in a pair of low-riding swim trunks watching me with overt amusement. He had a towel hanging off one arm, a pair of glasses perched on his nose, making him look attractive rather than trying too hard, and a grin that set off an adorable dimple.

"Um..." I didn't know what to say.

"I'm Hal Stevens." He extended his free hand. "I live on the second floor."

"Rowan Shaw," I said dumbly, sliding my hand into his. Though it was warm, I felt no spark, which should've been impossible, given the rather impressive body he had on display.

"You're the new tenant on the third floor, right?" Hal's smile didn't waver. "People have been talking about you."

"They have?" I was taken aback. "I totally tried to lift that garbage bag into the dumpster, but it was too heavy. The guy I saw down there said he would do it for me. If he didn't, that's on him."

Hal's grin widened. "People say you're from Salem." He had kind eyes as he inclined his head toward a patio table where a group of people were watching us with overt curiosity. "Come on. I'll introduce you to everybody."

I hesitated. "I just came up to look around," I said lamely.

"Well, now you're going to have a drink with us."

I felt out of place, but I was in an untenable position. I didn't want to come off as unfriendly. That would create a whole different set of problems if I wasn't careful. "One drink," I conceded as I fell into step with him. "I have to work tomorrow." It was a lame excuse. I didn't have to report for my shift until eleven o'clock. Given my difficulties with sleeping, I would be up five hours before then. I wasn't worried about missing my shift.

"Hey," Hal called out as we approached the table. "I found the new tenant. This is Rowan Shaw, and she seems a little nervous. Try not to scare her off."

I balked. "I'm not nervous." That was a total lie. In the

thirty seconds we'd taken to cross the roof, my hands had gone sweaty, and my heart rate had picked up two notches.

"Of course not." Hal didn't look convinced. "Rowan, this is Tyler Hamilton, Tad Lancaster, Emily Dwyer, Portia Prince, and Posh Spice."

The last woman introduced, a pretty brunette with curves that screamed boat model, glared at Hal with unrestrained annoyance. "How many times have I told you not to introduce me that way?" she demanded.

"I've lost count," Hal replied easily as he pulled out a chair for me. "Sit." His eyes were full of mirth. "It's okay. We don't bite. Posh is irritated with me, not you."

"Isn't that the truth," the woman in question muttered. She shook her head at him before smiling at me. "My name isn't Posh Spice. I didn't even know there was such a thing as Posh Spice until he started making jokes."

I was understandably confused. "Is your name really Posh?"

She nodded, her lips curving down. "Yeah, and I'm not talking to my mother. My real name is Posh Samuelson. Hal started the whole Posh Spice thing. I didn't even realize that the Spice Girls were a thing until I came here. When I asked my mother if she named me after them—I thought for sure it had to be a coincidence—she didn't deny it. Now, we're not speaking."

I didn't know if the story was funny or sad. It was likely both. "Well, Posh is still an interesting name," I hedged.

"It's a stupid name." Posh was having none of it. "I thought it was bad before I learned about the Spice Girls. Now, I'm having a crisis of faith and thinking about changing my name."

"Really?" I tried to picture myself in her position, wondering if I would go through the trouble of changing my name if I were in her shoes. The answer was yes. Posh was a weird name. "What name are you considering?"

"I was thinking I would stick with a *P* because that way, none of my monogrammed stuff will have to be tossed. So far, I like Piper and Phoebe."

"Which means we had to explain about *Charmed*," Hal said with a laugh as he accepted a cocktail Tyler handed him. "Thank you, honey." He lifted his mouth and accepted a kiss from the other man. "You take such good care of me."

My heart gave a little heave at the smiles they shared. Ah, true love. Then reality settled over me.

"Oh, that's why," I said.

"What's why?" Hal shot me a curious look.

"You're hot," I replied before thinking how I might sound. That was often one of my problems: I spoke before thinking. "That was the first thing I thought when I saw you. The second thing I thought was 'There's no sexual attraction here.' I thought maybe my hormones were off, but you obviously don't swim in my pool."

Hal let loose a delighted laugh. "I haven't heard it phrased that way, but you're right. I don't swim in your pool. If I did, there would most definitely be a spark."

"What would you like to drink?" Tad asked. He wasn't as good-looking as Hal but was just as well built. He had blond hair, which normally didn't do it for me, and green eyes lit with mischief.

"Oh, um ... anything is fine." I craned my neck to look toward the bar. "Is that an actual bartender on staff here?"

"Only on the weekends," Posh replied. "We're on our own on weeknights, but it's fine. As for what they're stocked with, it's no premium liquors. If you want something that costs more than twelve bucks a bottle, you have to bring it yourself. We're not picky, though."

"I'm not either," I reassured them. "Something basic like a gin and tonic is fine."

Hal made a face. "My mother called from her *Beverly Hills 90210* watching party and wants her drink back."

"I... What?" My eyebrows moved toward one another. "I don't think I understand."

"Hal is an encyclopedia of pop-culture references," Posh explained.

"I clean up on trivia nights," Hal confirmed.

"Ignore him," Posh continued. "If you want a gin and tonic, we won't judge."

"Speak for yourself," Tad muttered under his breath.

Posh shot him a quelling look, which was enough to send him shuffling toward the bar. "Tell us about yourself. Are you from Louisiana originally? You don't have any hints of an accent, at least not one that screams native."

"I grew up in Salem," I replied as I rubbed my sweaty palms over my capris.

"Salem, Massachusetts?" Posh's grin was lightning quick. "I've always wanted to visit there."

"You should," I encouraged. "It's a great town. I miss it a lot."

"Then why are you here?" Hal asked, grunting when Tyler landed an elbow in his ribs. "I didn't mean it in a rude way," he said quickly as he glared at his boyfriend. "I just meant you seem to be a little homesick. Why would you leave if you love it there so much?"

I was prepared for the question. "My mother died." I wasn't keeping her death quiet, just the curse. "My aunt is running the family store. I was feeling a little edgy, like I needed an adventure, so I decided to come down here for a bit. I'd always wanted to visit New Orleans, and I needed a break."

"Oh, that's sad." Sympathy rolled over Hal's handsome features. "Were you close?"

"Yeah." I tried to keep my voice from cracking. "It was hard at the end. My aunt suggested a change of scenery might do me good. When I started thinking about where I wanted to visit, New Orleans was on top of the list."

"So, you're not staying?" Posh asked as she reclined in her chair. "That's too bad. I think you fit right in with our little group. I'd hate to think your presence here is only temporary."

I held out my hands. "Nothing is decided. I have a job, and so far I like it, so we'll see how things go. If I do stay, I probably will have to consider buying one of the permanent units. The rent here is a little steep to stick with long-term."

"We all have permanent units," Hal confirmed. "The rent is high. How long is the lease you signed?"

"Six months. That was the shortest they had."

"That's why it's so expensive," Tad explained as he delivered my drink. "One gin and tonic." His lips quirked. "I'll keep the 'get off my lawn' jokes to myself until I know you better."

"Thanks for that," I said drily then sipped the gin, which was most definitely cheap. Since I was having only the one, I would have to suffer. "It's fine for now. I didn't want to pull the trigger on anything more permanent until I figured out if I can deal with the humidity."

Hal snorted, then sobered quickly. "Wait, you're serious."

"Yup." I bobbed my head. "I'm from the East Coast. Even in the dead of summer, we don't get humidity like this. I find I'm constantly grappling with a low-grade headache because of it."

"Seriously?" Hal shook his head. "I guess I didn't realize that was a thing. I'm sure you'll adjust."

"I hope so." I meant it. "I love the city. There's so much to look at. I love the food and the proximity to the river on one side and the Gulf on the other. I just hate the headaches."

"Have you tried not going outdoors in the afternoons?"

Posh queried. "That's when the humidity is worst."

"Yeah, but I don't relish the idea of hiding inside on my days off, when I want to be having adventures," I replied. "It's just something I'm going to have to come to grips with."

"Hopefully, you will." Hal's smile was sincere. "So, where do you work? We all work at different bars." He gestured at the various faces. "Most everybody is on Bourbon Street. Well, except for Tad. He's over on Royal at the Carousel Bar at Hotel Monteleone. He's fancier than the rest of us." The wink Hal tossed at the blonde told me they often messed around with one another.

"I work at Hex Appeal, over on Governor Nicholas," I replied. "I just started today. Well, I guess I started two days ago, but the first two days were training."

"Ooh." Posh perked up considerably. "You work at a voodoo store? How is that?"

"It's fine."

"That's the one with Madam Cleo, right?" Intrigue lit Hal's features as he leaned close. "It's impossible to get in for a reading with her. Do you think you can help us cut the line? We've been trying for months."

"I don't know. I can ask. I've only seen Madam Cleo twice. I work with her daughter, Toni, who is very nice. I'm sure she'll see if she can help me."

"Awesome." Hal exchanged a fist bump with Tyler. "We desperately want a couple's reading. She's the real deal. Those grifters down in Jackson Square are not the real deal, and we hate them."

"Totally hate them," Tyler echoed in agreement. "They told us we would never make it a year when we first got here."

"And we've been together three," Hal added. "We don't like the Jackson Square wenches."

"Not even a little," Tyler said. "They're total hacks."

I licked my lips, unsure what to say. Thankfully, Posh

swooped in to save me.

"So, Salem," she prodded. "Does that mean you're a witch?"

That was another one of those questions I was always prepared to answer. "Everybody in Salem is a witch."

She laughed, as I'd intended, but with a somber glint to her eye. "I'm being serious."

"My mother owned a witchcraft store," I replied. "She ran it with my aunt. I grew up working there. I think it's fair to say we embrace the whole witch mystique."

"But you're not there now," Hal pointed out.

"If I had a witchcraft store, I would never leave," Emily said, speaking for the first time. She seemed sweet but shy. "That's my dream job right there. Well, without the New England winters. I hear they're brutal."

"They can be," I agreed.

"Yeah, but at least up there, you don't have to worry about hurricanes," Tad argued. "They're often deadly down here."

"True," I agreed reasonably. "We have nor'easters, though. They can be just as dangerous, and when you add in the frigid temperatures that coincide with a power outage in the dead of winter, sometimes I think they're worse."

"I didn't think about that." Tad cocked his head, considering. "You guys have really good seafood though, right?"

I laughed. "Yeah. We have really good lobster. In fact, stuffed lobster is one of my favorites. You guys have good seafood down here, too, though. I've had the shrimp. It's good."

"Shrimp and grits?" Posh teased.

I hesitated then held up my hands. "I haven't gotten up the courage to try the grits yet. They look kind of gross, from what I remember the one time I had them as a kid."

"They are gross," Tad said with a scowl.

"Oh, don't listen to him." Hal tossed a dismissive wave in

his friend's direction. "If you get them prepared correctly, they're to die for. We'll take you to a good place for dinner one day this week. That way, we'll know you're getting the good ones."

Despite my reticence upon arriving on the roof, I found myself smiling. "That sounds fun. I work almost every day this week, though."

"We'll figure it out." Hal was firm. "You're one of the group now. That means you're stuck with us."

"We're like a cult," Posh agreed. "Once you get in, there's no getting out." She leaned back in her chair. "I seriously need to hear the skinny on Salem. It seems like a magical world, considering what we deal with here. You have to tell me absolutely everything."

"I'm not sure there's anything to tell," I hedged. "Salem is a relatively normal town except for the witch stuff."

"Yeah, it's the witch stuff I want to hear about."

"Fair enough." I got comfortable. "Should I start with the witches who dance naked under the full moon on the beaches during the summer or the ghosts that supposedly haunt the House of the Seven Gables?"

"Don't be ridiculous," Hal replied. "If there's a choice, you always go with nudity. It doesn't matter if we're talking women or men. Nudity always wins out."

"Okay, but I should warn you the cops were called."

"Even better. Lay it on me."

I couldn't help but smile as I launched into the tale. Jasper Bentley might've thought I was helpless and incapable of making friends. I'd showed him, though. I had new friends. That meant I was winning.

Not that it was a competition or anything. It most definitely wasn't that.

I was definitely winning, though. He simply didn't know it yet.

Five

I was up long before the sun. Sleep had never been an issue for me. Even right after my mother died, I managed to close my eyes and shut out the world. Sometime over the course of the past six months, things had changed. I couldn't put my finger on exactly when or why, but I'd gone from a person who got eight hours of sleep a night—that was pretty much *every* night—to one who struggled to get four or six. I was constantly tired.

Yet I could not sleep.

Instead, after an hour of staring at the ceiling fan as it lazily rotated above me, I got up and hit the shower.

Jasper had been right about the French Quarter sleeping in late. They partied until six o'clock in the morning most days—sure, those were only the diehards, but still—then things turned quiet until at least eleven. That allowed me to traverse Bourbon Street without having to dodge drunks or tune out the incessant noise.

I was lost in thought as I worked out what needed to be done if I expected to track down the source of the curse, and I didn't realize I was being approached until the individual was on me.

"Can you spare a dollar?"

I needed a moment to shake myself out of my reverie, and when I looked up, one of the city's many homeless individuals was watching me with unreadable eyes. That was one big difference between Salem and New Orleans. Sure, we had people who were down on their luck to grapple with, but it was nothing compared to this city.

"Oh, um, sure." I automatically reached for my purse.

Before I could unzip it, however, a blond woman appeared on my right. She had a cup of coffee clutched in each hand and seemed to be focused on the man rather than me. "How about you leave this nice woman alone, huh, Benji?" she prodded. "She's just out for a morning walk. She should be able to do it in peace."

I was caught off guard. "It's okay," I said automatically. "I don't mind."

"She doesn't mind," the man said, his eyes narrowing as he regarded the woman with something akin to annoyance. "Why don't you mind your own business?"

"Because you are my business." The woman extended one of the coffees in his direction. "Get some caffeine. Then I'll take you over to Oceana for breakfast. After that, we'll talk."

The man looked as if that was the last thing he wanted to do, but he grudgingly took the coffee. "I don't need breakfast," he groused. "I just need a few dollars to get a jump on the day."

"Well, you're getting breakfast." The woman was no-nonsense despite her round stomach. If I had to guess, she was pregnant. I would never have asked that question out of the blue, however. I'd learned my lesson at a young age on that one. "Head across the street. Gus is waiting there. He already has a table."

"Gus." The man—she'd called him Benji—wrinkled his nose. "I don't think I'm going to like this chat if it's both of you ganging up on me."

"Probably not." The woman's expression didn't change. "Go." She waited until the man begrudgingly shuffled away, to speak again. "I'm sorry."

After a moment, I realized she was talking to me. "You don't have to apologize." I meant it. "I was honestly fine giving him a dollar."

The woman's blue eyes were difficult to read when she shifted them to me. "If you'd done that, you would've been inundated with others wanting money, to the point where they would've surrounded you."

She inclined her head to an intersection about half a block down. There, six men stood grouped together, all watching us.

"I'm guessing you're new to New Orleans, huh?"

I hesitated then nodded. "How did you know?"

"Navigating these streets is difficult when you first get here. I know that better than most." She extended her hand. "Moxie Stone."

"Moxie?" I took her hand and shook it. "Is that a real name? I only ask because I met someone named Posh last night, and I'm still doubtful on that one."

She smirked. "It's not the name I was born with. It is my real name now."

"Huh." I pursed my lips, considering, then shrugged. "I like it."

She laughed. "I jokingly tell my fiancé it's not a name but a state of mind. As for Benji, I really am sorry." She glanced in the direction the man had disappeared. "He's been AWOL for a few days. I wasn't certain when he would show back up."

"Do you work with an outreach program?" I asked, thinking that was the only thing that made sense.

"No." She shook her head. "I own Moxie's Cantina. It's

located about four blocks that way." She gestured down Bourbon Street. "Benji is my father."

My mouth dropped open before I could stop it, then I struggled to recover. "Oh, well ... that's awesome. He seems like a great guy."

Her smile widened. "Oh, you're so cute. Are you from the Northeast?"

I was taken aback. "How did you know that?"

"Gus—that would be my fiancé—has taught me to read people over the past year. We own the bar together. You have manners coming out of your ass, but you're easily thrown. Plus, you just have that Boston thing going for you."

"Salem," I automatically corrected. "I live in Salem, not Boston."

She waited.

"Although they're, like, twenty minutes apart," I conceded after a beat.

Her eyes lit with amusement. "Well, that's something."

A current of unease rippled between us.

"I generally hate it when people offer up unsolicited advice," she continued after a beat. "I'm going to do that for you, though."

"Sure." I wasn't offended.

"Don't pull out money in front of them. I'm not saying it to be mean. I feed a group in Jackson Square every night. That's *every* night, rain or shine. Flashing money could get you hurt if the wrong person sees it. If you want to help, offer food. Most of them won't take you up on it because they prefer the brew, but the ones who are truly desperate will. You have to take those wins and ignore the losses. Otherwise, you'll drown in the sadness."

"That's probably a pretty good tip." Rueful, I dragged a hand through my hair. "Thanks for stepping in."

"No problem. We've been looking for him since he left the rehab facility he'd been living at for the past two months."

She looked so momentarily forlorn that my heart threatened to break for her. "I'm sorry."

"Oh, it's not the first time." She waved a hand dismissively. "My fiancé thinks I have unrealistic expectations, and he's right. When Benji fails, I'm the one who takes it the hardest. I need to stop doing that. He's never disappointed in himself. I'm the only one feeling that particular emotion."

That was an interesting observation. "I get it. Still, I think it's great that you obviously care enough to keep chasing him."

"Well, somebody has to do it." She briefly pressed her eyes shut, then loosed a breathy laugh. "Anyway, I should be going. It was nice to meet you." She stilled before crossing the street. "Do you need help with something? You seem as if you have something specific on your mind, and yet you also seem lost."

That was the understatement of the year. "I'm looking for a library, but it can't just be any library. I need one with local population records."

"Oh, yeah?" If Moxie thought that a strange request, she didn't show it. "Are you a genealogy student?"

"I'm just interested in the city's history. I love reading about family trees and stuff."

The lie slipped off my tongue. She was a nice woman, but I couldn't dare tell her about the curse. She would think I was nuts. Hell, I was fairly convinced I was nuts.

"There's a library over at the intersection of Common and Loyola. It's huge. I've been there before. I'm almost positive they have a genealogy section. I know because Gus said they expanded it, following Katrina. A lot of people were lost ... and the genealogy section allowed them to rediscover their roots."

"I can see that." My mind was already working. "Thanks for the tip." I pulled out my phone to google the intersection.

Moxie smiled kindly as she watched. "That way." She

pointed over my shoulder. "It's going to be about a ten-minute walk."

"That's okay. I have time to burn before work." I was already feeling better. "Thank you so much for the tip."

"Don't mention it." Moxie's smile was kind. "If you get a chance, stop in at the bar. Gus insisted on naming it after me, so you won't forget. Find me if you drop in, and we'll have a drink. I would love to hear about Salem. I've always wanted to go there."

I waved at her as I set off. "I'll do that. Thanks again for the tip."

"Don't mention it."

FINDING THE LIBRARY WASN'T DIFFICULT, but getting across the road, given the traffic, was a significant hurdle to clear. Once I was inside, however, I knew I'd made the right choice.

A cross woman—seriously, she had the personality of a rancid pickle when I approached the help desk—pointed me toward a quiet room in the library. She didn't bother explaining how to search for the information I needed, but I figured it out quickly enough. Then I dove in.

I didn't have much to go on. Michel—or Michelle?—was apparently a common name. If it was a last name, I had hundreds of records to sift through. If it was a first name, I had even more to grapple with. I didn't rule anything out and started sorting the information, figuring I should make a master list before whittling it down.

I worked hard, jotting notes down on a yellow notepad I'd purchased at a pharmacy across the road. I set a reminder on my phone so that I wouldn't accidentally forget when to pack up and leave—I didn't want to be late for my shift at the voodoo store in my first week—then I let the information wash over me. I was so lost in what I was doing that I jolted when my phone buzzed to remind me to head back.

I made a note on the notepad so that I would know where to start again when I returned, put everything away, then exited into the main library. I pulled up short when I recognized a familiar figure standing at the help desk.

"Jasper?" His name escaped—and way too loudly—before I realized I was drawing attention to myself.

Slowly, he turned. His eyes widened in surprise before a sly smile spread across his face. The woman behind the counter scowled when she saw me, and only then did I manage to put a name to her face.

Savannah. It was the woman who'd been with Jasper on the street the night before, the one who'd almost melted down when he separated to walk me back to my place. I should've recognized her, but she was dressed in standard street clothes rather than being decked out for a party. Also, truth be told, I'd been more focused on him than her the previous evening.

"Are you following me?" Jasper asked by way of greeting.

I narrowed my eyes. "I was here first."

"It was just a question. It seems a little coincidental for you to end up here if you weren't following me." His chest was puffed out as he leaned against the counter.

"Oh, don't let your ego inflate enough to ram you into the ceiling," I snapped as I slid my notebook into my purse. He really was insufferable. "I was here doing research. I don't care about you. Like I even knew you were here." I was feeling defensive, which frustrated me. I had no reason to feel that way, yet I was explaining myself like a teen caught breaking curfew.

"It was just a question." Jasper didn't look bothered by my reaction. "I just happened to be in the area. I wasn't expecting to see you."

"Well, I've been here for hours." I offered a lame half wave for Savannah's benefit. "Your girlfriend can confirm that if you're unsure."

Savannah smirked at the "girlfriend" reference, but the expression disappeared in an instant when Jasper snorted.

"She's just a friend," he said.

His back was to her, so he couldn't see the way her face fell. If she hadn't been so unpleasant, I would've almost felt sorry for her.

"What are you doing here?" He studied my empty hands. "Are you looking for something to read? I told you. That rooftop lounge of yours is way more entertaining than any book could be."

I glowered at him. "I'll have you know that I love to read. I was here doing something else, though."

"What?"

I ignored the question. "As for the rooftop lounge, you were right. It is amazing. I went up there and hung out last night."

"Really?" His eyes gleamed with an emotion I couldn't readily identify. "Fancy that."

"Yes, it was delightful," I agreed. "I met some new friends. You don't have to worry about me being antisocial."

"I wasn't worried. I just didn't want you to miss out on something fun because you were trapped inside your own head." The observation threw me, and hard.

"I'm not trapped inside my own head," I said.

Seriously, he didn't even know me. I couldn't believe he had the audacity to say something like that.

"I just moved here," I continued. "I needed to unpack."

"If you say so." He was completely ignoring Savannah at that point, which she clearly didn't like.

She rested a hand on his forearm and drew his attention to her. "We were talking about lunch," she prodded.

He frowned. "What? Oh, right. The guys are going to be over at the Fiery Crab for lunch in an hour. I said I would meet them there. I figured, since you were so close, you might want to join us." His eyes were back on me. "What about you?"

"What about me?" I asked blankly.

"Do you want the best fried shrimp basket you've ever tasted?"

Not expecting him to invite me, I was understandably thrown. "Oh, well... I have to get to work."

"I'm sure Toni won't care if you're late," Jasper pressed. "The food really is amazing. If you don't like fried food, they have this crawfish rice that's too tasty for words. Oh, and the sweet potato fries are to die for."

"It's a nice offer." Why he was extending it to me was a mystery. "I have to get to work, though. It will take me twenty minutes to get to the voodoo store."

"I'll call Toni," he offered. "If I tell her you're eating with us, she'll give you a pass."

"That's really not necessary."

Savannah's hand was back on Jasper's forearm. "You heard her. It's really not necessary. I would love a catfish basket, though. I try to limit the fried foods I eat—this body isn't going to maintain itself—but I make an exception once a week. Today can be my cheat day."

"Their catfish *is* amazing," Jasper agreed, not looking at her as he spoke. His gaze was solely for me. "How do you feel about po'boys? They have some good ones there."

"The food sounds awesome," I said. "I wouldn't mind checking it out another time. I really do have to go, though. I don't want to be late for work."

Jasper pushed himself away from the counter and followed me toward the door, leaving a glaring Savannah to stare at his back, stewing. "I'm going to give Toni grief for working you like a slave. That doesn't seem fair, given the fact that you've just arrived in town."

I tucked my dark hair behind an ear as I regarded him. "She hardly works me like a slave."

"And yet you're terrified of arriving late," he pointed out as he leaned close. "I'm going to give you a little tip."

His proximity did something to my stomach. I told myself I was just hungry—he'd been talking about food for five minutes straight, so that was to be expected—and forced myself to keep my expression neutral.

"If you've yet to experience a seafood boil in New Orleans, then you're missing out. I think you should come with me. They'll even take the heads off the shrimp at the Fiery Crab. They're conscientious if you have a weak stomach."

I made a face. "I don't have a weak stomach."

"You're a northerner. You all have weak stomachs. I can help you navigate that issue. The crab boil is amazing. Sure, it looks like you're eating a small monster from a Godzilla movie, but you'll get over that fast enough."

I tugged on my limited patience to steady myself. "I appreciate the offer—I really do—but I'm the sort of employee who likes to arrive on time and do my job. I don't take off willy-nilly during my first week because I'm hungry. I'm a diligent employee."

"Diligent, huh?" His lips quirked. "I don't know that we have a lot of those here. Start times are just a suggestion in New Orleans."

"Well, not in my world." I was firm on that. "I appreciate the invitation. I have to go, though. I'm sure I'll see you around again."

"It does seem to turn out that way, doesn't it?"

Unfortunately, shaking him was impossible.

"Have a nice lunch. Don't forget your friend." I pointed at a seething Savannah. "If you don't start paying attention to her, you're going to end up bleeding in an alley because she's going to hack off your manhood."

That only made him smile more widely. "Thanks for the warning. I appreciate it."

"Don't mention it."

Six

"I need a reading."

The woman who appeared at the counter like a furtive Karen ninja on uppers leaned in close as I was sorting hex bags. I wasn't big on my personal space being invaded. I wasn't a freak about it or anything, but I believed if you didn't know someone, a three-foot no-infringement rule needed to be maintained. That woman clearly felt otherwise.

"A tarot reading?" I asked as I moved away from the hex bags to retrieve the scheduling book. It was literally something one could buy at a random bookstore, but Toni had covered it with a leather binding, so it looked important.

"No, a children's book reading," the woman snapped. "Of course a tarot reading." Her eyes flashed with impatience. "I met a guy."

When she didn't expand, I merely blinked.

"A guy," she repeated after a beat. "He could be the one."

"Okay." I flipped open the book. "Toni is doing a reading right now, but she has an opening afterward if you want that. It should be about ten or fifteen minutes."

"What about Madam Cleo?"

"Madam Cleo isn't in today."

"Why not?"

Toni had warned me that the tourists would be upset when they found out her mother wasn't working full time. Apparently, Madam Cleo was a big draw, famous far and wide. We would have to put up with it until visitors adjusted to the new reality.

"She works only a few days a week now," I replied calmly. "If you want to wait for her, she'll be in Friday."

"Friday?" The woman's eyebrows practically popped off her forehead.

"Of next week," I added.

"I'm only in town for a few days." The woman's gaze turned dark. "This is just unacceptable. I need Madam Cleo. She's the only one who can solve my particular problem."

Toni picked that moment to exit the back room. The sound of the curtain sliding across the rod was a dead giveaway. The customer she'd been doing a reading for was a gushy mess as they appeared, but Toni's gaze was on the newcomer. She seemed to sense trouble.

"I really like what you told me about Linc," the woman with Toni said, enthused. "I'm going to give him another chance."

"Just because you picture sausage when you say his name, that doesn't mean he's a bad choice," Toni agreed gravely. "Besides, who doesn't love a good sausage?"

I had to press my lips together to keep from laughing at the way she delivered the line.

"Right." The woman clapped her hands like an excited high schooler. "Well, I have to meet my friends for lunch. Thank you so much for the excellent reading."

"You're welcome." Toni's smile was warm, but I could tell she'd already moved on and was focused on the woman across from me. "If you and Linc get married, just keep in mind that

Antoinette is a lovely name." She waited until the woman had left to focus on her next victim. "Are you here for a reading?"

The blonde appeared caught off guard. "How did you know that?"

"I know all and see all." Toni winked at me, clearly enjoying herself.

"She wants an appointment with your mother," I offered. "I explained the realities of Miss Cleo's present schedule. I'm not sure if she's ready to book an appointment with you."

Toni's expression didn't change. "It's okay," she told the woman. "If you're not ready to hear the truth, there's no rush. It's not as if you're making an important life decision today, is it?"

The woman shifted from one foot to the other, clearly uncomfortable. "I ... don't ... know."

"She thinks she might've met *the one*," I supplied. Not using air quotes took everything I had. I was from Salem, which meant I understood that people put endless faith in tarot readings. Personally, I'd never understood the appeal. Fate was what we made of it, not what others thrust upon us. Of course, I was suffering from a curse nobody else believed in, so I didn't have much room to talk.

"Here in town?" Toni queried. Her eyes were busy as they roamed up and down the woman's body. "You live in New Jersey, right?"

The woman let loose a theatrical gasp. "How did you know that?"

"It's one of my gifts." Toni shot me a knowing look. "If you want a reading, I have an opening now. If you want to wait for my mother, it's going to be a bit."

The woman chewed on her bottom lip for several seconds, then nodded. "I need to know if he's the one. He wants my virtue, and I can't decide if I want to give it to him."

Her virtue? I had to take another look at the woman. She

wasn't yet in her thirties, but she wasn't a teenager either. I had to think her virtue had been bestowed upon someone a very long time before.

"You're one of those revirginizers, aren't you?" Toni asked.

"How did you know that?" The woman was flabbergasted. "It's true, though. I made a bad decision prom night ... and then another bad decision graduation night ... and there might've been a hundred or so bad decisions in college. Oh, and then there was that time I met a guy outside the mall, and he told me he was recruiting for models, and I made that really stupid mistake and posed with the dildos ... which led to another really bad mistake. Other than that, my virtue is intact."

"Other than that." Toni managed a friendly smile, which looked as though it took effort. "I think if anybody was ever in dire need of a reading, it's you. We should talk. I really want to hear about this guy you met."

"Hiram."

"Hiram?" Then Toni did make a face, but it wasn't friendly. "How old is *the one*, if I might ask?"

"He's a young fifty. We belong together, though. He bought me a bottle of Dom Pérignon last night." She murdered the name but kept going anyway. "That means he's definitely the one, right?"

Toni looked pained. "Yeah, we need to talk." She gestured toward the curtained area. Her gaze fell on me as the woman disappeared beyond the barrier. "If Hiram shows up, kick him in the nuts."

I graced her with a saucy salute. "I think that can be arranged." Once they were gone, I went back to bagging hexes. As far as jobs went, mine held a lot of appeal. The curses still threw me, though.

I hummed to myself as I worked, my mind drifting to the research I was delving into. I wished I had more to go on, but it wasn't that easy. My mother had been lost toward the end. I was certain she had no idea what she was saying. The difference between Michel and Michelle was stark, however, and I had no idea which way I should be leaning. Rather than dwell on my issues—which were nothing compared to our new customer and her imperiled virtue—I set about organizing and cleaning. By the time Toni emerged with our tearful guest, I'd straightened up the entire storefront.

"Are you sure?" Tears streamed down the blonde's cheeks. "Are you sure he's not the one?"

"Hayley, I've never been more sure of anything in my entire life," Toni replied, her tone no-nonsense. "Just because he bought you Dom Pérignon and you both have names that start with an H, that doesn't mean that you're destined for a great love."

"Oh, I think you misunderstood." Hayley—knowing her name made her appear even younger in my eyes—looked momentarily hopeful. "I'm not suggesting he's my great love. I'm suggesting that he'll be the love I settle for. I mean ... he's, like, fifty pounds overweight and smokes cigars. He also drinks like a fish. He can't have more than twenty years in front of him, right?"

Toni blinked several times in rapid succession. "I don't know what you're getting at," she said finally.

"If he lives twenty years, he'll die when he's seventy. That's a good, long life ... for him. Women live longer than men. In twenty years, I'll be forty-five. He's rich. I'll get that money. Then I can find a hot pool boy and make him my true love."

"Huh." Toni slid her eyes toward me. "I see you've given this some thought."

"Oh, most definitely." Hayley bobbed her head. "Does that change things?"

"No. Don't let that man touch you." Toni vigorously shook her head. "I'm about to be blunt because you didn't pick up on any of the subtle hints I was offering back there. You should prepare yourself."

Hayley's eyes were wide, but she didn't say a word.

"Hiram is an asshole." Toni was matter-of-fact. "Worse than that, he's a predator. He's a dude with money—or at least he pretends to have money—and he basically hops from hot spot to hot spot so he can entice idiots into his bed. I'm guessing he puts in regular appearances at Daytona Beach. Something tells me he's here for Mardi Gras every year. I'm even willing to bet he's been to Salem, because pumpkin spice is like catnip for white girls in their twenties, and that's the sort of thing that would appeal to him."

Toni grabbed Hayley by her shoulders and stared directly into the woman's eyes. "I think your parents did you a disservice by making sex dirty. Now, I'm not going to pretend you weren't a little free with the love in college—seriously, the fact that one of the professors you slept with wasn't your professor and therefore couldn't give you an A should've been a red flag—but I'm not here to judge.

"You can't become a virgin again," she continued, shaking her head when Hayley opened her mouth to argue. "No. It's not possible. Not physically. Not emotionally. Just ... no. Also, the fact that your father gave you a promise ring and, in return, you agreed to remain a virgin until marriage is weird. That's some dopey-ass white people shit right there. You don't see Black people doing that, and there's a reason. It's stupid. You don't get engaged to your father to stave off hormones until marriage. I'm willing to bet your father was a freaky-ass pervert."

"That's what my mother says," Hayley agreed mournfully. "It was a really nice purity ring, though."

Clearly at the end of her rope, Toni gripped Hayley so tightly the blonde yelped. "Listen here. You're an adult. You might not act it, but you are. That means you need to become responsible for yourself. Do you know what that means?"

"Not really."

"It means you need to get a job."

"But Hiram..."

"No!" Toni wagged a finger in Hayley's face. "Hiram wants to stick his wick in you for thirty seconds of uninspired sex, maybe take a few photos, and then dump you. That's not really going to fix your sex problem, is it?"

Hayley's shoulders drooped. "No."

"Your real problem is that you're looking for an easy out," Toni said. "You want to find a man who will shower you with money, so you don't have to get a real job."

"What's wrong with that?"

"Oh, so much," I muttered under my breath.

Toni shot me a quelling look but didn't admonish me. Instead, she made an attempt at a smile as she focused on Hayley yet again. "You have to be responsible for yourself before you can link yourself with another person. If you're not, it creates an imbalance in the relationship. Do you want to marry a guy and have him make all the decisions about the relationship?"

Hayley hesitated then held out her hands. "I guess it depends on how rich he is."

"Yeah. That right there is why you're never going to get anywhere in life if you don't change your mindset." Toni rapped her knuckles against Hayley's forehead. "You're a smart girl who thinks she has to play dumb to get a man. The only men you're going to attract by doing that are the sort of men who should be left for dead in ditches and dumpsters."

"That's quite the picture," I mused.

Toni ignored me. "You have got to figure your own shit out before you let someone else in, and girlfriend, you're nowhere near close to figuring yourself out. It's going to take years at this point."

"Years?" Hayley looked anguished. "I don't have years to wait. I'll shrivel up and die if I have to wait years."

"Is this the sex thing?" Annoyance practically rolled off Toni in waves. "If so, get it together. You don't have to be a virgin again. I'm guessing that's something your parents foisted on you because they were afraid you were going to turn up pregnant and they would have to raise the baby. Of course, it's also possible your daddy was just a dirty pervert. Seriously, who wants to marry their daughter?"

Since that question was pointed at me, I merely shrugged. "I've never understood those purity ceremonies. They're what happens when the repressed take religion out for a ride and go down a one-way street the wrong way."

Toni blinked several times and grinned. "That is one of the best descriptions I've ever heard. I'm totally stealing it."

"Knock yourself out."

"As for you, Hayley, it's time to become the woman you were meant to be, not the girl who has unrealistic expectations about life. If you want your happily ever after, you're going to have to take control of things. Hiram is not an option. In fact, if you see him, you need to kick first and ask questions later. That dude probably has a drip line of Viagra hidden under his fancy-ass suits."

"How did you know about the Viagra?" Hayley asked, dumbfounded.

"I'm a genius." Toni didn't bother to hide her eye roll. "Do you understand what I'm saying to you?"

"Yes." Hayley's voice was small. "I don't think I like it, though."

"Well, you're going to have to suck it up. You have no choice."

"Fine." Haley scuffed her feet across the floor as she

marched dejectedly toward the door. She paused, one hand on the doorframe, and glanced over her shoulder one last time. "Are you sure about Hiram?"

"He's a dirty dog who just wants to hump your leg and make a mess," Toni confirmed. "He's never going to be your knight in shining armor."

"Right." Hayley didn't look in our direction again before exiting. The last glimpse we had was her trudging down the sidewalk in the direction of the Royal Sonesta.

"She's going to have sex with Hiram, isn't she?" I asked after a few seconds of silence.

"Oh, totally." Toni was blasé. "That right there is a messed-up girl who doesn't want to get better. That's the real problem with society. Nobody is born perfect. Nobody makes all the right decisions. You have to learn from your mistakes, though. That's a girl who is never going to learn."

I could see that. "Do you really think her father is a dirty pervert?"

"Dude, who marries their daughter? That's just wrong."

"Technically, I don't think it's an actual marriage ceremony."

"She said they exchanged rings and made vows. She's not allowed to give herself to a man until she's married. Her daddy said so." Toni's eye roll told me exactly what she thought of that.

"It's weird."

"It's gross and repressed." Toni's lip curled. "Seriously, what kind of sicko does crap like that? I don't even know what to say."

She wasn't the only one. "Do you think Hayley is a lost cause?"

"I think Hayley has some dark days ahead. She's going to have to pick herself up when the dust settles."

"Do you think she's capable of that?"

"Probably not. Never say never, though." Toni stared at the empty sidewalk a beat longer then turned back to me. "This place looks nice. You didn't have to do all that work, though. People buy no matter what."

I shrugged. "I wasn't doing anything else."

"Speaking of that, tonight when we close the shop down, you're coming with me."

As far as transitions went, that wasn't her finest offering.

"I'm not sure I understand," I hedged.

"I'm not letting you go home to hang out in that apartment alone. It's sad ... and wrong ... and pathetic."

I frowned. "I met some people there last night. They were almost completely normal and everything."

"Awesome." Toni shot me a thumbs-up. "That's good. You're going to meet some more people tonight. In fact, you're going to meet my people, and it's going to be excellent."

I stilled. "Your people?" I wasn't sure what to make of that.

Toni chuckled at my discomfort. "You're wondering if I mean voodoo people or Black people, aren't you?"

"Actually, I was kind of wondering if you meant lesbians."

She cocked her head, considering. "I can see that. Let's just say you're going to meet fun people and leave it at that. I'll let you figure out the rest of it on your own."

I knew arguing with her was a waste of time, so I was resigned. "Where are we going?"

"Frenchman Street."

"And what are we going to find there?"

"A magical wonderland of music and good food."

"Is that all?" I was understandably dubious.

"For now. Don't get worked up about it." She flicked my ear. "You're going to love it over there. Trust me."

Seven

The walk to Frenchman Street took longer than I'd thought. Since I arrived in New Orleans, the only time I'd left the French Quarter was during the ride from the airport. Otherwise, I'd been firmly entrenched in that area. Frenchman Street was in Marigny. It was only one block over from the French Quarter, but I was still excited to visit.

The second we stepped onto the street, I knew things were different. Depending on where you found yourself, the mood of New Orleans could shift wildly. Toni had told me that. Marigny felt old—even older than the French Quarter—but I absolutely loved the brightly colored buildings. I felt a kinship with the locals hanging out on front porches and on sidewalk chairs as we passed. Most of them seemed to recognize Toni on sight.

"Hey, Paul," she called out as we walked past a creole cottage decked out in turquoise walls and pink shutters. "How is life on the riverboat?"

Paul, who was smoking the sort of pipe 1980s grandfathers seemed to revere, shrugged. "I'm still alive."

"At least you have that going for you."

"Yup." He bobbed his head, his eyes drifting to me. "New friend?"

"Friend, yes. Not what you're thinking, though." Toni wagged her finger. "This is Rowan. She's working for me at the store."

"Ah." Paul nodded in understanding. "Is she new to the city?"

"Yup. That's why I'm showing her around the *real* New Orleans. I don't want her to think Bourbon Street is the norm."

"Good deal."

I was curious as we walked, my eyes darting left and right. I couldn't drink in the culture fast enough. "Did you grow up here?" I asked.

Toni nodded. "Yup. Two blocks that way." She pointed. "I live in the French Quarter now because it's easier, given how many hours I work, but this is still my home." She led me toward a bar, jazz pouring out through the open windows, where no sign designated its name, which struck me as odd. "This is my uncle Henri's place. He's my mother's brother ... and he's a trip. You'll like him."

I had no doubt that was true. "How come there's no sign on the bar?"

She shrugged. "Because it doesn't need one."

"Yeah, but how do people find it?"

Amusement lit her pretty features. "They just know where it is."

"But ... how?" I was legitimately confused. "Like ... how does a person who hears that Henri's bar on Frenchman Street is the place to be actually find it?"

"The locals know."

"But how does he expand his business? I can see people from Bourbon Street wanting to come over here. It feels more

"... authentic." That was the best word I could come up with to describe the vibe.

"Do you actually think the Bourbon drinkers want authentic?"

I held out my hands. "Why wouldn't they?"

"Because the tourists don't come here for authenticity. They want a show. Bourbon Street is a veneer."

"I kind of like it," I admitted. "Not at night, mind you, but when I walk the street in the morning, I find it relaxing."

"I think you're the only one who can say that. I get it, though. The real New Orleans is protected by the people who live here and love it. The veneer is for the tourists. We need it because that's how we make our money. We don't love the veneer, though."

That was an interesting opinion, one I filed away to consider later.

"What's the name of the bar?" I asked.

She laughed. "That's important to you, huh?"

"It's just weird. I can't imagine not having a sign."

"It's Henri's Place."

"Is that the actual name?"

"That's how everybody knows it. Does it matter if it's the actual name on the documents?"

"I ... don't know. I guess I'm just used to how things run in Salem. Everything there has a kitschy name. Witch's Brew. The Dark Cauldron. The Celtic. You know ... themed stuff."

"Is that the real Salem, though?" Toni looked legitimately curious. "When you go out to have fun in your town, do you go to those places?"

I hesitated and shrugged. "Honestly? The Witch's Brew is kind of fun, but only later at night, when the tourists go back to their hotels."

"Then that's your answer."

I was still puzzling things out when she led me inside the

bar. The wall of noise was deafening, and I cringed internally as I reared back. Toni, however, was in her element.

"There's my girl," someone sang out from behind the bar. There, a short man with a healthy midsection held out his arms toward Toni. "How is my favorite niece?"

"I think you say that to all your nieces, Uncle Henri," Toni replied as she leaned over the bar to hug him. "I'm good."

She motioned for me to move forward, which I did reluctantly. I felt out of place in the homey environment, which I knew was my hang-up, and couldn't quite shed my discomfort.

"This is Rowan. She's from Salem and just started working at the store."

"Really?" Henri's scrutinizing eyes shifted to me as he released his niece. "Salem, huh?"

I did my best not to appear too uncomfortable. "I'm afraid so." I held out my hands. "It's nice to meet you. This is a lovely place."

Henri blinked several times, then shook his head, a chuckle escaping. "Northerners."

Toni shot him a chiding look. "Leave her alone."

"Did I say anything?" Henri held up a hand and then flicked his eyes back to me. "Honey, if you want to fit in around these parts, you won't say anything is lovely. I happen to know my place isn't lovely. There's no reason to pretend otherwise."

"Seriously?" I didn't back down. "Everybody here obviously knows each other, adores each other, and the place is packed to the brim. How is that not lovely?"

The challenge clearly threw Henri for a loop because he moved his jaw left and right before responding. "I guess you have a point," he said finally.

Toni chuckled. "Don't be mean to her," she chided. "She's new and still getting the lay of the land. This is her first time out of the French Quarter. You should be nicer. Otherwise, she'll never leave the French Quarter again."

"Yeah, yeah, yeah." Henri waved a hand dismissively. "What will it be? Your first drink here is always on the house."

"Oh." I was caught off guard. "Um..."

"Try the Sazerac," Toni suggested. "You'll like it."

I had no idea if that was true. Since I was out of my element, however, I nodded. "I'll try the Sazerac."

Henri winked at me. "Good choice. I'll bring your drinks around when they're done. Grab a table."

Toni led me to the right, where a large rectangular table was already overflowing with drinkers. There, she proceeded to hug and kiss every single person as we made our way down the line. "This is Aunt Margie. That's my cousin Cole. He works at the aquarium and has a fish fetish. That's my cousin Lottie. She's looking for a man, and if she believes you're after the same man, she bites."

As she rattled off the names, I nodded, knowing I would never remember them all ... although the fish fetish made me curious. By the time we sat, I was exhausted. Henri pressed a drink into my hand ten seconds later and watched me expectantly as I studied it.

"What's in this?" I probably should've voiced the question before ordering, but it was only occurring to me right then, as the strong scent of liquor invaded my olfactory senses.

"Does it matter?" Henri watched me closely, seeming to wait for an answer that would reaffirm his initial assessment of me.

"Nope." I sipped the drink, doing my best not to sputter. It was strong. I was a White Claw girl, something I couldn't admit in New Orleans. I didn't deal with liquor all that often. I knew that if I wanted to fit in there, however, I wouldn't have a choice. "Awesome." I shot him a thumbs-up.

Henri stared at my hand for a full beat then burst out

laughing. "I just love it when you bring new friends here, Toni," he said. "You never disappoint."

"What did I say?" Toni's expression was stern. "She's new. Give her a break. Try to think how you would want to be treated if you visited Salem."

"Like that's going to happen." Henri made a face. "I have no interest in going north."

"I'm pretty sure you don't have any interest in going south, either."

"That's true." Henri's grin was quick and light. "Why would I ever leave paradise?" He ruffled Toni's hair, which clearly irritated her, then his eyes flicked to the door. "Well, if it isn't another one of your strays. I haven't seen this one in at least six months. I was starting to think he'd fallen off the face of the earth."

Curious, I angled myself to look at the door. The face I found there, the one beaming as the man shook hands with several people sitting at the bar, was a familiar one.

"Jasper," I said automatically.

Toni's gaze landed on me before drifting over to him. "That would be him," she agreed. She was thoughtful when she looked back at me. "You remember his name?"

"Oh, well..." I'd failed to inform her of our other interactions though I couldn't have said why.

Mentioning that he'd walked me home would've felt weird, and even weirder to bring up the incident at the library although that was because I didn't want to tell her what I was doing at the library in the first place.

"Oh, there's my new favorite girl," Jasper trilled when he saw me. His grin was wide and charming. "I haven't seen you since this afternoon, and I've been looking. I was starting to go through withdrawal."

I didn't look at Toni. I could feel her staring at me,

though, and I was grateful for the dim lighting that hid the shade of red I was certainly turning.

"You saw each other this afternoon?" Toni asked as Jasper hugged Henri, the two men exchanging what looked to be amusing words, given the smiles on both of their faces.

"I ran into him when I was leaving the library," I replied, grasping for a story that wouldn't make me sound like a crazy person. "I wanted to do some reading. I like history. He was there with his girlfriend when I was leaving."

"Girlfriend?" Toni screwed up her face into a dubious expression. "Since when do you have a girlfriend?" she demanded of Jasper as he joined us at the table.

"Oh, I don't do girlfriends," Jasper replied with a laugh. "Who said I had a girlfriend?"

Toni jerked her thumb at me.

"Savannah," I insisted, hating how shrill my voice sounded. The music was loud enough that I hoped it would blunt the edges of my sharp response.

"Savannah Morton?" Toni rolled her eyes. "Are you messing around with her? Seriously?" She gave Jasper a dirty look. "Why would you possibly be hanging with her?"

Jasper offered a nonchalant shrug. "She's not so bad."

"She's a walking billboard for chlamydia."

"Yes, but that's one of the good venereal diseases," he said as Henri delivered him a drink. "You can knock it right out with a dose of penicillin. You can't hold the chlamydia against her. That's judgmental and mean."

"In my world, chlamydia is not a thing," Toni argued.

Jasper pressed a finger into her cheek. "We're not all lucky enough to be lesbians, my little voodoo queen."

Toni slapped his hand away, but I didn't miss the smile curving her lips. Jasper clearly irritated her, but in a brotherly way. She was genuinely fond of him.

"You'd better get yourself over to the clinic if you don't

want to go crazy," she said. "Chlamydia drives you crazy, right?"

"That would be syphilis."

"You know way too much about VD." Toni shook her head. "Remember what I told you," she told me. "He's fine to look at, but don't touch unless you want your lady parts to grow mold."

"No lady parts ever grow moldy when I'm around," Jasper countered. "I'm gifted in that department."

"You're a tool." Toni lightly cuffed the back of his head. "What are you even doing over in this part of town? I thought you were trolling Bourbon Street for conquests these days. That's what Arnie Lenox told me."

"Arnie Lenox is a moron," Jasper replied. "All that glue sniffing he did when we were in elementary school has come back to haunt him. He can't even cross the street without getting hit by a car these days. It's happened twice in the last three months."

"I heard he was doing that to make money," Toni argued. "He offers to take a payout from the drivers, so they don't have to turn it over to their insurance."

"And you somehow think that makes him smarter?" Jasper drawled.

"I can see your point." Toni huffed out an annoyed growl. "You still haven't answered me. What are you doing in my neck of the woods?"

"Taking a break," Jasper replied simply. His gaze had wandered to the band on the small stage. "Not every night needs to be a party night. Sometimes, I just like to relax." He winked at me when he said it.

Toni's gaze briefly drifted to me as if she was suspicious, then she relaxed in her chair. "It's nice you still come around. Uncle Henri likes you even though you got caught with Cousin Ally in the back room that one time when we were in college."

Jasper was the picture of innocence. "Hey, she chased me."

"I didn't see you running too hard."

"That room is small. I would've smacked into a wall. This face is too handsome to get marred for life."

"If you say so."

Jasper slid her a sidelong look and patted her shoulder. "Try to unclench. I know family is difficult, but your family is mostly okay. You're lucky to have them. I would trade my Aunt Irma for ten Cousin Allys."

"Your Aunt Irma is worse than the hurricane that had her name."

"Right? Now you know why I like hanging out here."

"If you say so."

Toni's eyes were back on me, and avoiding her stare was difficult. When I did, I accidentally snagged gazes with Jasper, who was watching me with overt interest. I didn't know what to say to either of them, so I focused on the music.

The night had taken a turn I wasn't expecting. I had no idea how things would work out in the end.

"GOOD TIMES." JASPER STOPPED AT THE bar long enough to hug Henri once the band was finished and the crowd started thinning out. "There's a reason I like coming here. You always deliver."

"You come here when you need to rest your man parts," Henri shot back. "Don't pretend I don't know what you're doing. You only visit when you've had enough of your own games and need a mental break. Then you disappear for weeks, sometimes months, at a time."

"You make me sound like a dog," Jasper complained.

"Is that the wrong comparison?"

"Oh, I'm hurt." Jasper mock clutched at his heart. "And here I thought I was your favorite."

"My favorite what?"

"Whatever category I slide into for you."

"Well, I guess you're not my least favorite."

Jasper winked, then turned his attention to me. Toni was busy saying goodbye to her relatives, and I was debating the best way to get home.

"Did you enjoy your first night of real jazz?" he asked.

"It was great." After two Sazeracs, my cheeks felt as if they were on fire. I was feeling a little buzzed too. That didn't bode well for the long walk ahead of me. "Do you think I can get an Uber out here?" I was already thinking ahead.

"It's only a twenty-minute walk from here to your place," Jasper pointed out.

"Yeah, but I'm not sure it's safe. I'm a little ... woo-hoo." I twirled a finger near my head. "Those drinks packed more of a punch than I was expecting."

"She's an amateur," Toni offered as she joined us. "I should've taken that into consideration when I brought her here. Now, I need to get her home."

"That's not your responsibility," I said automatically. "I can call an Uber."

"It's not safe for you to take an Uber alone from this neighborhood," Toni countered. "It's definitely not safe enough for you to walk the entire way alone."

"She doesn't have to walk alone," Jasper offered, catching me off guard. "I'll walk her home."

"Do you even know where she lives?" Toni asked dubiously. "That's quite the hike for you."

"I don't mind." Jasper's tone was light and airy. "I need to sober up a bit, myself. I'm plenty together enough to walk with her. By the time I get her home, I'll be sober."

Toni didn't look convinced, but she was a bit tipsy also.

"Okay, I'm going to trust you with her. No funny business, though." She jabbed a warning finger in his face. "I know all and see all ... and I will shrink your manhood to pretzel-and-raisin territory if you do anything weird."

Jasper involuntarily shielded his crotch area. "Oh, geez. Now, I'm going to have nightmares."

"Good. That way, I know you won't pull a you and try to get her in bed. That won't end well by the way. Just ... keep it in your pants."

Jasper shot her a dirty look. "You make it sound like I'm some uncontrollable sex fiend. Good grief."

"Aren't you?" Toni arched a challenging eyebrow. "Don't be a pain for once. Walk her home, and be a gentleman."

"I'm always a gentleman."

"Be way more gentlemanly than that."

Eight

"You don't have to walk me home."

Jasper's insistence on being gallant was making my stomach clench. On top of that, it made me uncomfortable. Toni had told me about his reputation for a reason. I had to think that reason was that she believed me susceptible to his charms. She didn't know about the curse, of course. Sure, she laughed when I mentioned it. She thought I was joking, though. I wanted to keep it that way.

What she couldn't know was that I'd hardened my heart against all men. That was the only option I had, given all that had happened.

"It's fine." Jasper waved off my discomfort and lifted his nose as we moved into the French Quarter, inhaling deeply. "Do you smell that?"

My forehead creased in confusion. "What?"

"That smell."

I sniffed the air. "I'm don't smell anything."

"Are you sure? New Orleans has a unique scent. No other place has it."

"Urine and beignets?"

He belted out a gregarious laugh. "You're funny."

"I was being serious."

"Only Bourbon Street smells like urine, and that's because of the tourists." The way he said it made me think he wasn't any fonder of the tourists than Toni.

"Bourbon Street definitely smells like urine. That's only before they clean it, though. After they clean it, it smells like something else."

"Have you seen the crews cleaning Bourbon Street in the morning?"

I nodded. "I like to watch. It's ingenious how they do it."

"How so?"

"Well, it's a system all in itself." I hadn't realized just how tipsy I was, but I took two tries to get onto the sidewalk after crossing the street. I opted not to comment on that, hoping Jasper wouldn't notice. "They're like modified golf carts, only bigger. Some of them have water tanks. Some have brushes. Then they have these big scoop things, almost more like huge windshield wipers, and they use them to collect all the trash."

"I've seen them," Jasper noted. "I'm surprised you have. They're out early."

"I can't sleep." I didn't realize I was going to say that until it was already out of my mouth.

"Just in New Orleans ... or ever?" Jasper looked legitimately interested.

"It's not just New Orleans."

"You're an insomniac?"

"I never used to be. It's more of a recent thing."

"Since your mother?" He phrased it as a question, but he had a knowing look on his face.

"I guess." I averted my gaze.

He had a way of looking at me that made me distinctly uncomfortable, as if he could see through me, which was disconcerting on a level I wasn't familiar with.

"You can talk to me about her, you know." Jasper's voice was soft. "You don't have to keep it all bottled up inside."

"I don't know what there is to talk about. I loved her. She was fine until she wasn't. When she got sick, she went fast. It was ... difficult. I'm happy she's no longer in pain, so there's that, at least. At the end, there was nothing but pain."

"I'm really sorry about that." He sounded sincere. "I mean ... really sorry. I can't imagine having to go through that."

I wanted to change the subject to something else, anything else. "I take it your parents are still alive?"

He nodded. "Yup. Jennifer and Jack Bentley are both alive and kicking ... and making my life more difficult than is necessary."

"How so?"

"They're just ... them." He laughed hollowly. "I love them—don't get me wrong—but they're very involved parents."

"There are worse things."

"Like not having parents. I get it. I don't wish them gone or anything. They're just ... overbearing."

"You work for them, right?" I found myself interested in his life although I couldn't say why. But focusing the conversation on him was a way to kill time as we cut our way across the French Quarter.

"Yup. They own Murder, Mayhem, and Magic Tours. Have you heard of them?"

"I have. I see the signs everywhere. You guys offer ghost tours, right?"

"And voodoo tours. The murder-and-mayhem tour is my favorite. That's the one I tend to lead although we all jump around and fill in for one another."

"Do your parents still run the tours?"

"They do about three tours a week. They like them. They're older now, though, and want to fill their time with other things. My mother is taking a pottery class. She's determined to open her own shop at some point. My father is a golf fanatic. They want to keep one foot in the door at the business but also do their own things."

"Isn't it better that they're not constantly looking over your shoulder? I would think that separation would be good."

"It would be. Unfortunately, I have a brother and sister who have both inherited my parents' busybody tendencies."

That made me laugh. "Well, we all inherit something from our parents."

"True."

"What did you get from them?"

"I got my mother's free spirit and my father's obsession with word puzzles."

"Oh, yeah? You're a fan of word puzzles, are you?"

"Yup. I order those books with like thirty different types of puzzles, and I spend at least an hour a day working on them. That's my quiet time."

That was something I had trouble picturing, yet it made sense in a weird way. We all had something we liked to focus on alone each day. That was his thing. Weirdly enough, it was one of my things too. "I have a bunch of those books. When I can't sleep, which is always, now, I spend an hour in bed doing them before I take off to start walking."

His gaze was keen as it moved onto me. "Why can't you sleep, Rowan?"

"I don't know. I just ... can't." I held out my hands and practically tripped over my own feet when I upset my balance.

Jasper caught me before I could fall into a nearby building. "Slow down there, honey bear," he drawled with a flirty grin.

I was starting to understand that was his default expression, which wasn't necessarily pointed at me. That made sense because he was a tour guide. Flirting would mean more tips.

"There's no rush to get home," he said.

"Sorry." I was sheepish. "My feet feel heavy."

"That's probably all the Sazerac you drank."

"Yeah, I should've stopped one cocktail before I did. That's always my downfall."

"In New Orleans, that's not considered a downfall. It's simply the way of the world."

"I can see that."

"You didn't answer my question, though," he prodded. "Why can't you sleep?"

"I don't know." That was the truth. "Before my mother died, I was someone who never thought about sleep. I was out seconds after my head hit the pillow, and I slept straight through for eight hours. It was like clockwork."

"But after, things changed."

"Yeah." I felt weird talking to him about that, yet it felt natural at the same time. *It's probably the alcohol*, I told myself. It always loosened my lips. *What else could it be?* "It happened the first night after she was gone. I fell asleep hard—a day spent crying will do that to you—and I assumed I would sleep for ten or twelve hours.

"We'd been sitting vigil by her bed for the last few days, and I was only sleeping in bursts," I continued. "Once she was gone, when she no longer needed me, I expected my body to demand a long bout of sleep."

"That's not what happened, though," he surmised.

"Nope." I shook my head. "I woke up at two o'clock and couldn't get back to sleep. I blamed the grief. It kept happening, though. Every night, I would fall asleep fine. Several hours later, I would bolt awake and never be able to get back to sleep. I took melatonin, of course, tried several other over-the-counter sleep aids. Nothing worked."

"Did you go to a doctor?"

I nodded. "Yes, and they said there was nothing wrong with me. They suggested I should see a therapist and talk things out."

"Did you?"

"I gave it a try. I spent six months talking to someone. It didn't help. By that time, the curse had completely taken over my life. I got distracted and wandered away from the therapy. It wasn't helping me sleep anyway."

I didn't realize what I'd let slip until I glanced at Jasper and found his brow furrowed in concentration. He looked as though he was trying to solve a puzzle. This time, though, it wasn't a word puzzle—it was me.

"What?" I asked defensively, one hand flying to my mouth. "Is there something on my face?"

He shook his head. "No, I'm just trying to ... um ... I have a question."

"I'm not getting naked for you," I replied automatically. "Toni warned me about your reputation. There's no way I'm going to be another notch on your bedpost."

He scowled. "Not *that*—although screw Toni. She gives me a hard time when it's not warranted. It's not like I'm a user. I'm just a free spirit."

"Like your mother."

"Yes. I'm young and not ready to settle down. I don't think that's such a terrible thing."

"Me either." That was the truth. "As long as you're upfront with your conquests, I don't see what the big deal is. I'm simply saying that I'm not going to be one of your conquests."

"Did I ask you to be?"

"No."

"Then stuff it." He wagged a chiding finger although amusement danced in his eyes, telling me he wasn't all that upset. "That's not what I was asking about."

I was drunk enough to be confused. "I forgot what we were even talking about," I said honestly.

He snorted. "And that's another reason I'm not going the route you suggest. You're not together enough to consent."

"I'm together enough to not consent. That's what I'm doing. I'm not consenting."

"Fair enough. I'm not pushing you."

The conversation lapsed into awkward silence, something I found unbearable. I was never comfortable with awkward silences. Since Jasper was a chatty guy, I expected that to be rectified ... and quickly.

Unfortunately, the silence dragged on too long, and I felt an overwhelming urge to fill it, so I did. "Besides, you wouldn't want to conquest me. Wait ... is that a thing? Can you conquest someone? That might not be proper grammar." I tilted my head to one side. "It doesn't sound like a thing, and yet it might be a thing. I'm going to let it go."

"Good idea," he said. "Why wouldn't I want to conquest you? Does it have something to do with the curse?"

I almost tripped again, but his hand on my arm stopped me.

"Stop doing that," he growled. "You're making me a nervous wreck. I would hate for you to scar that pretty face by smacking it into a brick wall."

"Oh, you think I'm pretty?" I batted my eyelashes.

"I think you're a lot of work," he countered. "I guess it's good you're pretty to go along with all that work. I'm being serious, though. What's the deal with the curse?"

That time, I didn't stumble. I was still confused. "How do you know about the curse?"

"You've mentioned it twice now."

"No way." I vehemently shook my head. "I would never."

"Well, you did. Watch your hair." He brushed my hair back from my sweaty face. "It's going to get in your eyes if you're not careful."

I tried to ignore the way my skin hummed when his fingers

brushed against me. "What were we talking about again?" I asked after another silence stretched for years.

"The curse, and I'm not going to forget you said it, so you might as well tell me." Jasper was firm. "Why do you think you're cursed?"

"Because I am." The answer was as simple as that.

"I grew up in New Orleans. Curses are a normal thing here. You don't have to be afraid to tell me. I want to hear about it."

"You don't." I focused on the ground so that I wouldn't trip. "It makes me sound pathetic."

"I'm sure it doesn't."

"Oh, but it does."

"Try me." He was demanding.

"Why do you care?"

"Because you intrigue me. There's something about you that makes me want to help you ... although I have no idea why."

For some reason, his words warmed me in a way that shouldn't have been possible, given my man fast. My mind wasn't exactly firing on enough cylinders to figure it out, however. "I don't need help."

"Oh, I know. You're strong and self-sufficient."

"I am."

"I get it. I still want to know about the curse."

"Are you sure?" I had zero good-judgment skills to fall back on right then. They'd all disappeared in a haze of Sazerac.

"Tell me."

I did just that. I didn't know what was coming, but everything spilled out. The bad dates were easy to explain. I'd grown adept at telling those stories, and for a laugh, at that. I didn't stop there. I also told him about my mother and what she'd said in the moments before her death.

"So, that's it," I said as we appeared in front of my apartment building. "I didn't believe her when she told me, thought she was delirious from the pain meds, but I'm well and truly cursed."

Jasper's only initial response was to stand in front of me and blink.

"Thank you for walking me home," I said upon realizing he wasn't going to speak again. He likely thought I was a loon. Thankfully, I was too drunk to care. I wouldn't even remember the conversation in the morning. "I appreciate you going above and beyond to protect my virtue. Good day, sir." I offered up a saucy salute before turning to leave.

"Hold up." He grabbed my arm before I could walk away, his expression impossible to read as he searched my face.

"What?" I asked dumbly. "What are you looking at?"

"I was trying to decide if you were messing with me."

"About what?"

"The curse."

"Oh, I would never mess with anybody about the curse. It's too sad ... and pathetic ... and just so stupid." I sputtered out a laugh. "Seriously, how did this become my life? I'm freaking cursed. How does that even happen?"

"I don't know." His expression was impossible for me to read.

"Don't bother calling the men with white coats," I warned. "I'll lie and say there's no curse if they show up. I'm not an idiot, despite what the story I told you might suggest. I know it sounds ludicrous. There's no other explanation, though."

"It sounds like an ordeal," he hedged.

"Yup."

"I would like to help you."

"With what?"

"The curse."

"How are you going to help?"

"I'm not sure, although this is New Orleans. If we can't find a solution for a curse here, there's no solution to be found."

"That's why I'm here. I happen to agree."

"Good." Jasper brushed my hair away from my forehead again. He looked unbelievably intense. "Are you okay to make it up to your apartment alone?"

"Yup." I shot him a thumbs-up. "I'm A-OK."

His lips tilted up at the corners. "You're drunk as hell is what you are. I'm going to talk to Henri about the Sazerac. He needs to tone it down for the newbies."

"He doesn't care about that. He hates the tourists. He'll probably laugh when he hears how drunk I got."

"We all have issues with the tourists," Jasper hedged. "We don't hate them, though. We definitely don't hate you."

"Because I'm just a temporary transplant." I tapped the side of my head sagely. "I've got it."

"That, and you're too cute to hate. You are going to be hating yourself in the morning, though. You need to drink some water before bed, maybe take some Advil."

"I'm perfectly fine."

He didn't look convinced. "I'll check on you in the morning. What unit are you in?"

"I just told you that I'm immune to your charms," I reminded him. "There's no way I'm telling you my apartment number."

"I'll bring coffee and beignets in the morning when I check on you."

I chewed on my bottom lip, uncertain. "I do like beignets."

"I'm a charming houseguest," he added. "I promise I don't have designs on your virtue."

"That's probably good. With my track record, you'll find yourself on the FBI's Most Wanted list if you're not careful."

"I just want to help with the curse."

"Why?" The curiosity was too much for me to ignore. "Why would you possibly want to help? You don't even know me."

"It's another puzzle," he replied. "I love solving puzzles."

"Oh." I nodded. "That makes sense."

"There's no reason we can't have coffee and beignets when solving the puzzle. What unit are you in?"

"6F."

"Then I'll see you in the morning."

"Yup. Yup." I turned back toward the building, desperately needing to pass out. "Thanks for walking me home."

"No problem. I'll see you in a few hours."

"Maybe I'll sleep tonight. The Sazerac might be like a magical elixir."

"For your sake, I hope so."

I didn't glance over my shoulder as I walked. I wasn't coordinated enough. For some reason, I knew he watched me for the entire trek.

I took twice as long as normal to find my unit—I walked in the wrong direction twice—and when I made my way into the bedroom, I grabbed a pair of pajamas from the dresser, and promptly fell facedown onto the bed. I didn't get a glass of water. I didn't rummage in the bathroom for Advil. I just passed out ...and immediately forgot I'd told anybody about the curse.

That would come back to bite me, and sooner rather than later.

Nine

My head was pounding when I woke up the next morning, and the light filtering through the shades was bright enough to blind me. My stomach clearly thought my bed was a Tilt-A-Whirl on top of everything else, and I had to battle back three waves of nausea before I could even consider climbing out of bed.

Then another sort of pounding started.

"What in the hell?" I stomped to the apartment door, ready to dole out death and destruction to anyone who would dare make that much racket at such an early hour. When I yanked it open, I pasted my best do-you-want-to-die look on my face and came face to face with Jasper.

"Hello, sunshine," he drawled as he took in my mangled hair and puffy face. "Got dressed up for me, did you?"

I glanced down at my outfit, frowning when I realized I was in oversized flannel sleep pants—hey, they're a thing where cold winters are—and my Drink Up, Witches T-shirt. I didn't speak initially because I was having trouble finding the right words.

"Speechless, huh?" Jasper asked after a beat. "I have that effect on women. Don't get down on yourself for it."

I touched my tongue to my top lip and considered how I wanted to respond.

"You could've at least put on a bra," he added. "I mean ... that is considered polite when entertaining guests."

Mortified, I checked to see if he was right—by looking, not touching—and grimaced when I realized I was indeed sans bra. "What are you doing here?" I asked in a raspy voice when I finally found the strength to speak.

"Um ... I'm here to help you."

"Help me with what?"

He held up a takeout bag from Cafe Beignet, which was right around the corner. "Hangover food. I'll have you on your feet in no time."

"I'm on my feet." That was a dumb thing to say, but my mind wasn't firing on all cylinders. "How do you even know where I live?"

"I've walked you home multiple times now, including last night."

"Yeah, but that just tells you what building I'm in, not where I live."

"You told me what unit you lived in."

That's unlikely. "I don't tell strangers where I live."

"I'm not a stranger. We're old friends now." He pinned me with a serious look. "Are you going to invite me in? There's a woman standing in an open doorway at the end of the hall, and she looks as if she wants to call the police."

"Mrs. Sanderson," I said. "She's on the building watch committee."

Jasper cocked an eyebrow. "The building watch committee?"

"It's like the neighborhood watch, only for the building."

"Ah. I understand." His expression told me he didn't, but

he clearly didn't care enough to press the issue. "I have a mocha latte and two full orders of beignets. It's guaranteed to chase that hangover away."

I was caught. I didn't particularly want to invite him in—I still had no idea how he'd found my unit—but the scent of the coffee and beignets were making my mouth water. Never in my life had I wanted something more than what he was offering right then.

"Fine." I held open the door and ushered him inside. "I want that coffee, though."

He smirked as he stepped into my inner sanctum, his eyes scanning everything in a few seconds. "This place is sterile," he announced as I ravenously dug into the bag, which I'd taken from him. "You don't live here."

I frowned as I shoved a powdered-sugar delight into my mouth, then proceeded to make one of my mother's top five don't-be-rude mistakes and talked with my mouth full. "I'm pretty sure I do. My bank account can back me up if you don't believe me. The rent is fairly steep."

Jasper's frown grew deeper. "That's not what I meant. It's just ... there's nothing of you here."

"I don't understand."

"Where's your favorite blanket?"

"I don't have a favorite blanket."

"Everybody has a favorite blanket. Mine is fuzzy and has little bears on it."

I was still slow, the hangover essentially making me crawl through quicksand to keep up with him, but the bear thing was hard to picture. "You have a fuzzy blanket with bears on it?"

"Yes." Jasper didn't look bothered as he bobbed his head. "My mother got it for me on my seventh birthday. The bears are wearing hats."

"So it's like a safety blanket."

"See, you're trying to insult me, but it doesn't work. I happen to love my blanket, and I'm secure enough to admit I want it with me when I'm feeling sick. You have no blanket, though."

"No." I shook my head as I sipped the latte. "I was never much of a blanket person. My mother did get me an electric blanket when I was thirteen, but it lasted exactly three days before it caught fire and stank up the entire house."

"Wow. You really are cursed."

I froze as I reached for another beignet. "What now?" I asked when I could form words. *Just like me to let something slip when drunk.* I had a big mouth when liquor was involved, and I wasn't ashamed to admit it. Well, mostly.

Okay, I was totally ashamed of how big my mouth was. That was neither here nor there, though. I had bigger problems at present.

"Your curse," Jasper replied, not missing a beat.

"What curse?"

His eyes narrowed, telling me he was thinking things through. "The one where you date the worst guys in the world and it always ends badly for them and you," he said finally. "I personally like how many guys you've dated who have had the cops searching for them, but that's not important right now. What is important is that I'm going to help you end the curse."

I was so lost that I didn't know what to do. I chose my words carefully. "Um ... I think you're mistaken."

"No, I'm not. You told me all about the curse last night when we were walking home."

Seriously, Sazerac is the drink of the devil. *I'm never having it again.* I had to find a way out of this situation. He probably thought I was a loon. He'd most likely called in reinforcements—ones wearing white coats and carrying straitjackets—and they were gearing up that very second to burst through my door.

"Then I was mistaken," I offered. "Clearly, I'm an idiot when drunk. I never should've said that stuff to you. I apologize ... and it won't happen again." It was a dismissal, plain and simple.

Jasper didn't get up to leave. Instead, he continued staring at me.

"What?" I demanded after several seconds, my erratically beating heart the only sound I could make out.

"I'm just trying to figure you out," he replied.

"I'm clearly a bad drunk. There's nothing else to figure out."

He snorted. "Right."

"It's true." I felt defensive and exposed and maybe a little sick again, given the way I'd inhaled the beignets. That was not a good combination.

"While I think it's entirely possible someone would make up a story like that—I grew up in New Orleans, and that's not even the nuttiest thing I've heard today—I don't think you're the sort of person who would make up something like that for attention. You were deadly serious last night."

"I was drunk and stupid."

"And yet still serious." His eyes were contemplative. "I don't want to tell you your business."

"Then don't."

He barreled forward. "But I'm uniquely qualified to help you."

I was officially exasperated. "I don't need help."

"You're cursed. Of course you need help."

"I was drunk when I said that."

"True, but I think you meant it." His eyes softened. "I'm not messing with you. I really do want to help. You can trust me. I mean... I brought you the nectar and ambrosia of the gods to cure your hangover. That should be some sort of indication of who you're dealing with."

I wanted to crawl into a hole and die, but I was also intrigued. "The nectar and ambrosia of the gods?" I demanded finally. "Who says things like that?"

He chuckled. "My sister. She reads this urban fantasy angel stuff. There's a bunch of sex thrown in there to go along with the mythology. That's the stuff she really likes, but she'll never admit it. Because of her, I know things."

At a loss, I leaned back on the couch and pinched the bridge of my nose. "Most people think I'm crazy. They don't believe in curses."

"I'm not most people."

"You most definitely aren't," I agreed. "The thing is, I don't think I can talk about this."

"You talked about it last night."

"Again, I was drunk ... something I will not be doing again for the rest of my life."

Jasper's chuckle was like a warm blanket. There were no bears on it, but that didn't make it any less divine. "Ah, the morning-after 'I'm never drinking again' pledge. I'm a big fan. I've made it myself a time or two ... or ten. You'll get over that eventually."

"I'm still not sure why you're here," I admitted as I grabbed another beignet. Despite my mortification—which was profound—I found myself intrigued by his presence. "Why do you want to help me?"

"I'm a helpful guy."

"Why really?"

He worked his jaw, then held out his hands. "I don't know that I have an answer sufficient to your question."

"Then give me an insufficient one."

"I find you fascinating."

"Oh, I'm not going to be another notch on your bedpost,"

I growled. "I'm on a man fast, and that's not changing for the foreseeable future."

He smirked. "A man fast?"

"That's what I said. You heard the stories. At least you said you did. If you were me, would you trust your instincts with men, given the crapstorm I've been trapped in over the course of the past year?"

"Those stories were pretty out there," he replied. "I think you're being too hard on yourself, though. Anybody can pick a dud here or there. I know I have."

"Oh, really?" I cocked an eyebrow. "Name one dud you've picked that's equal to the duds I've picked."

He screwed up his face in concentration, giving me the impression he was really thinking it out. After a few seconds, he snapped his fingers. "Chrissy Dunlap."

When he didn't expand, I arched an eyebrow. "Who is Chrissy Dunlap?"

"She's this girl I dated about three years ago."

"Dated or bent over a bench in Jackson Square after hours of drinking?"

His lips quirked. "First off, Jackson Square is locked after dark. There is no bending people over benches. Secondly, don't believe everything Toni tells you. I have a reputation—I would never say otherwise—but that doesn't necessarily mean the reputation is earned."

I didn't believe that for a second. "What did Chrissy Dunlap do to you that was so terrible?" I asked, redirecting the conversation to something that was at least entertaining.

"She pretended to be pregnant when I broke up with her."

That wasn't the response I was expecting. "Seriously?"

"Seriously." He bobbed his head. "We spent three months together. I genuinely liked her at first and then found our goals in life didn't mesh."

"Meaning?"

"Meaning that I wasn't ready to settle down. She told me four weeks in that she expected a ring by our six-month anniversary. I spent the next two months trying to break up with her."

"Trying?"

"Yes, she wouldn't accept the breakup. I told her it was over. She cried. Then she would stalk me to wherever she figured I was hanging out that night. If I happened to be talking to a woman, she would corner her and tell her how I was a heartbreaker who used women. If that didn't work, she would tell them she was pregnant."

"She sounds deranged." I rested my feet on the coffee table.

"Oh, she was a little something special. She even went to visit my parents to tell them I'd gotten her pregnant and was refusing to take care of her and the baby. That is not the sort of thing that goes over well in my family. We're responsible folks."

I tapped my bottom lip and considered the story. "That's rough," I said finally. "It sounds like she had legit mental issues, though. I don't want to make excuses for her, but that's the type of woman who needs medication."

"It certainly is." Jasper bobbed his head. "I still know the pain of dating a dud. That's what I'm trying to point out."

"While I appreciate the story, I still don't understand why you want to help me on this." I opted for honesty. "I mean ... you don't even know me."

"I know you."

"Not well."

He shrugged. "I happen to like a good hard-luck case, and that's exactly what you are. Your luck is the worst if even a quarter of those stories you were telling last night were true."

"I have no idea what stories I told you, but there was no reason to embellish, so I doubt I did. They're all true."

"Well, then I definitely want to help you. Besides, I can use your curse story when running a tour. It needs a happy ending before I can tell the story, though."

I balked. "I don't want people knowing about this."

"I won't use your real name. Besides, I thought the plan was to find someone to lift the curse and then go home. You won't even know who is talking about you because you won't be here."

He wasn't wrong. Still, the notion of people whispering my name and laughing—even long after I was gone—made me feel icky. "I want a fake name, and I get to pick it if you're going to use my story."

He chuckled. "I think that can be arranged."

"Fine." I didn't see that I had much of a choice because Jasper struck me as the sort of guy who wasn't going to give up under any circumstances. "You can help me solve my problem. I mean ... you know the area, right? You know the ins and outs of finding people. It's your city. You might be able to actually help."

"Oh, your faith in me is touching." He clutched at his heart in mockery.

"Don't push it," I warned. "I can only put up with so much today, and I'm already at my limit."

"Yes, your hair suggests that you passed your limit some time ago."

I instinctively reached up to touch my hair and frowned. I'd forgotten what state I'd been in when he knocked on the door. "I guess that's my cue to take a shower. I mean... I'm assuming you want to start looking for ways to end my curse today."

"I'm thinking that's the best way to go," he agreed. "I thought we would start at one of the older cemeteries. We can turn it into a learning experience for you as we look."

I was confused. "A learning experience?"

He nodded. "New Orleans has a rich history. There's no reason I can't introduce you to that history while also working to solve your problem."

"But ... why?"

"Why not?"

I didn't have an answer for such a simple question. "I'll get showered and changed." I pushed myself to my feet. "Don't go through my stuff when I'm getting ready. I hate it when people invade my personal space."

"I have no intention of going through your stuff, mostly because you have no stuff. Seriously, this place is stark."

"It's an apartment," I shot back as I padded down the hallway. "I have all the stuff I need."

"Yeah, I'm thinking we might hit up a few shops when we're out today too," he said. "I mean ... a splash of color on the walls wouldn't kill you."

"Whatever floats your boat. I'm too hungover to argue."

"That's the spirit."

I paused with a hand on the bathroom door. "Just be forewarned, I'm serious about the man fast. If you think this is a way to get me to change my mind, it's not going to happen."

"Believe it or not, I can control my hormones. I'm here to help you with the curse. Nothing more."

I wanted to believe him, so I nodded. "I'll be ready in twenty minutes."

"I'll be waiting."

Ten

"How are we feeling?" Jasper was all smiles as he led me through the streets.

I had no idea where we were going. He seemed to know, which was all that mattered.

"I think I'm going to make it." I sipped my coffee—we'd stopped at another spot along the way—and studied the area. I couldn't remember ever being there before, but that didn't mean anything. I hadn't been in New Orleans overly long.

"Good. I would hate to have to deal with the coroner on top of everything else." He offered up a wink. "So, I've been giving it a great deal of thought, and I have an idea for where we can start."

He walked up to a machine and fed his credit card into its slot. It looked like an ATM but clearly wasn't. A quick look at our location filled me with worry. "Are we getting on a bus? I don't have time for that. I have to be at work at one."

"No bus. Better." His grin was wide as he directed me toward a bench. "Have you been on the streetcars yet?"

Despite myself, I found I was intrigued. "No. I've seen

them on the news and stuff, in all the photos people post when visiting. I didn't even know where to find them."

"Well, here you go." Jasper pointed at the tracks that veered off in different directions. "We're going to the Garden District. Have you been there yet?"

I shook my head and sipped. "No. It's supposed to be cool, though."

"It's very cool. The Garden District is one of my favorite places in the city. Well, other than the French Quarter. I'm also a big fan of Bywater."

"What's in Bywater?"

"Some of the coolest street art you've ever seen. They graffiti the buildings and sidewalks. Heck, they paint the roads. It's like an entirely different world over there."

"So you're basically saying you get off on graffiti."

He smirked. "It's not graffiti. It's art."

"In Boston, it's called graffiti."

"It's different in Bywater. I promise. I'll show you."

"If you say so." I rubbed a hand over my shorts. Early in the day, the heat was already starting to build, and I was feeling sweaty. "What do you think we're going to find in the Garden District?"

"A cemetery."

"I'm no expert, but I don't think a dead person is going to help me break the curse. I need someone who is alive."

"Oh, are you sure?" Sarcasm was a weapon he wielded easily. "I never would've guessed that was the case." He flicked my ear as though we were old friends, earning a scowl. "This curse has been in place a long time, right?"

I nodded. "According to my mother."

"It's entirely possible that the woman who supposedly cursed your family is dead. That doesn't mean we can't find a solution."

"You say 'supposedly' as if you don't believe me." My

voice was laced with accusation. "I didn't ask for your help. I can do this on my own."

"No, you can't. Also, I didn't say I didn't believe you. It's just, well, in the Quarter, everybody says they're cursed. Very few people actually are. I didn't mean to say you weren't cursed."

"That's good because I am."

"Of course you are."

I slid him a sidelong look. "Just out of curiosity, why do you believe I'm cursed if you doubt everybody else?"

He shrugged. "You're a very pragmatic person. You wouldn't say you're cursed if you're not. You also don't tend to jump to random conclusions, and last night aside, you don't tend to get drunk on a nightly basis as far as I can tell."

"Never again," I growled darkly. "Sazerac is clearly the devil's nectar."

He smirked. "You're an amateur in a professional milieu. You'll adjust. As for the curse, let's just say that you've piqued my interest."

"Meaning?"

"Meaning I've always wanted to break a curse. Think how well that will go over on my tours."

I thought that made sense—kind of. "Well, at least you have a reason."

"Definitely." Jasper inclined his head toward an incoming streetcar. "That's ours. Are you ready to see something fantastic?"

Even though my hangover was still hanging on, I found myself excited. "I have always wanted to see the Garden District, even before I knew I was coming here. I've seen it depicted in movies, and it's fabulous."

"It's even better in person. Trust me." He held out a hand. "At the very least, even if we don't find anything, we'll have a fun adventure to cure your hangover before your shift at the store."

He had a point. "Okay." I placed my hand in his. "I really am cursed, though. You need to remember your boundaries if you don't want to end up in jail or something. It will be bad."

"Duly noted. I will totally remember my boundaries."

"It's for your safety."

"And I'm nothing if not obsessed with my own safety."

He was being sarcastic again. I didn't care.

"Show me something magical," I said.

"Rowan, prepare to be amazed."

"IT'S CLOSED."

I couldn't contain my disappointment when we approached a wrought-iron gate on Coliseum Street and found the sign waiting for us. Jasper had been right about the ride on the streetcar. It had been fun while also allowing me to see parts of the city I'd yet to lay eyes on. The fact that we couldn't actually see the cemetery after all the buildup was a blow, however.

Jasper's smirk never diminished as he reached into his pocket and came back with a key ring, which he jangled enticingly. "You're forgetting one thing."

"What's that?"

"I give tours. That means our tour company has a key. I grabbed it before leaving this morning."

"Oh." I was taken aback. "I guess I didn't realize you had keys to the cemeteries."

"We give many different kinds of tours." He searched through the keys until he found the one he was looking for and fitted it into the lock. "I prefer the French Quarter tours. They're more my speed because they normally include bar visits, and this is the sort of city where the tourists want their guides to drink with them. My sister likes the cemetery tours, though, and largely sticks to them."

"Huh." I watched as he pushed open the door and inclined his head. "So ... we're just allowed to wander around without supervision?"

He leaned close, perhaps too close as I could feel his breath on my face. "Technically, I'm your supervision."

I blinked twice, then shook my head, hating that my suddenly traitorous heart was excited at his proximity. "That is a terrifying thought."

"Totally." He pulled back. "Come on."

I was still leery when I entered. What we were doing felt illicit somehow. The second I was inside the walls and got a gander at what we had all to ourselves for the morning, however, all the reservations I was feeling disappeared in an instant. "Oh, holy... Wow."

He chuckled as he locked the gate behind us, giving it a good tug to make sure it had latched. "The cemeteries here live up to the hype. This happens to be my favorite one for several reasons."

"Are you going to give me a history lesson?"

"Do you want the whole spiel?"

I nodded.

"Okay, then." He started down the sidewalk, picking a leisurely pace. "This is Lafayette Cemetery Number One. It was founded in 1833 and was inside what was once the City of Lafayette. It's still in use today and is notable for the architecture and the layout, which is in a cruciform pattern for funeral processions."

My eyebrows drew together. "Cruciform?"

"Like the crucifixion. It's a cross."

I angled my head to look. "Huh."

His smile grew larger. "Do you watch a lot of movies?"

"Kind of," I hedged. "I don't know that I would watch the sort of movie that might be filmed here, though."

"*The Vampire Diaries*?"

"I've seen a few episodes."

"There were some filmed here, as well as the movie *Double Jeopardy* with Ashley Judd and *Interview with the Vampire*."

"Oh, cool." I added a little skip to my step as I looked around. The mausoleums were unbelievable, and some of the statues spotting the area as decorations took my breath away. "That is really neat."

"It is. This is one of my favorite cemeteries."

"What's your absolute favorite cemetery?"

"That would be St. Louis Cemetery Number One. That's the oldest and most famous cemetery, and it's also where Marie Laveau was supposedly laid to rest as well as Delphine LaLaurie ... although that depends on which legend you believe. Other people believe she was buried in Europe. My favorite thing in the cemetery is this garish pyramid that Nicolas Cage bought to be his final resting place."

That sounded fantastic. "How come we're not visiting that cemetery?"

"Because this cemetery has something that one doesn't. If we can't find answers here, I have every intention of taking you over there on another day. Heck, even if we do find answers here, I'll take you over there. I have no doubt that you'll fall in love regardless." He definitely had my attention.

"What does this cemetery have that the others don't?"

"I think you need to see it." He grabbed my hand. It was a friendly gesture rather than a romantic one, yet a little jolt ran through me, sort of a current of emotion I couldn't put a name to. If he felt the same thing, he didn't show it. "Come on."

The cemetery was bigger than I'd envisioned, but when we finally got to our destination and I saw what had caused him to bring me here, my heart skipped a beat. I read the huge plaque on the front of the biggest mausoleum in the grouping. "Michel. That's the name my mother said."

Jasper bobbed his head. "I remembered this mausoleum in the middle of the night. It woke me from a dead sleep."

"How come?" I moved closer, entranced.

"Probably because you had just told me your grand tale of being cursed."

I was rueful. "How hard did you laugh on your way home?"

"I didn't laugh."

"Oh, come on." Even though it was happening to me, I still found the situation funny. "If I were in your position, I totally would've laughed."

"Well, I didn't." He looked sincere. "I don't know you very well, Rowan, but you look as if you have the weight of the world on your shoulders sometimes. I think it's more than a curse, but you're clearly serious about this ... and I want to help you if I can."

I chewed on my bottom lip as I turned back toward the mausoleum. "I didn't believe my mother when she told me." That was hard to admit. "She was dying and in so much pain at the end. I thought it was the medication."

"I can see that."

"I asked my aunt about it after the fact. She said Mom was serious. I laughed as if it was the funniest thing I'd ever heard. She never did, though. It wasn't until several months later, when I recognized the pattern as my life started falling apart, that it occurred to me it might be real."

"And what did your aunt say then?"

"She didn't say all that much. She just said that she didn't believe when she was my age either. She thought my grandmother was just looking for attention. I never knew my grandmother—she died before I was born, and I've only heard stories—so it didn't register either way whether it was true."

"But now you believe."

"Now I believe." I dragged my eyes to his handsome face and found nothing but earnest sympathy waiting for me. I'd expected to find mischief, maybe even a little bit of amusement at my expense. That wasn't present, though. "Do you think I'm crazy?"

He shook his head. "No. I think you're unbelievably strong."

"That doesn't mean I'm not crazy. Abraham Lincoln was strong, and people still thought he was crazy, what with the ghosts he claimed to see and stuff."

Jasper cracked a smile. "Yes, well, the word 'crazy' can be used in a myriad of ways. In this particular instance, I don't think you're crazy. All those stories you told... They're too much for one person to bear. So even if you're the only person who believes in the curse, at the very least, it's true for you."

I nodded as I stared at the crypt again. "Do you think she's in there?"

"I think we have a name," he cautioned. "Michel is going to be a common name in this city. We can't even use voodoo to narrow it down because it's going to be a common name in voodoo circles as well."

"Plus, we don't even know if it's Michelle the girl's name or Michel the surname that we're looking for."

"There's that, but even in her weakened state, I have to think your mother was pointing you toward something you could track. That makes me think it's the surname."

"Are you just saying that because it's going to be an impossible task if it's the female name?"

"No. I choose to have hope." He tapped the end of my nose in a playful manner. "Michel is a common name. We're not talking millions of people, though. If we narrow the time period to when your grandmother would've been alive—perhaps focusing on the years between her sixteenth and forty-fifth birthdays—then it might not be as difficult as we're envisioning to narrow down the Michel we're looking for."

I brightened considerably. "I hadn't even thought about that part of it. You're smart."

"I'm a genius," he readily agreed. "I figured we would start with the people in this crypt."

"Just out of curiosity, if Michel is such a common name, why would you focus on this crypt? I mean ... couldn't the Michel we're looking for be in any cemetery?"

"Yes, but I wasn't lying when I said this cemetery had something unique." He tugged lightly on my hand and pulled me to the right. "Do you see that there?" He inclined his head toward a plaque on the wall.

I leaned closer. "It lists the names of the people in the crypt," I surmised. "Wouldn't there be records of that elsewhere too?"

"Yes, but it's not just the names that interested me. It's that symbol there. Can you see it?"

I had to squint to make out what he was indicating. "It looks like two small coffins flanking an altar with a cross," I said finally.

"Yeah. That is called a veve. It's a religious symbol that can be traced back to Africa, but it's especially steeped in Haitian Vodou lore. That particular veve belongs to Baron Samedi. He's the loa of the dead and the husband of Maman Brigitte."

"So the presence of this veve proves this particular family was into voodoo," I surmised.

"In the most simplistic of terms," he agreed. "I've always been fascinated by the loas. Some of them are a lot of fun. Baron Samedi was always my favorite. In addition to being the loa of the dead, he was also famous for being able to cure mortals of any disease or wound. Most importantly for us, however, he was also into black magic ... which involves hexes."

Realization dawned on me. "You think whoever this Michel person is might've been attracted to the loa stories."

"It makes sense, right?"

"Right." I bobbed my head. "How do we chase the information, though? Like ... how do we narrow it down?"

"I have an idea on that front too." Jasper pointed a charming grin at me. "I have a friend. He's very into genealogy, especially the genealogy of the Haitian immigrants in the area. He's Haitian himself and is working on a book. I think he might be able to help."

"How much do you think that will cost?" I was already doing the math in my head. "A genealogy expert can't be cheap."

Jasper shot me a narrow-eyed scowl. "I just said he's my friend. He won't want money."

"Oh, I don't feel right about that." I shook my head. "If he's going to help us, he should be rewarded for his time."

"You are so much work," Jasper growled under his breath. "I've got this covered. Have a little faith, huh? I won't lead you astray. This guy is my friend. I'll ask him if he can point us in the right direction. There's no harm in asking."

"I guess not." I was still uncomfortable asking someone I'd never met for a favor. Then something occurred to me. "This is a really good lead. Thank you for bringing me here."

"You're welcome." He squeezed my hand. "Come on. Let's take a wander around the rest of the cemetery while we're here. We'll take photos of the names on the plaque on our way out, but there's no reason you can't enjoy yourself for an hour and take a one-on-one tour of the rest of the place while you're here."

I nodded and grinned. "I would like that. I love a good

cemetery, and this one is so different from the ones we have up in Salem."

"So let's look around." He tugged me away from the mausoleum. "New Orleans is a place that proves there's beauty in death. Let's take a breather and enjoy that beauty."

I'd had worse offers. "Show me what you've got, Mr. Tour Guide."

"I thought you would never ask."

Eleven

Jasper walked me to Hex Appeal after I stopped at my apartment long enough to change for work. I'd told him that wasn't necessary, but he simply waved me off. We'd come up with a list of names to research, and he sent them off to his genealogy friend while waiting in the living room. He was all smiles as we set off across the French Quarter.

"I'll keep in touch," he promised as we turned onto the street that led to the store. "As soon as I know something, you'll know something."

Since my hangover was completely gone, my head clear, I recognized a need to say something. I struggled with what that should be, however, so much so that when I slowed my pace, he looked concerned.

"Are you feeling okay?" He pressed a hand to my forehead. "You're not sick, are you?"

"I'm not sick," I assured him. "The hangover is mostly gone and everything. It's just... I feel the need to tell you again that you don't have to help me. This is my thing. It doesn't have to be your thing."

Jasper's expression was hard to read. "And I told you that I want to help."

"But you have so many things to do, so many women to enthrall."

He smirked. "If I can come up with a genuine curse story for my tour, it will all be worth it."

I didn't believe him. He was volunteering his time for other reasons. I didn't call him out, though. That seemed unnecessary.

"Well, thanks anyway. I expect you to change my name if you use my story. I already told you that, right? I don't want to be forever known as the pitiful witch from Salem who brought countless men to their knees—so they could be cuffed—through a voodoo curse. I'm thinking that will ruin my rep, should I ever want to start dating again."

"Oh, you'll start dating again." Jasper sounded sure of himself. "This is just a momentary blip."

"Here's hoping." I gave him a little salute and then started for the store's front door. "Thanks again."

"Yeah. Just one more thing." He snagged my wrist lightly to get me to stop. "I know you're embarrassed to tell the truth to people because ... well ... it's so very weird."

"Oh, why would it be embarrassing to tell people I'm cursed? That's just crazy talk."

He smirked. "I want to remind you that you're in New Orleans." He inclined his head toward Hex Appeal. "Curses are part of the deal here. I'm guessing you haven't been lucky enough to stumble across one of the homeless people who remove curses for money. They've got an entire racket going. Nobody will laugh at you if you tell the truth."

I arched a dubious eyebrow. "Nobody?"

"Okay, well, most people," he said. "The woman in there right now... She's going to be one of the people who listens."

I knew what he was getting at, and strangely enough, I

understood what he wanted. "She's already given me a job," I pointed out. "I don't think unloading the rest of my problems on her is exactly fair. I mean ... she's dealing with her own set of problems. She's taking over a store for her mother. That's stressful in and of itself."

His gaze appraised me. "That would've been you if your mother had survived," he surmised. "You would've had to take over for her at some point."

"Yeah. I was dreading that." My heart constricted for reasons I couldn't identify. "Now, I don't have to worry about that. My aunt is easygoing when it comes to store stuff."

He nodded, pressing his lips together. A lot seemed to be going on beneath his tough guy exterior, but he kept that in check. "Toni will be the best friend you've ever had if you let her. She's tough as nails and has always been comfortable in her own skin. That's why people are drawn to her."

"That doesn't mean she's open to other people dumping all their problems on her."

"No, but in this case, I don't think your problems are as big as you think they are. Sure, they're big to you, but nobody else feels the weight of them like you do."

"Tell that to the guys doing time."

His lips quirked. "I guess it's fair to say that it's rough for them," he hedged. "You didn't cause them to go to jail, however. You just drew guys who were already destined for jail to you. Do you see the distinction?"

"Yes, but I'm still guessing they blame me."

"That's on them." Jasper was firm. "Just ... consider what I said. Toni is an amazing person. She'll help you, and you don't have to make yourself small in the process."

I was taken aback. "What do you mean?"

"I get the feeling that you've gone your entire life without making a ripple. You're the type of person who wants to make things easier for everybody else, including your mother and aunt. That's not necessary. You don't have to make yourself smaller than you are. Just be you."

That was the first time anybody—including my mother—had ever called me on my tendency to make sure I wasn't responsible for the emotional tsunami of others when it made landfall.

"I'll think about it," I said finally, wondering what else I was supposed to say. "I'm not sure I can bear the thought of burdening someone else with my problems."

"You had no problem burdening me."

"Yes, well, I blame the Sazerac."

His grin lit up his entire face. "It is the devil's drink."

"Totally." I waved at him as I climbed the stairs. "Thanks for everything. Again."

"It was fun. I'll make sure to get you to St. Louis Cemetery too. I guarantee you're going to fall in love with that one."

"That sounds fun." I was still smiling to myself when the door shut. Thankfully, except for Toni, the store was empty. "I'm not late, am I?" My eyes flitted to the clock on the wall to be certain.

"You're not late," she reassured me from behind the counter. She was going through a ledger, but curiosity lined her face as she focused on me. "I saw you through the window."

I was confused. "Doing what?"

"You weren't technically doing anything. I was more intrigued by who you were with than what you were doing."

Discomfort rolled through me. "You mean Jasper."

"Yeah. Um... I told you about him, right?" She looked pained. "I don't want to stick my nose in your business, and I certainly don't want to talk poorly about Jasper behind his back. The good news is that I tell Jasper to his face that he's a dog, so I'm not worried about that. The other stuff, though..."

"We're not doing what you think," I said as I moved to the

corner behind the counter to grab one of the logo aprons we wore as part of our uniforms. They were pocketed and allowed us to carry business cards and matchbooks to dole out during our shifts. "Like ... it's not a romantic thing."

"No?" Toni didn't look relieved. "What is it if it's not romantic?"

I shuffled from one foot to the other, my stomach squirming. "I might've let something slip to him last night when he walked me home from your uncle's bar. He was intrigued enough to show up with breakfast this morning. It's not a big deal, though."

"Oh no." Toni wagged a finger. "You can't say something that vague and expect me to let it go. What did you tell him?"

Jasper's words came roaring back to me, and I sighed. "You're going to think I'm crazy."

"Quite possibly." Toni bobbed her head and waited.

"Fine." I had no choice but to tell her. "I'm cursed."

"Yeah, I know. You have bleeding tragic taste in men. We really need to figure out a way for you to pick up on the red flags before you have sex with them. Sex just complicates matters."

"Oh, I didn't have sex with all of them," I said hurriedly. "Not even half of them, really."

"It was a joke." Toni rolled her eyes.

"Oh, right." I was really off my game and blamed the hangover. "Here's the thing. Um ... the thing is..." I licked my lips. Telling her was harder than I thought it would be. The Sazerac had loosened my tongue the night before, but that wasn't an option at work. "I wasn't joking about the curse. I wasn't being funny or exaggerating. I really am cursed. It was passed down to me from my mother."

Rather than laughing, Toni knitted her eyebrows and waited.

"My mother told me on her death bed," I continued. "She

was cursed, and her grandmother before her was as well. My aunt is cursed. We're unlucky in love. I don't just have a bad picker when it comes to partners. I'm always destined to pick wrong."

"Yeah, I'm going to need more than that."

I was gratified Toni wasn't laughing in my face, which was enough of an opening to launch into the sordid tale. Explaining everything to her took a solid thirty minutes—including pauses long enough to wait on two guests—and when I was finished, she was dumbfounded.

"Wow."

"This is the part where you call the men with the white coats and straitjackets to come get me, right?" I asked, resigned. "I would really prefer if you would skip that part and just fire me."

Toni's pretty face screwed up in confusion. "Why would I fire you?"

"Because I'm clearly crazy for believing a story like this."

"Um ... look around." She gestured toward our surroundings. "We're in a voodoo store. We wouldn't have a business if curses weren't real."

"Wait, so you really believe in curses?"

"Of course I do. Voodoo is totally real. Not everything we do here is real, but that's beside the point. Voodoo is most definitely real, and I've seen a few creole curses that would curl your hair. Well, maybe not *your* hair. That stuff is *Beverly Hills 90210* flat, if you know what I mean. Other people, though... Yeah, curly hair can be a real curse."

The statement was absurd on the face of it and made me laugh. "You don't have to placate me." I sat wearily on the stool behind the counter. "I get that I sound like a nut."

"You do sound like a bit of a nut, but not to me. Other people will totally think you're a nut, though, so be careful who you tell this story to. I'm not one of those people."

"You're not?"

"Nope."

Relief I thought out of my reach washed over me. "Well, then I guess Jasper was right. He told me I should tell you."

"Jasper told you that, huh?" Toni didn't look impressed. "What else has Jasper been telling you?"

"Not much. I only let the truth about the curse slip last night when he walked me home. Apparently Sazerac and secrecy don't mix."

"Hell, girl, I could've told you that."

I grinned. "He wants to help because he's looking for a curse story for his tour."

"Is that a fact?"

"That's what he said."

"Uh-huh. And did he need to reach up your shirt to check if you were wearing a bra while he was helping you? Because—and no joke—Jasper once told a tourist that he was part of the Breast Cancer Prevention team for New Orleans, and within five minutes, he had her asking him to touch her boobs. He's that good."

I choked on a laugh and shook my head. "He hasn't put his hands on me. He hasn't even intimated that's what he wants. I warned him it wouldn't be welcome even if I wasn't cursed. He seems fine with it."

"Of course he does." Toni rolled her eyes. "Not that I don't trust him or anything—I don't, for the record—but how exactly has he been helping you?"

"Well, this morning, he brought coffee and beignets to cure my hangover. Then he gave me my first ride on the streetcars. We went over to the Garden District, which is just as beautiful as everybody says. Because he's a tour guide, he has a key to get into Lafayette Cemetery. Once there, he took me to a mausoleum. It had the name Michel on it."

Toni's eyes went wide. "Like the same Michel that cursed your family?"

"Obviously, we don't know. He says he has a friend who is good with genealogy, and he's going to zero in on the years when it makes sense for my grandmother to have been cursed."

Toni waited a beat, then held out her hands. "And that's it?"

"That's it."

"Huh." She rolled her neck until it cracked. "The mausoleum was a good find. I'm impressed. I've never seen him work this hard to get under anybody's bra before."

"Maybe he's telling the truth. Have you ever considered that?"

"No, and here's why." Toni rested her elbows on the counter and stared directly into my eyes. "I've known Jasper my whole life. He's not a bad guy. In fact, he's a very good guy. He has a heart of gold, and he's always willing to volunteer time and money to help others."

I blinked several times, confused. "So, what's the problem?" I prodded finally.

"The problem is that Jasper lets his dick do all the thinking for him. No matter what a great guy he is—and he is a good guy—he's a terrible boyfriend. He can't commit, and he doesn't want to settle down. That means he's not the right match for you."

I couldn't contain my laughter. "I told you the story about the guy who got his wang stuck in a glory hole in the restaurant bathroom on our first date, right?"

Toni made a disdainful snorting sound and rested a hand on her chest as though she was having trouble catching her breath. "You did not tell me that, and I totally want to hear more. I can guarantee that you'll never catch Jasper doing that. He doesn't need to. He's always had a way with women. Heck, if he played for the other team, I'd have no trouble believing he would have a way with men too."

I could see that. "There's nothing romantic going on between us," I insisted. "He wants a funny story for his tours. I want to solve my little problem so maybe one day I can have a kid and not raise it alone. It's not a big deal."

Toni searched my face, then nodded on an exhalation. "Okay. You're a smart woman. You know better than to fall for a pretty face. I just want to reiterate that Jasper can't help himself from doing the things he does. He likes the attention. He has a big family, and he's always liked competing with his siblings for attention from his parents. If you ask me, his parents always cared about each other more than their offspring, but that's neither here nor there."

She held up a hand to silence me before I could interject my opinion. "I'm not done." She turned grave. "I like Jasper. Heck, I love the idiot. I'm not his target audience, though. He can have a friendship with me, and it's really just a friendship. I've never witnessed him do that with another woman. Either he crushes their spirit, or they were never that interested to begin with. There's no middle ground with him."

I didn't know what to say. I had only one argument, and she didn't seem to be hearing it. "I'm really not interested in dating—or anything else, for that matter—right now. He's helping me. There's not going to be any hanky-panky between us. There won't be anything else, either. You don't have anything to worry about."

Toni stared hard, then nodded. She seemed to be over the idea of arguing. "Okay, you're an adult. You get to make your own decisions. I've done my due diligence and warned you."

"And I've taken the warning to heart. I am not going to fall in love with Jasper Bentley and end up with a broken heart. It's not in the cards."

"Good." She tapped her fingers on the counter. "Now, as

for the curse, I might have a few sources I can tap regarding the name Michel. Most of my mother's friends have lines that run way back in the voodoo world. Somebody must know something about the name Michel."

"Do you think you can ask around?" I ruthlessly tamped down the hope threatening to overwhelm me. "I mean, I know the odds are long. I'll take anything at this point, though."

"I'll ask," she promised. "At the very least, we might find another line to tug. That can't possibly hurt."

"Definitely not."

"Okay, then." Toni pushed herself away from the counter. "We're agreed. You're not going to keep things from me any longer, and you're not going to let Jasper talk you out of your panties."

"We're agreed on both those topics," I said. "No sexy time with Jasper, and no more keeping my curse to myself. It's a brave new world."

She managed a smirk. "You're a bit of a weirdo," she said after a beat. "You know that, right?"

"Oh, I'm well aware."

"Just checking."

"Thanks for your concern."

"Don't mention it." She tapped her chin. "Now, let me decide who I should tap for information. I have a few options. One of them has to know something that can help us. It's just a matter of who."

Twelve

Work was fun. I found I liked Toni a great deal. Over the course of my shift, she told me a few stories about Jasper that made me laugh out loud. I recognized the stories were meant to keep me away from him—and I appreciated the effort—but she really didn't have to worry. I was off men for the foreseeable future. Even if I wasn't, Jasper wouldn't be a consideration as anything more than an entertaining party guest.

Despite that, when I left the store shortly before ten o'clock, I was surprised to find the sidewalk outside the door empty and wondered if the pang in my chest was disappointment—hard to tell. I'd expected Jasper to magically materialize, something I'd come to associate with him because he'd done it more than once, but he was nowhere to be found.

"Huh." I stared a beat longer, then shook my head.

Jasper did have a life of his own, after all. He'd offered to help me because he was intrigued by what I was doing. That didn't mean he was intrigued by me. Disappointment wasn't warranted.

Yet I couldn't shake the feeling that I'd missed out on something during my walk home.

I avoided Bourbon Street because I was too tired, only crossing when I hit Conti and was heading past the revelers. The music playing from Cafe Beignet was raucous, and even though we weren't in peak season, so many people were dancing in the street that I had trouble telling one individual from the next.

By the time I got to The Annex, I was tired. I told myself the smart thing to do would be to head back to my apartment and sleep off the dregs of my hangover. Truthfully, however, I no longer felt sluggish despite the alcohol I'd imbibed the previous evening. I was feeling pretty good. That was probably why I took the elevator to the roof of my unit instead.

Just seeing what everybody was doing couldn't hurt, I told myself. I would just pop my head in, say hello to anybody who looked familiar, then be on my way. To my utter surprise, however, a dance party seemed to have kicked off on the roof. I saw Posh right away—she was shaking her hips and having a good time with a guy I didn't recognize from behind—and she screeched when she saw me.

"Rowan, I wasn't sure you would come," she said, hurrying in my direction. The flush of her cheeks told me she was drunk. "I bet Jasper you would—and now he owes me fifty bucks—but I honestly wasn't sure. Here you are, though." She threw her arms around my neck as I tried to figure out what she'd actually told me. It felt like a lot even though it was likely very little in the grand scheme of things. I shifted my eyes to the man she'd been dancing with and almost fell over when I realized he was Jasper.

"Oh, hey." I felt unbelievably stupid.

"Hey." He dragged a hand through his hair, which looked to be wet from sweat, and offered me a charming grin. "Did you just get home from work? I thought for sure you were hiding in your apartment. That's why I knocked as hard as I did."

"I just got home from work," I confirmed. "Toni and I closed together."

"I'm going to have to talk to her about working you like a dog." Once Posh released me, Jasper rested a hand on the back of my neck and flicked his eyes toward the bar. "What do you want?"

What I wanted was an explanation for his presence. Instead, I kept my smile in place. "A gin and tonic is fine. Thank you."

"Okay, *Grandma*." He shook his head. "Just for the record, gin and tonic is for old people. You should try something young and fun."

"Go with a flirtini," Posh volunteered out of nowhere. If she was bummed about losing her dancing partner since Jasper was focused on me, she didn't show it. She was already making eyes at another guy on what they'd deemed the dance floor.

"What's a flirtini?" I asked blankly.

"A Shirley Temple martini, in essence," she replied. "It's pink and pretty."

I was about to tell her that wasn't my speed but changed my mind. "Why not, huh?" I flashed a smile at Jasper. "I will have a flirtini."

He winked at me with exaggerated slowness. "That was your preview of the flirt part," he explained when I remained rooted to my spot.

"Good to know." I hooked an arm through Posh's and dragged her away from the dance floor. "You should have some water before you do anything else."

Posh snorted, clearly amused. "This isn't amateur hour. I know what I'm doing."

She was probably right. That didn't stop me from dragging her away from another potential dance partner. "You'll thank me tomorrow if you don't make a fool of yourself in front of that guy."

"Who? Are you talking about Oaks?"

I blinked several times in rapid succession. "That's his last name, right?" I asked finally.

"No. Oaks Thornton. He's lived here about a year now." Her eyes drifted back in the guy's direction. "Isn't he dreamy?"

"Not with a name like Oaks." I forced her to sit at the table with the others, who seemed amused by her chirpy arrival. They didn't look nearly as concerned as I felt. "Is she allowed to throw herself at Oaks?"

Tyler laughed at the question. "Oh, you're adorable." He poked a finger into my cheek as though to prove it. He looked lit. "This is totally normal for her. She's going to stare at him all night, maybe dance with him once or twice, and then she's going to sneak back to her apartment before he can make a move. It's par for the course."

"Huh." I was fascinated despite myself. "Why does she do that?"

"Because he's her dream guy," Tad replied from across the table. "You can't ever be cool and collected with your dream guy. It's against the rules."

"You learn something new every day," I told Jasper as he joined us with drinks. The pink one he slid in front of me was as bright as a bad lipstick shade I'd once seen. Curious, I leaned over the rim and sniffed.

"It's just a pink martini," Jasper said as he sipped his drink. "I watched the dude make it. He added grenadine and maraschino cherries. It's fine."

It looked fine. Actually, it looked delicious. Still, I was

tentative as I sipped. "It's pretty good," I said finally, offering a grin. "Who knew I would be a flirtini fan?"

"I think he knew." Tyler jerked his thumb at Jasper. "How come you didn't tell us about your boyfriend when we were hanging out the other night? That feels like a gross oversight on your part."

"Oh, he's not my boyfriend," I replied automatically. "I'm on a man fast."

"Is that like a low-carb diet?" Posh asked. "If so, your poo is going to stink thanks to a limited diet at some point."

I blinked, unsure what to say, then glanced at Jasper. His head hung low, his shoulders shaking with silent laughter.

"It's not funny," I complained to him.

"Are you saying your poo doesn't stink?" he teased. "If so, I'm going to call foul. You're a magical being, Rowan Shaw, but you're not that magical."

For a moment, I got lost in the twinkle of his eyes. He was a happy guy, always smiling and having a good time, which made him one of those effortlessly beautiful people. Sure, he was handsome on a superficial level. However, his willingness to embrace new people and his ability to seamlessly fit in with anybody and everybody somehow enhanced his appeal.

"Let's talk about something else," I suggested as I shook myself out of my reverie. "Does anybody have any good gossip?"

"I have gossip about Oaks over there," Tyler offered, his eyes narrowing as he focused on the man in question, who was dancing with a petite blonde in such a way that suggested they would be taking their leave for some private time before long.

"Wait ... his name is Oaks?" Jasper looked thoroughly puzzled. "What sort of name is that?"

"It's a rich person's name," Tyler replied. "Rumor is that his parents are filthy rich developers and they sent him ahead to scout New Orleans because they plan to revitalize a bunch of buildings and make a name for themselves in the city."

That was an interesting theory, yet I was instantly dubious. "Um ... if they're rich, wouldn't they put him up in a nicer place? Like, why not rent an Airbnb in the Garden District or something? We were over there this morning, and the houses are amazing."

"You were over there?" Tyler switched his eyes back to me.

"Jasper and me," I replied before thinking. "He took me on a cemetery tour."

"Did you, now?" Tyler's lips quirked as he leaned back in his chair. He looked to be gearing up for a vigorous round of teasing. "I thought Lafayette Cemetery was closed these days."

"Jasper has a key," I volunteered, studying Jasper's face when he poked my side. "What? Is that a secret?"

"Kind of," he replied with a laugh although he didn't look all that agitated. "I'm not technically supposed to be boasting about it."

"Oh, well, it's okay." I patted his arm, my brain momentarily fuzzing when I felt the muscles he had going for him under his shirt. "You didn't brag. I did the bragging for you."

"That's a weird date," Tad noted. "I've never heard of a guy trying to get into a woman's pants through a cemetery tour."

Jasper remained calm as he took another sip of his drink. "I wasn't trying to get into her pants," he replied. "I just wanted her to see the cemetery. She's never been out of Salem."

"I've been out of Salem," I replied. "Don't make me sound more bumpkin than is necessary."

Jasper's lips curved up at the corners. "I just wanted her to see it. When she goes back north, I want her to have a bevy of memories to call on. I'm guessing her life up there is very different from her life down here."

"Depending on who you talk to, I don't have a life in either place," I mused, more to myself than anybody else.

"We're going to change that." Jasper patted my knee under the table, sending a little jolt through me.

You're on a man fast, I reminded myself. *Don't let his charm trick you. It will end badly.*

"Let's get back to Oaks over there," Jasper instructed. "I have to agree with Rowan. If he's from a rich family, why would they send him here to do reconnaissance?"

"Maybe they want him to hang out with the common folk," Tyler suggested. "You can't make money off the backs of the little guy if you don't know what makes them tick."

"Good point." Jasper bobbed his head. "I still don't know if I'm buying it. That being said, he's got hoity-toity hair."

"And muscles for miles," Posh said with a drunk giggle.

Everybody at the table laughed. The night was nice, and I liked my new friends. Sure, I wasn't in it for the long haul, but that didn't mean I couldn't embrace my new life for the time being. *Fun is fun, right?*

"WHAT ARE YOU DOING OVER HERE?"

Jasper found me sitting on one of the pool loungers, sipping a bottle of water shortly before one o'clock.

"Huh?" I glanced up from my phone and smiled at him. "I was just running the name Michel and adding potential names to my research list."

"You keep a list?" Jasper lowered himself into the chair next to me. He had a bottle of water in his hand, which meant he was likely sobering up before heading out. "Why am I not surprised?"

"Yes, I'm anal retentive," I agreed. "Alert the media. I'm sure everybody will be shocked to hear the uptight girl likes making lists."

"I don't think you're nearly as uptight as you think you are," he countered. "You might be a little rigid—there's nothing wrong with that—but you like having a good time. You should embrace who you are. Don't make excuses."

"I wasn't making an excuse. I was simply telling the truth."

"Uh-huh." He didn't look convinced. "Speaking of the truth, how was work with Toni? Did you tell her the truth like I suggested?"

"Actually, I did," I confirmed as I lowered the phone to my chest. "Not for the reasons you told me to, though."

"What other reasons are there?"

"She saw you drop me off. She thinks there's something going on between us."

"Ah." Jasper tipped his head in understanding as he leaned back and stared at the pretty night sky. "She's worried about you, isn't she?"

"She thinks you're going to run roughshod over my heart. I had to explain about the curse to get her to back off. Obviously, she thinks I'm a moron who can't think for myself."

"I doubt that's what she's thinking," Jasper countered. "How did she take news of the curse?"

"She was surprisingly open to the possibility. She says she'll help too, at least to the best of her ability. She's not sure what she can do other than ask around, but she's more than happy to do that."

"Good." Jasper took another sip. "When you told her you weren't interested in me, did she believe you?"

I might've sworn his voice had an edge to it if that hadn't been a ridiculous notion. When I glanced in his direction, however, I found his face relaxed. He looked as though he didn't have a care in the world.

"She said she understood you were protecting me," I replied, forcing my eyes back to the moon. "She seemed to think your reasons for helping were weak, but I reminded her I was a grownup who was capable of making her own decisions. That didn't stop her from telling me ridiculous stories about your checkered dating history throughout the shift, though."

"What checkered dating history?" Jasper sounded offended. "I am a dating god."

"Did you really once borrow gold paint to pretend you were a human statue to hide from a woman you ghosted after having sex with her?" I asked.

Jasper frowned. "Of course she would tell you that story."

"That's a lot of effort to go through to ditch a woman."

"First off, Elle was a ... what's the word I'm looking for?"

"Disappointment?"

"No. She was a nut. She told me she loved me after we had sex one time. I knew it was a mistake to let her spend the night. I was too drunk to listen to that little voice inside my head that kept warning me of trouble, though. That was the date that broke the camel's back, so to speak. I never do drunken hookups at all now."

I was understandably confused. "Wait ... she told you she loved you after you had sex one time?"

"Yes. It was disturbing. I had to trick her to get her out of my apartment. Then she proceeded to follow me around the Quarter when I was doing tours. The paint was an effort of last resort."

"I've seen those guys who paint themselves and pose for hours," I mused. "You're far too antsy to pass as one of them for more than five minutes."

"I just needed to lose her that day. Once I did, I convinced my parents to tell her I was mentally unstable and also cut off from any family funds. That was enough to scare her away."

"That's a bummer." I meant it. "Are your parents rich or something?"

Jasper held out his hands. "'Rich' isn't exactly the word I would use. They're comfortable. We make a good living from the tour company. Elle made certain assumptions. Either way, it doesn't matter. I learned a lesson, thanks to her." He paused a beat. "Actually, I learned two lessons."

"And what lessons did you learn?"

"No drunk hookups. Also, that paint doesn't come out of certain cracks without work. Those statue guys are to be revered as gods, given the amount of work they put into that gig."

I couldn't swallow my giggle, which made his smile wider. "I guess that's good to know," I said when I recovered.

"I love to learn," he agreed. "Speaking of that, I talked to my friend, the genealogy expert. He's agreed to meet with us. He's open to dinner tomorrow. I didn't commit because I wasn't sure what your work schedule looks like."

"I have tomorrow off," I replied. "I can totally do dinner with him, especially if he can help." I found myself feeling hopeful for the first time in months. "Thank you for doing this, Jasper."

He offered me a wink as he stood. "I'm having fun. I'll call you when I have a time tomorrow."

"Sure." I nodded. "Are you leaving?" The disappointment I'd felt earlier in the night returned with a vengeance.

"I am. I need some sleep. Don't worry, though." He offered another wink. "This isn't goodbye forever. You will see me again."

I made a face. "I wasn't worried about that."

"Oh, I know better." He wagged his finger. "You adore me. Don't worry. It's perfectly normal. Everybody who meets me adores me. It's my curse."

All I could do was roll my eyes. "Be careful walking home."

"Be careful avoiding the tree dude." He pointed toward Oaks, who was still on the dance floor. "If you think I would be bad for your man fast, he would be ten times worse."

I had no idea what he was getting at. "I have zero interest in that dude," I reassured him. "He's so not my type."

"Good to know." With that, he was gone, leaving me with just my water.

"What a weirdo," I muttered to myself.

Thirteen

I was fresh out of the shower and drinking coffee when Jasper knocked on my door the next morning. I arched an eyebrow as I studied his ready smile, then allowed him inside.

"Did we have plans?" I was understandably confused.

"I'm not done with my tour. I thought I would show you around the French Quarter today."

"What about your friend?"

"That's dinner tonight. You have a whole day off work—as do I—so I thought it best to show you the joys of my hometown."

Such a weird thing to say. "The joys of your hometown?"

"You heard me." He didn't back down.

"I thought I would just laze around today. You know, be a bum."

"You could do that, or you could let me show you around."

"Because it will be joyful?"

"Yup."

I blew out a sigh. "Fine. It seems weird to me, but you probably know all the good places."

"I know the best places," he agreed. "Besides, I can definitely provide better coffee than that." He made a face as he looked in my mug. "That's not real coffee."

The idea of real coffee did have me frothing at the mouth. "I need ten minutes to get dressed."

"Take as much time as you need." Jasper snagged the mug and dumped it into the sink. "I'll do your dishes."

"That's really not necessary."

"I might as well make myself useful."

I stared at his back as he started the water, a million arguments on the tip of my tongue. I didn't use any of them. Really, what was the point? "Ten minutes. Then I'll be ready for however much joy you can dish out." I only realized that what I'd said could be taken in a variety of different ways when he shot me a wicked look. "Don't be gross. I'm definitely still on a man fast."

"Oh, I don't want to break your man fast. I just like watching you get embarrassed."

"Fair enough."

TWENTY MINUTES LATER, WE WERE IN line at Cafe Beignet. Jasper ordered coffee for both of us and some beignets to share. Then we got comfortable at one of the metal tables to make our plans for the day.

"So, I don't want to be obnoxious with the tour stuff—some people don't like that—but I do have the sort of information that makes history buffs drool," he said. "I need to know before we start how many nuggets you want me dropping on you."

That was an interesting way to start our day.

"I actually like historical stuff," I admitted as I sipped my latte. "I go on the Salem tours at least once a month even though I already know everything they have to offer. It's still fun."

"Okay." He broke a beignet in half and studied me. "Are you delicate?"

My eyebrows moved toward one another. "As compared to what?"

"As compared to someone who wouldn't be delicate? Like ... are you okay hearing the gruesome stories? Do you like murder-and-mayhem stuff? Do you want to hear about the city's voodoo history?"

"Oh." I bobbed my head in understanding. "I get what you're saying. I want to hear it all. I don't get squeamish when it comes to that stuff."

"Awesome." He nodded approvingly. "You picked the right guide for today's excursion if you're not squeamish. I'm the best guide in the city for a reason."

All I could do was shake my head. "You have a very high opinion of yourself."

He winked. "I've found that's better than having a low opinion of yourself."

"Probably." I grabbed a beignet. "Where are we starting?"

"I figured we would head over to the LaLaurie Mansion. Do you know what that is?"

"Only because I've watched a few seasons of *American Horror Story*."

"Well, the real story is vastly different. It will give you nightmares."

"Is that a good thing?"

"Most definitely."

Finding his enthusiasm contagious, I let a giggle escape. "Okay, well, as soon as we're done here, I'm ready."

"Good. I like it when my audience is enthusiastic."

Something told me he would settle for nothing less than applause.

"You'd better live up to the hype," I said. "If not, I'm going to leave a scathing Yelp review."

He turned imperious. "Oh, I'm going to knock your socks off."

For some reason, the statement sent a chill up my spine, and likely not for the reasons he was anticipating.

"Show me what you've got," I said.

"Gladly."

"THE LALAURIE MANSION THAT DELPHINE LaLaurie lived in is not the building you're looking at now," Jasper explained once we were in front of our destination.

While impressive, the house itself wasn't like the mini mansions seen in modern subdivisions or on lakefronts.

"That house was burned down by a mob in 1834 and remained in a dilapidated state for four years before being rebuilt in 1838."

"I read there were a lot of misconceptions about her," I noted as I studied the second-floor patio area. During the walk over, Jasper had explained that the current inhabitants of the house absolutely hated when people wandered by their property. In theory, I could understand that. In reality, I figured it went with the territory when buying a house with such a sordid past.

"That's true." Jasper bobbed his head. "The problem we run into when reciting stories from the time period is that a lot of them were cited without proof. So, Jeanne deLavigne, for example, wrote in *Ghost Stories of New Orleans*—a book printed more than a hundred years after the mansion burned down, mind you—that those who'd responded to the 1834 fire found male slaves naked and chained to walls, eyes gouged out, fingernails pulled out by the roots, and so on."

I cringed involuntarily. "Lovely."

He chuckled. "It made for a great story. The problem is none of the reports of the time included those details."

"Would they have?" I was honestly curious. "Like ... would they have gone into the nitty-gritty details of what was found in the house? I'm guessing the newspapers covering the incident back then would've held back some of the more salacious details."

"I think you're probably right. That only enhances the problem, though. We have no idea of what's true and what's not."

"Okay, tell me what's absolute fact."

"What's fact is that Delphine LaLaurie was married three times." Jasper rubbed his hands together as though relishing the telling of the story. "Although I guess I should start at the beginning. Her family held prominent positions in New Orleans back in the day, including an uncle who was governor of the Spanish American provinces of Louisiana in the late 1700s.

"She was four when the Haitian Revolution erupted, and that made a lot of Southern slaveholders nervous for obvious reasons," he continued. "It's been theorized that's one of the reasons she did what she did, because she'd villainized slaves in her head as a child."

"I'm sure she had help from the adults in her family when it came to that," I mused.

"Probably." He was in his element. "Her first husband was a high-ranking Spanish royal officer. She was pregnant with their daughter when he died in Havana. Her second husband was a prominent banker who she had four children with, one of whom died as a child, which wasn't unheard of at the time.

"Her third husband was a doctor," he went on, his expression shifting to far-off whimsy. He clearly enjoyed telling a story, something I found strangely alluring. "Her third husband was much younger than her. She bought this property we're standing in front of, in her own name, separate from her husband, and built the first mansion. She was known as a bit of a fireball.

"One interesting tidbit about her is that she petitioned a district judge for separation of bed and board from her husband about seven years after they married." Jasper's eyes lit with amusement as he turned back to me. "Do you know what that means?"

"Not exactly," I replied. "I can guess, though. Basically, she wanted to live under her own roof and not have sex with her husband. Back then, it would've been considered her duty to do both."

"Very good, my cute little witch." He tapped the end of my nose, causing me to frown. "Her children with her previous husband testified on her behalf and said he mistreated her. The judge granted the request, but the separation didn't stick because her third husband was at the mansion the day of the fire."

"Tell me about the fire." I was intrigued despite myself. I knew what I was about to hear would be horrible, yet I was morbidly fascinated.

"You're getting ahead of yourself," Jasper warned. "For starters, you should know that there's debate about how Delphine treated her slaves. Some people say that her slaves were 'singularly haggard and wretched' in appearance. Other people say she was polite to Black individuals in public.

"Records from back then record the death of twelve slaves at the Royal Street mansion," he continued. "There's no cause of death listed. Also, I would be remiss if I didn't mention that court records show she freed two enslaved individuals ... although those instances happened thirteen years apart. On the flip side, her mistreatment of slaves was supposedly an open secret, and a local lawyer actually sat her down for a talk about how she was supposed to treat her slaves."

My stomach constricted with discomfort. "I don't like talking about this as if it were normal."

"I don't either, but it's part of the story." He rested a hand on my shoulder. It was warm and heavy enough to make the butterflies in my stomach stop flitting around because of the story and start in earnest for other reasons, including fluctuating hormones.

"There's another story about a child slave who neighbors said fell to her death from the roof while trying to flee a whip-wielding Delphine," Jasper offered. "I think it's fair to say she wasn't a pleasant woman. The day of the fire, when the police and fire marshals arrived, they found a female cook chained to the stove. She said she'd set the fire as a suicide attempt. She also said that enslaved people taken to the uppermost room in the house never came back."

"This is where things get terrible," I assumed.

He nodded. "Bystanders asked for the keys to the slave quarters, and Delphine refused. They wanted to make sure nobody would burn to death in the fire. They broke down the doors anyway and found seven slaves who had been mutilated. Even during the event, Delphine refused to make excuses or apologize. She basically told the neighbors to mind their own business."

"She sounds like a true humanitarian." I wrinkled my nose. "I'm guessing the neighbors always knew there was something wrong with her and never said anything."

"Is that so different from what happens with serial killers today?"

"I guess not." I playfully bumped a hip against his. "Finish it out."

"The story of abuse spread quickly," Jasper said. "Because

of that, a mob descended on the house and completely destroyed it. Officials dug in the yard and found more bodies. Unfortunately, Delphine escaped during the mob violence. She fled to Alabama and then ultimately took refuge in Paris.

"Now, here's where things get iffy," he continued. "In a letter one of her sons wrote to his brother-in-law, he suggested Delphine wanted to return to New Orleans. This would've been in 1842, so years after the fire. Her children supposedly refused to agree and forced her to stay.

"As to rumors of her death, they vary wildly. Some people say she died in a boar-hunting accident in France. In St. Louis Cemetery Number One, a local sexton found a cracked plate that had her name on it. It gave the date of death as 1842, the same year she supposedly wanted to return. French archives say she died in 1849, however."

I waited for him to expand. When he didn't, I prodded him. "And what do you believe?"

"I believe that evil never dies."

"Oh geez." I gave his shoulder a hard shove. "Don't run your tour stuff on me. I want to know the truth."

He captured my wrist before I could shove him again and tugged me nearer. We were close, with almost no room between us, and my breath caught in my throat when I realized how warm he was against me.

"Um..." I licked my lips, suddenly uncomfortable. My head told me this was a terrible idea—even though I had no proof anything was actually happening—but my heart decided to lodge a formal complaint with my head.

He didn't immediately respond, instead touching the tip of his tongue to his top lip. His fingers appeared out of nowhere, close to my face, but I didn't flinch. Instead, I watched in surprise as he brushed my hair back. The intent in his serious gaze was impossible to ascertain.

"Why did you want to tell me this story?" I asked finally, my throat dry.

"I'm not sure." His voice was raspy. "I guess maybe I wanted you to know that there are worse things than a curse."

"You mean mutilation and slavery? Yeah, I figured that out myself. That doesn't mean I'm not keen to end the curse."

That earned a smile. "What if you're not cursed?"

I hadn't expected that question, especially right then. "What else could it be?"

"Grief."

I was taken aback, meaning I literally forced myself to take a step back and increase the distance between us. Once our bodies were no longer touching, I found I could breathe again. I could also think. "I don't understand what you're saying. If this is about my mother, of course I'm grieving. She was my mother. My grief didn't cause me to imagine a new reality, though."

"No?" Rather than backing down, Jasper continued pressing. "Isn't it possible that you convinced yourself it was wrong to be happy in the wake of your mother's death? Heck, maybe 'happy' is the wrong word. Maybe you wanted to make sure you didn't have a good time. She was your mother. I can see you convincing yourself that laughing, yukking it up with your friends, even dating someone who might be a good fit, all of those things could be seen as a betrayal."

I narrowed my eyes. "I didn't ask you to be a part of this."

"Don't." He sounded pained. "I told you I want to help."

"And yet here you are trying to convince me that I'm crazy."

"That's not what I'm trying to do."

"I'm not crazy," I insisted. "It's not like this happened once and I freaked out. It happened multiple times. She told me about the curse on her deathbed. There had to be a reason.

She wouldn't just say something like that without cause. That was her last thought. It means something."

He didn't respond immediately. An emotion I couldn't quite identify lurked in the depths of his eyes, yet he didn't explode and tell me I was a nut. Ultimately, he simply nodded with a sigh. "It sounds to me as if you've been through it."

"I'm not imagining it."

"I know." He held up his hands in supplication. "I wasn't trying to upset you. I just don't think that blaming everything that's gone wrong in your life on a curse is healthy."

"When did I do that?" I was officially offended. "I'm not pretending that my life is terrible. It's not. My life is good."

"Other than the curse."

"Yes."

He pursed his lips, as if debating himself, then nodded. "Okay. I'm sorry I brought it up."

I didn't believe him. "You don't need to stick with me. I realize it's my fault for getting drunk and blabbing—I really should've followed my first instincts and hid in my apartment every night because I knew how this would end if I opened my mouth—but I don't expect you to follow through on this if you don't want to be here. I'm grateful for your help, but you can walk away at any time."

"I don't want to walk away," he said hurriedly. "I also don't want you spending all your time alone in your apartment. This city can be your best friend if you let it. You don't need to be alone. I don't want that."

"I'm just looking for answers." I chose my words carefully. "I don't expect you to have them. If you doubt me—and you clearly do—then maybe we should end this partnership now. I'm appreciative for the genealogy guy you found. If you want to walk away after we talk to him, though, I get it. I'm not here to force you to chase something you don't believe in."

"I believe in you," he said, taking me by surprise. "That's

enough. I'm sorry I tried to force your hand that way." He looked earnest. "My sister has been warning me for years that I have a tendency to want to fix problems that don't necessarily need to be fixed. I'm bad at listening and being supportive. I constantly want to provide a solution even though that's not always my place."

Surprisingly, I understood where he was coming from. "I don't want you to be uncomfortable. I get that I sound like a wack job. I honestly feel I have no choice but to chase this, however."

"Then I'm going to chase it with you." He offered a smile. "I told you I want a good curse story for my tour. That still stands."

I was hesitant but nodded as I blew out a breath. "So, where to next?"

"How do you feel about pirates?"

That wasn't where I was expecting him to go, yet I laughed all the same. "Johnny Depp or Orlando Bloom?"

"I'll let you choose."

I cocked my head and gave it some real thought. "I think I'll go with Orlando Bloom."

His eyes lit with mirth. "People say I look like Orlando Bloom."

I burst out laughing. "People lie."

He made a face. "Oh, let me have my fun. I can totally look like Orlando Bloom if I want to."

Since I didn't disagree, I merely nodded. "Take me to see the pirates."

"Your wish is my command."

Fourteen

Jasper was a surprisingly good tour guide. He was gregarious and cheeky, and on top of that, he knew his stuff. Our trip took us around the entire French Quarter, ending at the riverwalk.

"We're meeting Charlie at Tableau," he explained as we stared out at the rapidly flowing Mississippi. "It will only take us ten minutes to walk there."

"It's beautiful here," I noted. "It's different than Salem, the energy I mean, but it's still fantastic. Both places have a lot in common, but there are big differences too."

"Such as?"

"Well, the booze, for one. Nobody gets rowdy drunk in Salem unless it's Halloween. Most of the bars shut down at midnight unless it's a weekend night in October. The bars here don't seem to shut down at all."

"Oh, that's not true," he teased. "Some of them shut down from four o'clock to eleven o'clock in the morning. That's siesta time."

I laughed, which I'm sure he'd intended. "I guess that's true."

He was quiet for a long beat, then fixed me with a serious look. "Do you like one place more than the other?"

That was something I hadn't given a lot of thought to. "I miss the ocean in Salem," I said finally. "You guys have the Gulf here, but it's not in walking distance, from what I can tell."

"No. Definitely not."

"In Salem, I live about five blocks from the store. About six blocks from that is Derby Street, which leads right to Salem Harbor. There are a lot of little rivers intermixed through there and restaurants right on the water. I love that area. It's my absolute favorite."

"What's your favorite place here?"

"I don't think I've been here long enough to find a favorite place. The riverwalk is great. I like Jackson Square. The Garden District is beautiful. I'm not comfortable enough yet to find a favorite place."

"Do you think you will find a favorite place? Before you go, I mean. You plan on returning to Massachusetts, right?"

I nodded. "Yeah. I don't have much choice. I inherited my mother's half of the store. I can't just abandon my aunt to run it herself."

"Have you asked her?"

"Who?" I was momentarily confused.

"Your aunt. Have you asked her if she would be okay with you abandoning your half of the store? Maybe you could sell it to her or something."

On the face of it, that was the most ridiculous thing I'd ever heard. The trip to New Orleans was supposed to be temporary. It *was* temporary. Still, part of me yearned to make it, if not permanent, at least long-lasting.

"If I tell you something, do you promise not to tell anybody else?" I asked finally.

He nodded, no hint of a smile on his face, for once. "Lay it on me."

"When I think about Salem, I remember my mother. Not in a bad way or anything, but whenever I turn a corner, I expect to see her, whether it's making a fuss over the *Bewitched* statue because she hated it or having a good time with the witches during the annual jam-making festival. She's everywhere, like I'm breathing her. There's very little me there that's not filtered through her."

"Maybe that's why you feel suffocated."

That was like a fast slap on a naked cheek. "I don't feel suffocated." The response was reflexive, something I didn't notice until he arched a challenging eyebrow. "I didn't say I felt suffocated," I insisted.

"Okay." He held up his hands. "It was just an observation."

"That I feel suffocated when I'm up there?" I had somehow turned shrill, and I didn't like it.

"Rowan, I wasn't trying to upset you," he said calmly. "You just seem to breathe so much easier here even though you think you're cursed. When you talk about Salem, your shoulders droop, and you get this look of sadness on your face."

"I lost my mother."

"And that's a terrible thing. I just want you to be happy, and you're never happy when you talk about Salem. Do you think it's possible that you're staying there for her? Because if that's the case, you need to know that it's not necessary. You're allowed to live your own life."

I had no idea what to make of what he was saying. "Salem is my home," I repeated. "That's where my life is. Well, that's where I hope my life will be when we get rid of this pesky curse."

He nodded after a few seconds. "Okay, then." He held out

a hand for me to take. "Let's head to dinner. Charlie is a good guy. I'm hoping he can at least give us a direction to look."

I took his hand without thinking, his warmth instantly fighting off the chill that had settled over me. "I hope so. I feel as if I'm not getting anywhere, and it's driving me crazy."

"We'll find answers." He sounded sure of himself. "Trust me. Things always work out how they're supposed to."

CHARLIE DUTTON HAD ONE OF THOSE smiles so bright that it could signal ships to shore. He was sitting at a balcony table at Tableau when we arrived and immediately hopped to his feet when he saw Jasper.

"There you are, you rogue," he said, heartily clapping Jasper on the back as they embraced. "I haven't seen you in months. Where have you been hiding yourself?"

"I haven't actually been hiding myself anywhere," Jasper replied as he pulled out a chair and motioned for me to sit. "I've been busy with work. Mom and Dad are doing only a few tours a week now, and they pick and choose. They've delegated most of the organizing to us kids, and we're not exactly known for our organizational skills."

Charlie chuckled as he sat. "How is your lovely sister, Maria? She's always been such a gem amongst the roughage that is the rest of your family."

Jasper shot him a dirty look. "You can't hit on my sister. You know I don't like that."

"I wasn't hitting on her. I was asking about her."

"I'm not answering questions about my sister. That's all there is to it." Jasper was stern before turning his attention to me. "This is Rowan Shaw. She's the woman I was telling you about."

"Hello." Charlie grinned at me as he extended a hand. "I

can't believe somebody actually reined in this Romeo. It must be some sort of French Quarter miracle."

I was taken aback. "Oh, we're not together."

"You're not?" Charlie didn't look convinced. "Okay, I guess I'm confused. I thought you were working on some project together because you're a couple."

"I met Rowan through Toni," Jasper explained. "She's working at the shop."

"Ah, Toni." Charlie took on a whimsical expression. "She was supposed to be the love of my life."

I was really confused. "What, now?"

"Charlie and Toni went to a few dances together in high school," Jasper explained. "Charlie fell in love. Toni realized she was gay. We all blame Charlie for us losing her from the dating pool."

As he was speaking good-naturedly, I didn't take offense on Toni's behalf. "Did the other guys give you grief for being the one who made Toni realize she was gay?" I asked.

"Oh, the ribbing was terrible." Charlie's expression was forlorn. "They banned me from dating the hot girls for a full year after that. I could only go after the tourists or the B-list team because they didn't want to risk me turning anybody else."

I frowned. "That's not how it works."

Jasper let loose a jovial chuckle. "He knows. He's just messing with you. He's not naturally funny, so when he finds a bit that works once—even if it was from years ago—he refuses to let it go."

"Yeah, that's not how it is," Charlie shot back.

"That's exactly how it is."

The server picked that moment to interrupt. We ordered cocktails to start then entrees when she delivered the drinks. After that, we turned to serious matters.

"So, Jasper was vague when he said you needed my

services," Charlie offered. "He felt you should be the one to tell me what's going on, Rowan."

My mouth was suddenly dry. I'd been expecting having to explain why I wanted the information. Telling a stranger I was cursed was more difficult than admitting it to a co-worker or drunkenly blurting it to an acquaintance. "Oh, well..."

"She's cursed," Jasper volunteered.

I slapped his knee. "You need to ease into it," I hissed. "He's going to think I'm crazy."

Jasper snorted. "Please. This is New Orleans. Everybody here is crazy in one form or another. He doesn't care about the curse."

"Au contraire," Charlie drawled. "I love a good curse. What are the specifics of this one?"

"Well?" Jasper nudged me with his elbow when I didn't immediately respond. "Give him the list of guys who you've dated and wished you hadn't."

I wanted to kill him.

"Fine. I'll tell him." Jasper's slow grin told me that was what he'd wanted all along. "Basically, she's dated ten guys in the last year, and they've all ended up in prison. She thinks she's cursed."

My mouth dropped open. "That's not how it went. You're totally going off the rails with the story."

Charlie looked deeply amused. "Don't take offense, Rowan," he chided. "That's what he does. He likes to get a rise out of people."

"It's not like that at all," I insisted. "He's leaving out the whole part where my mother told me on her deathbed that the family was cursed."

"That would seem like an important tidbit," he acknowledged.

Since I had no other choice, I filled him in, doing my best to be clinical rather than emotional. I couldn't exactly remember how the conversation with Jasper had gone, so I wanted to make sure I didn't ramble or come across as deranged. When I was finished, Charlie's expression was unreadable.

"Is that it?" he asked gravely after a few seconds of silence.

I nodded. "Yes."

To my utter surprise, he burst out laughing. "Wow."

I was appalled. "Excuse me?"

"Just ... wow." He swiped at tears as they leaked from the corners of his eyes. "That was quite the tale."

I was officially offended. "I think I should go."

As I moved to stand, Jasper grabbed my wrist. "Don't." He shook his head. "He's not laughing at you. It's just... That story is amazing. I think you've told it so many times you've lost perspective on how amazing it is."

"You think the disaster that is my life is amazing and that I shouldn't be offended?" I demanded.

"I think that you're sensitive to the subject and careful not to tell people you're cursed for a reason," he clarified. "Don't get worked up. I swear Charlie will be able to help." He pinned his friend with an expectant stare. "Isn't that right?"

"Oh, I definitely want to help." Charlie nodded. He was still smiling, but he was no longer leaking happy tears. "I also don't want you thinking I was making fun of you because I wasn't. It's just... That's a terrible run of luck."

"It is," I agreed, slouching in my chair. "I didn't believe my mother when she told me we were cursed. I thought she was making it up. Obviously, she wasn't, though. All she gave me as a hint was the name Michel—or Michelle depending on if it's a first name—and then pointed me toward New Orleans."

"Just out of curiosity, were there ever times you thought you were cursed when you were dating in high school or anything?" Charlie queried.

"Not really. Although I almost lost my virginity to Dalton

Comstock the night of senior prom, and in hindsight I should've had more questions when he told me that they were all supposed to be that size. Thankfully, I thought better of it at the last moment and waited until college."

Jasper shifted on his chair. "Big or small?"

"Small. We're talking pencil eraser. I couldn't understand why everybody said sex was such a big deal. I don't even think I would've known it had happened if we'd gone through with it. You can understand my confusion when my next boyfriend and I actually did it and he was hung like a porn star."

Jasper's chuckle was warm and light. "Wow. I never understood how confusing it must be for girls of a certain age until right now."

"You grew up with a sister," Charlie pointed out. "It's not as if she couldn't have filled you in on the basics."

"Don't go there," Jasper warned. "Maria is still a virgin."

"Yes, a twenty-five-year-old virgin in the French Quarter," Charlie intoned. "It sounds perfectly feasible."

"Shut up." Jasper turned morose. "What about the name Michel? I have to think it was a last name because if it's a first name, we're never going to get anywhere."

"I think it's a last name too," Charlie said as he leaned back in his chair. Suddenly, he was all business. "I think she was talking about Lisette Michel."

I looked at Jasper to see if the name rang a bell, but his face was blank.

"Who is she?" he asked.

"For a good twenty years, she was the head voodoo queen on the block," Charlie explained. "She owned a store on St. Peter, not far from Pirate's Alley. She was the most popular draw in the area. Katrina wiped out her store, though, and some insurance snafu made it so she couldn't rebuild. After that, she retired to Bywater."

"I'm not saying I doubt you, but why do you believe it's

her?" Jasper had draped an arm over the back of my chair and was idly tracing his thumb over my bare upper arm.

I didn't even think he realized he was doing it. Why I didn't shift or ask him to stop, I couldn't say. It felt nice, so I let him keep doing it.

"How long ago did you say you believe this curse was enacted, Rowan?" Charlie asked me.

"I don't have a definitive timetable," I replied. "I just know it was my grandmother. I'm guessing we're talking at least fifty years, though."

"The timing makes sense," Charlie explained. "Fifty years ago would've been when the Paranormal Festival Brigade was a thing."

"Ah, right." Jasper bobbed his head.

I blinked several times. "Did he just explain something?" I demanded, earning a laugh.

"The Paranormal Festival Brigade was a yearly get-together of sorts," Charlie explained. "Think of it like a boat expo without the boats. People in the paranormal trade—think the witches of Salem, the ghost hunters of Savannah, the voodoo queens of New Orleans, et cetera—would descend on New Orleans for one week a year. They would trade stories, sell their wares, and generally carouse it up."

"Huh." I rubbed my cheek. "I didn't know my grandmother, but the stories I've heard lead me to believe she would've loved that sort of thing."

"Lisette was a central figure when it came to hosting," Charlie explained. "She was one of the main organizers. She was also known for having a temper and ... um ... spreading her love around with various vendors and guests."

It wasn't hard to ascertain what he was saying. "You think my grandmother and this Lisette woman fought over a man," I surmised.

"It makes sense, doesn't it?" Charlie asked. "I mean ... you have a love curse on you. Lisette was known for cursing people left and right if you believe the stories. The guy who made the final decision on her insurance claim after Hurricane Katrina ended up with blisters on his dick and could never get it up again."

My eyes went wide. "What, now?"

Jasper shifted on his chair, shielding his crotch. "I never heard that story. Can the voodoo queens really give you dick blisters?"

I rolled my eyes. "Maybe you should stop running through women. Then you wouldn't have anything to worry about."

"Shush, you." Jasper shot me a quelling look. "It was a simple question."

Charlie snorted. "Are you sure you're not together? I mean... I'm getting a vibe. I won't tell anybody if you are. I won't ruin your reputation, Jas, but you act like you're together."

"We're not together," I reassured him. "Jasper is just helping me in exchange for the story to use on a tour when I'm gone."

"Uh-huh." Charlie's expression was disbelief, but he didn't push the matter. "Lisette still works out of her house over in Bywater. It's sporadic—mostly, she sells potions and does card readings—but I've heard she's only gotten more cantankerous with age. I've never actually had the pleasure of crossing paths with her in person."

"Do you think she would be willing to sit down with us?" Jasper asked.

"I don't know." Charlie's shoulders hopped. "That's going to have to be something you guys figure out. I've heard enough stories about her that I'm not comfortable getting anywhere near her. If even half of them are true, you could both leave that meeting with new curses."

That was disconcerting. Still, I wasn't about to be dissuaded.

"I have to try." I was firm on that. "I didn't come all this way to sever the curse just to turn around because the enemy is formidable."

Jasper's lips quirked. "That was a little dramatic."

"Just a little," Charlie agreed. "It might work in your favor, though. Lisette likes true believers if the rumors are to be believed. She might take pity on you if you show her deference."

"And if I don't?" I asked.

"Then she might decide to double down and make things worse."

"I figured." I was resigned. "So, deference it is."

"Yeah, that's the route I would take."

"At least we finally have a lead."

Jasper winked at me. "I told you I would come through. That will teach you to doubt me."

"Yes, lesson learned. You're nothing if not reliable."

"Well, don't say it like that. I'm not boring or anything."

"I'll try to come up with another way to describe you by the time we leave."

"Great. I'll be waiting with bated breath."

Fifteen

"What do you think?" I asked Jasper as we walked down Conti Street. We were still a block away, but I could hear the revelry on Bourbon Street and knew it would be too loud to talk when we got there.

"I think it's a solid lead." Jasper looked lost in thought, more focused on where he was walking than anything else. "I'm going to talk to my mother."

As far as transitions went, that wasn't what I was expecting. "What, now?"

"My mother."

"Yes, you said you're going to talk to her." I was confused. "What are you going to talk to her about?"

"Hmm?" He finally dragged his eyes to me and stared for what felt like a really long time. "Oh," he said, blinking himself back from wherever he'd gone. "Some context would probably be good, huh?"

"Maybe just a little," I hedged.

"I'm going to talk to my mother about Lisette Michel."

If I'd been confused before, that was nothing compared to what I was currently feeling. "I don't understand. What do you think your mother can do? Unless... Does your mother know Lisette?" I figured he would've mentioned that before if it were the case, but I was still hopeful he'd simply decided to hold his cards close to the vest.

"I don't think my mother knows her, but never say never," he replied. "I'm actually interested in knowing if she's ever heard stories about Lisette."

That's when realization dawned, and I felt like an idiot. "Oh, right." I bobbed my head. "Your mother knows all the players in the area. She might be able to help us."

"I don't know if she knows *all* the players. New Orleans is a big city. Sure, the French Quarter isn't all that big, but it's still packed with people. Then when you include all the other boroughs, well, it's definitely a lot of people. We used to have a voodoo tour, though. This was a long time ago. It's possible my mother crossed paths with Lisette back in the day."

"That would be helpful," I admitted. "Now that we finally have a name, I would be lying if I said I wasn't a bit nervous."

He laughed. "Do you think she's going to curse you or something?"

"According to my mother, she's already cursed me. I just don't want to make matters worse."

"Given your taste in men, I'm not sure they could get any worse. The only thing you have going for you at this point is that you haven't tried dating Scott Peterson."

My eyebrows knitted. "Who?" I asked after a beat. The name wasn't familiar.

"He was that guy who killed his pregnant wife and dumped her body in the ocean," Jasper replied. "You know, he had a mistress and claimed his wife disappeared walking the dog or something."

"I guess I don't remember it."

Jasper offered a dismissive wave. "It happened a long time ago. The only reason I remembered the name is because I saw a *Dateline* episode on it last night before I went to sleep. I like watching those shows when I'm zoning out."

I brightened. "I do too."

"You do?"

I nodded. "They remind me that no matter how bad the dudes I've been dating are, there are way worse guys out there."

"Right?" Jasper solemnly dipped his chin. "When you compare your dating history to the guys hanging out with the *Dateline* crew, you're hardly cursed at all."

For some reason, that struck me as funny, and I started to giggle.

"I'm being serious," he insisted. "You could do way worse. Like, this one guy, he used to like to eat live butterflies before going on dates. He thought the innocence of the butterfly would hide the fact that he didn't have a soul."

I frowned. "Are you sure you're not making that up? That sounds like something you read and imagined was on *Dateline*."

"Oh, no." He was insistent. "The guy was a freak. Your guys were nowhere near as freaky as him."

"True story."

I was still smiling when we arrived at Bourbon Street. The driving beat of the music caused me to shut my eyes briefly. As much as I loved the French Quarter, Bourbon Street was something else entirely.

"This is my least favorite spot here," I admitted as I quickly sidestepped a guy trying to reach around and grab my ass.

Seeing what was happening, Jasper slapped the stranger's hand away and shot him a dirty look. "Manners!"

The drunk in question shot Jasper a sheepish smile. "Sorry, dude. I didn't know she was yours."

"It doesn't matter if she's mine or not." Jasper was firm.

"It's just good manners not to grab a woman's ass. Don't be a douche."

"Sorry." The man shot me a sheepish smile. "It won't happen again." He mimed crossing his heart. "Well, unless you want it to happen again."

I forced myself to keep my smile at bay. That would only encourage him, after all, and I didn't want my amusement to serve as tacit permission for him to touch women against their will.

"Do you want it to happen again?" he called out as he moved down the sidewalk. "If so, I'll be right over."

I let loose a sigh as the guy switched his attention to a willowy blonde. "Ours was a fleeting love," I drawled.

Jasper smiled and held out a hand. Confused, I stared at it.

"Come on," he prodded, shaking it. "I'm going to take you for a drink."

"To one of these places? Um, no. I love your city, but I hate Bourbon Street. I won't be partaking in this brand of fun."

"You won't be partaking?" Jasper rolled his eyes. "I love how you talk all fancy and stuff. That must be a Boston thing, huh?"

I'd never really considered that. "I guess," I said. "It doesn't seem abnormal to me. Like, I don't consider it fancy."

"Well, it's fun, whatever it is." He shook his hand again. "Come on. I didn't say we were drinking on Bourbon Street. I know a place right down the street. I promise you're going to like it."

I hesitated. "Are you trying to get me drunk?"

He barked a laugh. "No. I'm trying to get you to loosen up a little bit. It's been a long day. You finally got some answers. There's no reason you can't have one cocktail to celebrate. Besides, it's early."

I exhaled heavily and slid my hand into his. "Okay, one drink. You'd better not be taking me to a seedy place, though."

"I guarantee it's not seedy. Trust me."

I NEVER WOULD'VE KNOWN THE BOMBAY Club was such a cool place if Jasper hadn't decided that was our destination. I'd passed the entrance multiple times but mistaken it for a hotel entrance. Once inside, I realized it was a tunnel of sorts. The hotel entrance—a very old hotel if I wasn't mistaken—was to our right. Farther down, however, a set of huge wooden doors welcomed us.

Still dubious, I poked my head inside. I was fully ready to veto the place until I saw the bar. It was huge, dark wood practically glowing under the mood lighting, and candles burned at every table.

"This looks like a seduction location," I told Jasper, who was focused on me to gauge my reaction.

He chuckled. "It's got some of the best mixologists in the Quarter, and it's quiet enough to hear ourselves talk. I like the pomp of Bourbon Street because that's what keeps my family fed. That's what keeps the tourists happy. This place speaks to my soul, though."

His tone was stirring. "I guess we can have a drink here," I said begrudgingly, although being inside made me want a strong cocktail. "No funny business."

He caught the finger I wagged at him. "You're in luck. I left my clown costume and floppy shoes at home." He led me to a table, waving at a bartender as he held out a chair for me. Once settled, he handed me a cocktail menu.

"Don't go for the first thing you see," he ordered. "Read all the drink descriptions. Some of the drinks they make here are real gems. If you have questions, hit me up. I think I've tried them all at this point."

"A drinking problem is nothing to brag about," I chided.

He laughed again. "I didn't try them all in one night. I do come in here at least once a week. Isn't that right, Chet?" He pointed the question toward the bartender he'd waved at when we picked our table.

"Yes, Jasper is a frequent visitor," Chet agreed. His smile was gregarious, but a hint of curiosity also lurked in his eyes. "And who might you be?"

"This is Rowan Shaw," Jasper replied before I could. "She's working for Toni at the store and is new to the area. She joined us from Salem, which makes her a real-life witch."

"Is that a fact?" Chet's grin widened. "You're working for Toni, huh? Ah, she broke my heart." He pressed his hand to his chest. "I was in love with her in high school. Even after I found out I didn't have the right parts to entice her, I was still hoping she was just confused. I never got over it."

"Believe it or not, you're not the first person to tell me that today," I said as I studied the menu. Jasper was right about it being eclectic. "I don't even know what to order. They all sound amazing."

"Well, what do you like?" Chet put coasters down on the table. "Are you a vodka person? Do you prefer tequila?"

"I'll drink almost anything."

"Gin?"

I nodded.

"Do you like blackberries?"

"I do."

"How about this?" He tapped on my menu. "The Blackout Brambles. It's got muddled blackberries, and they enhance the drink, so it's perfection." He offered a chef's kiss by way of proof.

"I'm sold." I grinned at him. "When you come back, I want you to tell me stories about Jasper when he was in school. So far today, we've crossed paths with no less than eight former schoolmates, and they all had stories about him. I'm keeping a running tally."

Chet barked out a gregarious laugh. "I think that can be arranged."

"I'm sure you have some at the ready for whenever Jasper brings his conquests here," I added.

"Oh, Jasper doesn't bring his dates here." Chet turned serious. "This is the place he goes when he doesn't want to be Jasper the Magnificent but rather Jasper the Guy Who Had a Long Day at Work. This is his sanctum, which means you must be pretty special for him to bring you here."

I was caught off guard. "Oh, um, we're just working on a project together." The words tumbled out.

"Sure." Chet gave me an if-you-say-so grin. "What will it be for you, Mr. We're Working on a Project Together?" he asked Jasper.

"I'll have the Meet Your Maker," Jasper replied. If he was bothered by Chet's assumption, he didn't show it. "I'm thinking it's a bourbon night."

"You've got it." Chet offered us a friendly wink before setting off for the bar.

"Do you know everybody in the Quarter?" I asked Jasper when the waiter was gone. "I mean ... seriously, we haven't gone anywhere today where you haven't known someone."

"The French Quarter is often full of tourists," he acknowledged. "The locals all know one another. We're kind of a secondary family because sometimes it's like we're in the trenches when it gets busy here, and we need each other to stay sane."

"I never really thought about that," I admitted. "It makes sense, though. We're the same way in Salem except we have two tourist seasons."

"How does that work?"

"Well, the Halloween season starts in September and lasts

through the beginning of November. That's all the stuff you see on television. In the summer, given our location on the water, we get overrun by a lot of boaters. It's a different sort of tourist season."

"Your tone tells me you don't like the boaters." Jasper leaned back in his chair. "Is there a reason?"

I hesitated then lifted one shoulder. "Sometimes, money comes with a certain attitude. I don't like the attitude. What's interesting about New Orleans is that I haven't seen anybody with that attitude. I think that's why I like it so much."

"You should try hanging around in Uptown. You'll find that attitude everywhere up there."

"Oh, yeah?" I pursed my lips. "Or maybe I'll just stay in the French Quarter. I think these are my people."

"They're my people too." He planted his feet on either side of mine under the table. "So, tell me about yourself, Rowan Shaw. I want to know everything."

"I already told you about the curse."

"I don't want to hear more about the curse." He was serious. "I want to hear about you. We have cocktails coming, and I want to hear absolutely everything."

"You'll be bored."

"Something tells me I won't."

"But I think you will."

"Try me. We won't know until you try."

With a sigh, I nodded. "Okay, but don't say I didn't warn you."

"SO, DID YOU REALLY DECLARE COSTUME DAY sexist in middle school?" Jasper asked as he walked me back to my apartment hours later. One cocktail had turned into three, and the conversation that followed was the sort of thing unbelievable first dates were made of. None of my dates, mind you

—and that certainly wasn't a date—but the stories had flown freely, and at one moment, I felt as if I'd known him my entire life.

"I did." I solemnly tilted my head. We'd stretched the three drinks over two hours, so I wasn't tipsy. I felt somehow giddy, though, something I couldn't explain. "It was Salem, so of course all the girls dressed up as witches. It's totally sexist."

"Uh-huh." Jasper's eyes lit with amusement as he stared down at me. We were at the front door of the building although he didn't seem in a hurry to say his goodbyes and go on his way. "Did you ever think everybody just dressed up like witches because those were the costumes that were handy? I mean ... it's Salem. I'm guessing everybody in Salem has a witch costume, just like everybody here has something that can be thrown on in a pinch for a Mardi Gras party."

"No, it's sexist."

"Well, at least you can form an opinion." He leaned closer, his eyes on mine, and exhaled heavily. I could feel his breath on my face, and mine clogged in my lungs.

What is he doing?

"You should probably go now," I blurted out of nowhere, my heart hammering. His proximity, which had felt natural before, had me tongue-tied. "Thanks for walking me home."

"Of course. I'm a gentleman." He didn't pull away.

"You're not leaving," I pointed out a few seconds later, something akin to panic licking at my skin. "Don't you think you should go?"

"Probably. I just..." His lips brushed against mine out of nowhere. It was the softest of touches, to the point where I almost thought I'd imagined it. Then his tongue slipped between my lips for a quick search before retreating again. When he pulled back to stare into my eyes, he seemed conflicted.

"What was that?" I demanded, hating how breathless I sounded. "I told you that we're not doing that."

"Because of the curse, right?" He didn't move away from me, instead invading my space further.

"Because of the curse," I confirmed.

"What happens when you're no longer cursed?"

I wondered if he was hanging around waiting for that moment. The possibility hadn't even occurred to me. I decided to go with the truth. "Nothing, because I'm not a one-night-stand girl and you're not a relationship guy."

"How do you feel about a week-long stand? I mean ... it doesn't have to be one night."

"Maybe not for you, but it means something to me."

"What does? Sex?"

I nodded. "I need to feel a connection with someone. I won't waste that connection on a guy who's just going to walk away." I reached out to grab his wrist as he took a step back. "I like you. I do. You're funny, and you go out of your way to make me laugh. It's okay that you don't want to make a connection. You're not ready yet. That doesn't make you a bad guy."

"But it makes me the wrong choice for you, even for a short period of time, because you don't do temporary," he surmised.

I swallowed hard and nodded. "I can't. I know myself. I'll grow attached to you. I'll want more. Even though you've told me I can't have more, I'll be crushed when you're gone, and I'll blame myself. It will be the curse all over again."

"A new curse?" He arched an eyebrow.

"Or an old curse rearing its ugly head." I was rueful. "I'm not a temporary girl. Realistically, I know every relationship I get into isn't going to last forever, but I at least like to know that's an option. With you, it's not."

"No, I guess it's not." He blew out a sigh, ruffling my hair.

"I'm going to blame the cocktails. Chet always makes them too strong."

I grabbed on to the olive branch he was extending. "Yes, let's blame Chet. This is clearly all his fault."

"I'm going to give him a piece of my mind." Jasper took a shaky step back. "I might do it right now."

As long as he removed himself from my space so that I wouldn't accidentally lose my head, I didn't care where he went. "Give him hell for me too."

"Okay." Jasper's smile was wan as he dragged a hand through his hair. "Are you okay to get upstairs?"

"I'm fine."

"Okay. Good. Um ... great." He started to walk away then stilled. "I'll be in touch after I talk to my mother. I'm certain she'll have dirt on Lisette."

"I'm looking forward to the dirt." That was all I got out before he started across the road.

Part of me wanted to apologize one more time, but that was unnecessary. I hadn't done anything wrong. I was simply protecting my heart. He couldn't be angry about that.

Sixteen

"How is the curse going? No boils on your girl parts, right? Those are the worst."

Toni was all smiles the next day as she rested her elbows on the counter and watched me dust the Marie Laveau statue located on the display table at the center of the store.

"Boils?" I made a face. "That's just ... so gross."

"I'm right there with you. That's why I'm glad I'm not the one who's cursed."

"You should be glad. Being cursed is zero fun."

"Oh, I don't know." Toni shook her dark head. "You have some pretty good stories to go with that curse. Who doesn't love a good story?"

"The woman dating scammers and future prison inmates," I replied, not missing a beat. "As for boils, I seem to be missing those right about now."

"Are you complaining?"

"Not even a little." I went back to dusting. The statue was one of my favorite pieces in the store, and it always drew my eye.

"Are you any closer to solving your little problem?" She looked legitimately interested. "I mean... I could still ask my mother. She'll probably give me grief for not knowing the answer already—she thinks I've fallen down on my education—but I'm willing to take one for the team. You were kind of wishy-washy when I offered before."

I wasn't opposed to asking Cleo questions, should the situation come to that. However, since I knew how uncomfortable Toni was asking her mother for help, which was why she hadn't followed through after the first offer, I decided to table that option ... at least for the time being. "You don't have to. Jasper's friend gave us a name last night, and we're going to pursue that."

"Jasper's friend?" Toni arched a curious eyebrow.

"Yeah. His name is Charlie Dutton."

"Charlie?" Toni snorted derisively. "Exactly how is he proving helpful?"

I hesitated, suddenly unsure. "Jasper said he was a genealogy expert."

"Oh." Toni's face twisted into an expression I didn't recognize. "I forgot he was into that stuff. I guess it makes sense."

I exhaled heavily, relieved. "So, he's not a moron, right?"

"Charlie? I guess it depends on what you want to use him as an expert for. Genealogy would be a topic he knows a few things about. He was always into that stuff when we were in school. He bought parchment paper and made family trees for all of us. I thought he was just bored for a bit, but then I realized he really liked it. I gave the one he made me to my mother. She still uses it to this day."

"He had nice things to say about you."

"Yeah?"

I nodded. "He said that you broke his heart when you announced that you were attracted to women."

Toni snickered. "He did not say that."

"He did. In fact, he's not the first one to mention that to me. Jasper has introduced me to several people who have said the exact same thing."

"And what's that?"

"That they were in love with you and their hearts were crushed in a vise when you came out."

"Huh." Toni rubbed a cheek. "I have trouble believing Charlie ever had a crush on me. He was much more interested in books than girls ... or boys, for that matter."

"Just because he lost himself in genealogy on a regular basis, that doesn't mean he didn't like you." I opted to be pragmatic. "Not all teenage boys are like Jasper. Er, how I imagine Jasper likely was at that age," I said quickly. "He probably had confidence for days. That's just how he's built. Not everybody is like that, though."

"How were you in high school?" Toni leaned against the counter, arms crossed. "I picture you as popular, maybe even a cheerleader."

I choked on a laugh. "Um, no." I swung my head hard left and right. "I was much more like Charlie. I always had my nose buried in a book. I didn't even have a date for junior prom. I went by myself, but only because my mother insisted that it wasn't okay to miss out on a big memory."

"Oh yeah?" Toni cocked her head. "When was your first boyfriend?"

"Not until college." I thought back to the young man in question. "Ted Kingsley. My mother hated him although she went out of her way to pretend otherwise because she didn't want to dissuade me from dating. I heard her and my aunt making fun of him one night, though. They kept equating him to Ted Bundy ... and I don't think they were doing it to be funny."

Toni's chuckle was light. "It sounds to me like you've always had bad taste in men. What was Ted's problem?"

"I don't think he had a problem. I mean ... he was just a guy. My mother said he was a narcissist, that whenever there was a mirror in the room, he was always drawn to it. I never noticed that, though."

Toni's lips were pressed tight.

"What?" I asked, suddenly self-conscious.

"Nothing." She shook her head. "Did you lose your virginity to Ted?"

"Yeah." I frowned at the memory. "That was the worst forty-eight seconds of my life. Well, at least until that point."

Toni's eyebrows hiked up her forehead. "Forty-eight seconds? You timed him?"

"There was a clock on the nightstand."

"And you counted?"

I held out my hands. "It wasn't like the books I was reading at the time."

"It's never like the books. Tell me your mother didn't send you out into the world believing it was going to be like a romance novel."

My need to defend my mother was fierce. "Oh no. She was big on having 'the talk' once every six months, starting when I turned twelve. At first she stressed I wasn't old enough but that she wanted to be open. By the time I made it to college, she changed things up and suggested that maybe I was getting too old to wait."

That made Toni laugh. "Most parents stress that 'virgin until marriage' thing ... even though they know it's not realistic."

"Not in Boston. It's pretty liberal there. Plus, well, it's Salem. People have attitudes about female sexuality being squashed there. I mean ... the Salem witch trials influence almost everything in that area."

"Huh." Toni seemed legitimately intrigued. "I never thought of that, but it's kind of cool. I bet there's a lot of female empowerment stuff going on there."

"Oh, definitely." I smiled at the mention of home. "You would love it there."

"I bet. Maybe after you lift your curse, I'll take a trip up there." She hesitated then pressed forward. "You did find a guy who could last longer than forty-eight seconds at some point, right?"

"Oh, yeah. Skip Pendleton. He was really good in bed ... which he proved by spreading his talent around the campus. I thought he was my boyfriend, but it turned out I was only one of five or six girls to believe that."

"Ugh." Toni made a disgusted face. "That is ... not good."

"Yeah. He sucked." I grinned for no discernible reason.

"Why is that funny?" Toni looked horrified.

"I was just thinking about how I found out. He was sleeping with my roommate, and we all got mono together. It was delightful."

"You have a twisted sense of humor." She rolled her eyes. "Seriously, though, I'm starting to think you might be on to something with this curse business. Have you ever had a good relationship?"

"Sure. Well, I mean ... I haven't found 'the one' yet, but I've had relationships that didn't go poorly. Johnny Conners and I dated for six months without a single bit of drama."

"Oh, yeah? What happened to Johnny?"

"He switched schools after he was caught plagiarizing a term paper."

Toni's mouth dropped open. "You just told me there was no drama with him."

"There was no drama with him and me together, as a couple," I clarified. "He was a total loser. He didn't cheat or anything, though. Given my track record, that truly is a win."

"Ugh. Have you ever considered that you're not cursed but have bleeding tragic taste in men and that's your true problem?"

"What do you think got me through college?"

She smirked. "What did Charlie say?"

"He said he was brokenhearted when he realized you were gay but that he still held out hope it would be a phase."

"Not *that*. What did he say about your curse? Does he have any ideas on who this Michelle might be? That's a very common first name."

"That's why we're focusing on Michel as a last name. He did come up with something. Lisette Michel. Apparently, she had a big presence in the voodoo circuit back in the day."

Toni's face immediately fell. "Lisette?" She pressed a hand to her abdomen. "Holy crap. I didn't even think about her. It makes sense, though."

"You know her?" Hope kindled as I pulled away from the statue. "Please tell me she owes you a favor and we can nip this little problem in the bud by the end of the day."

Toni shot me an apologetic grimace. "Sorry, your luck isn't that good."

"Oh, I know."

"I do know of her," Toni hedged. "She's not a nice woman."

"Tell me about her." I was resigned to hearing horror stories, but I needed to get ahead of this if I wanted to ever lay claim to a life that couldn't be described as a travesty.

"I met her when I was a kid." Toni took on a far-off expression. "We used to have picnics with all the local practitioners. They were over in Bywater, at Crescent Park. I remember because they were a lot of fun. I got to hang with the other kids, and there was always good food. Then, at night, they would have a big bonfire, and everybody would get naked and dance under the full moon."

"We do that in Salem too. Well, the nature witches do. My mother was never a fan although when she decided I was frigid, she tried to get me to go to one of the dances because she said I needed to unclench. I never did."

"I can't tell if you're being serious."

"I totally am."

"I once met a guy who said that he believed song lyrics should mean something, that every lyric had to be truthful. He was a big fan of the antiwar stuff of the seventies. He was not a fan of the Beastie Boys, however. He said that fighting for your right to party was insulting to those who came before us."

I blinked several times in rapid succession. "Um … what does that have to do with this conversation?"

"I don't know. It just popped into my head. I'm curious about the naked dancing, though. Is that really a thing up there?"

Suddenly, I was thrown off my game. "Not if it's not really a thing down here."

"Yeah, I was trying to be funny."

"Well, good job." I shot her what I hoped would pass for an enthusiastic thumbs-up.

"Right." Toni didn't look convinced. "Back to Lisette. She has a rotten reputation. She's the reason all the picnics went away. She was in charge and kept getting in beefs with other priestesses because she was a territorial bitch on wheels. My mother hates her."

"Do you think it's possible she cursed my grandmother? I mean … the way Charlie described it, Lisette threw annual events. It's entirely possible my grandmother traveled down here for one of those events and somehow got on the wrong side of Lisette."

"If the stories I've heard are true, almost everybody ended up on the wrong side of Lisette," Toni noted. "This is the first time I ever heard she might be responsible for a love curse, though."

"Do you think I'm looking in the wrong place?"

She hesitated then held out her hands. "I honestly don't know. If I were you, I would keep chasing this angle. I would be careful, though. You don't want to make things worse. There's little Lisette loves more than fighting with people. Just because she might've cursed your grandmother, that doesn't mean she won't be more than happy to curse you again and make things ten times worse."

I hadn't considered that, but it made sense. "Jasper says he's going to try to find an address. Apparently, she lives in Bywater although I'm not sure where that is."

"It's not far. It's within walking distance." Toni's lips swished back and forth. "It's not like the French Quarter," she said finally. "You need to be careful."

"Is it dangerous?"

"No. It actually used to be when I was a kid, although I don't remember it being anything other than what it is now."

"And what is it?"

"An artist community. It's a close-knit neighborhood. The neighbors all look out for one another. It's being gentrified, which makes the locals bitter. They don't like that the Baton Rouge businessmen have come in and torn down the older homes so they can put up condos and bring in more part-time residents."

"And Lisette lives there?" That didn't make a lot of sense to me.

"I'm not sure. Did Charlie tell you she lived there?"

"Yes."

"Then he probably knows. He keeps up on all those things." She hesitated then continued, "Don't go down there alone. Take Jasper with you. He's a pain, but all the locals will know his parents. They might even know and love him."

"Oh, well, I'm not sure how much time I'll be spending with Jasper," I hedged.

Toni's eyes gleamed with suspicion. "And why is that?"

I considered lying but discarded the notion almost immediately. Toni had been good to me. I wasn't going to repay her with disloyalty. "Because ... um ... there might've been a slip last night."

"Oh, you slept with him." Toni's expression told me exactly what she thought of that possibility. "I told you not to flirt with him. He's got a magic penis or something. Even women who are determined to protect their virtue fall for his crap. I don't know how he pulls it off."

"I didn't sleep with him," I reassured her. "It's just ... we stopped at the Bombay Club on the way home after dinner last night. I had a few drinks. That led to a kiss."

"A kiss?" She arched a brow and waited.

"Yeah." I was still angry with myself for having let it happen. "When we were finished, I told him it couldn't happen again."

"And he just accepted that?" Toni was clearly dubious.

"He did. He knows about the curse. I also explained that, even if there was no curse, I wasn't a one-night-stand girl. When I finally do get the chance to engage in a relationship that's not destined for failure, it won't be with a guy who doesn't want something real. I've learned my lesson on cads, and I've learned it the hard way. He's a nice guy, but I don't want something empty."

Toni stared hard as if trying to see inside my soul. Ultimately, she nodded. "He really is a good guy." She wrung her hands. "I don't want to say otherwise because it's not fair to him. He's been a good friend to me ... more than once. He's just a terrible boyfriend."

That made me laugh. "Has he ever been a real boyfriend? I'm betting not."

"I don't think so." Toni was rueful as she shook her head. "I keep expecting him to stumble across a woman who will knock him for a loop for a change. It hasn't happened yet, but I think it will eventually. When he finds her, he's going to fall head over heels. He's loyal to a fault. He'll be a good husband and father. I just don't know when he's going to finally grow up and embrace that possibility."

"Well, he's a man. He doesn't have the same biological clock ticking down that we do. He can afford to be wild and untethered well into his forties if he feels like it. I don't have that luxury."

"Are you sure you're not falling for him?" Toni looked tortured at the thought.

"I'm sure." I meant it. Or maybe I just hoped I did. "He's very charming. He's a lot of fun. I like hanging out with him, but only as friends. I blame that blackberry bramble drink for slipping up. I've been feeling a little lonely. It won't happen again."

Toni looked as though she wanted to press things further, but she nodded eventually. "It's good that you recognize his faults. He doesn't mean to break hearts left and right. He simply can't seem to help himself."

"Well, if it's one thing I don't need, it's a broken heart. I think I have enough to deal with otherwise. Jasper Bentley is not going to mess up my head. I know exactly what I'm doing here, and I'm focused."

"Good." Toni exhaled heavily. "I'm glad. He's a good guy. He's just not the guy for you."

"Oh, I've already come to that conclusion myself. You don't have to worry. I've got everything under control."

I just had to make sure I kept my eye on the prize. I was finally getting somewhere. Letting my forward progress be derailed by a man wasn't going to happen, period.

Seventeen

I tried calling Jasper when I was finished with my shift, but he didn't pick up. I knew he had his own job—although I'd never actually seen him do it—so I decided to brave the wilds of Bywater alone. To save money, I walked. That turned out to be a mistake because I was a dripping, sweaty mess when I got there.

The area itself was delightful, however, and I gladly bought a huge bottle of water and walked the streets to cool down. I'd never seen anything quite like what I found there. The art was breathtaking. That was the best word I could come up with to describe it. I was absolutely floored by the murals, colorful houses and businesses, and even the sidewalk art adorning every corner.

"Wow." I thought I was alone when I said it, but when I looked to my left, I found an older woman watching me with mirth. "Sorry." Suddenly, I felt like an outsider in their insulated community. "It's just really colorful."

The woman chuckled, her white teeth blinding against her dark skin. She carried a covered cup and gestured toward a bench in the shade. "Sit down."

I was taken aback, wondering if she was about to warn me to get out of her space. That didn't seem out of the realm of possibility. In my laid-back khaki capris and simple black shirt, I'd never felt more out of place. "Um..."

"I'm not going to bite you," the woman reassured me. "It's hot, and you're very red. I'm afraid you're going to pass out. You need to take a breath."

"Oh." I wiped a forearm against my forehead and sat down. "It's hotter than I realized," I admitted, searching for a topic of conversation that wouldn't make me sound like a moron.

"Northerner, huh?" Amusement twinkled in the depths of the woman's eyes, but I knew that "northerner" wasn't a compliment here.

"How did you know?" I asked ruefully, sipping my water. "Is it my outfit?"

"Your outfit makes you look like a tourist, and not the ones who get drunk and obnoxious on Bourbon Street every night. You look more like the mothers who bring their children here, thinking they're going to give them a dose of culture ... only you don't have any little ones."

"Right."

"I'm Ruby, by the way. Ruby Sanders." She extended a hand.

I took it without hesitation. "Rowan Shaw."

"Rowan?" Ruby's forehead creased. "That's an interesting name."

"I'm from Salem. Massachusetts, not Oregon."

"Ah." Ruby nodded in understanding. "You're a witch."

That wasn't a question, but I smiled all the same. "That seems to be the general consensus. My family owns a witch shop in Salem, so I guess that's an apt enough description."

"Do you not consider yourself a witch?"

I opened my mouth to answer, then snapped it shut, really

considering my answer for a change. "I don't know what I am," I said finally. "I think, maybe, I'm still figuring that part of it out."

"Which is why you ended up here." She nodded knowingly. "I get it. New Orleans is a great place to find yourself."

"I didn't know I was trying to find myself until I got here." My voice was soft. "I always thought I knew. It turns out I didn't." I had no idea why I was telling her that, but I couldn't seem to stop myself. Perhaps she had the sort of face that exuded trustworthiness and knowledge and maybe a little something else I couldn't put a name to.

"What happened to make you lose yourself?"

"Oh, I don't know that I'm lost. I just don't think I ever found myself in the first place."

"That's even worse." Ruby sipped from her cup. "Rum," she said to my unasked question, grinning like a madwoman about to embark on an adventure. "It's New Orleans, so it's allowed."

"I wasn't judging you," I blurted. "I didn't know people carried rum around in cups like that until I came here. Now, I'm almost used to it."

"You'll be one of us before you know it."

That made me laugh. "This is just a stopover for me. I have a business to run with my aunt. I'll have to go back."

"Maybe." Ruby didn't look convinced. "How did you find yourself over here? I only ask because most of the tourists stick to the French Quarter ... and sometimes the Garden District. It's only those individuals with NOLA in their souls who find Bywater."

I considered lying. Honestly, I didn't want to admit the truth to that kind woman. Ultimately, I decided to hedge my bets and toe a line somewhere in the middle. "I'm looking for somebody. It's someone who I believe knew my grandmother.

She's supposed to live over here, although I'm not entirely certain where."

"Your grandmother was from here?"

"No. I believe she visited. I didn't know her. She died a long time ago. She came for some sort of paranormal conference thing. I guess ... well, I guess I was just looking for a touchstone. I'm not doing a very good job of explaining myself."

"It's okay," Ruby reassured me. "I get it. You lost your momma."

I stilled, my heart rolling painfully. "How...?" I trailed off.

"How did I know?" Ruby's smile was kind. "You're marked by sadness. It pretty much rolls off of you in waves. I can see it when I look at you ... although there's a light trying to peek out from inside. I can see that too."

"Oh, yeah?" I was amused despite myself. "What sort of light?"

"I don't know." She offered a one-shoulder shrug. "I don't think it's important that I know what the source of the light is. I think it's important that you know."

"I didn't even know there was a light."

"Oh, you would've seen it eventually." Ruby reached forward and patted my knee. "The light will reveal itself to you when you least expect it. And your momma, that woman you're missing something terrible even as you try to find who you're supposed to be without her? Yeah, she's going to find a way to lead you to the light."

"That's a pretty tall order," I noted, "what with her being dead and all."

"Dead isn't gone."

"Are you saying she's haunting me?"

"In a sense, but that's not what I meant. The dead are never truly gone as long as someone remembers them. Your momma is still in your heart, so she's not gone. She lives through you."

I wasn't much of a crier, yet I found my eyes burning with unshed tears, my throat thick. "I guess that's an interesting way to look at it," I said when I was reasonably assured I could speak without my voice cracking. "For now, I just want to find Lisette Michel. I don't suppose you know her."

"Oh, everybody in these parts knows her." Ruby's smile faded. "She's the one who knew your grandmother?"

"Yes. I was hoping to get to meet her."

Ruby ran her tongue over her lips, considering, then blew out a sigh. "She's over on Pauline Street. She lives in a gray house with purple storm shutters and a pink door."

That sounded both divine and hideous. "Seriously?" *It can't possibly be this easy.*

"Seriously," Ruby confirmed. "Don't be surprised if she doesn't welcome you with open arms. Past associations aside, Lisette isn't known for being one of the friendlier faces on the Bywater Welcome Wagon."

"Do you guys actually have a welcome wagon?"

She smirked. "More or less. It's sort of a crawfish boil wagon more than anything—they're a community thing—but Lisette doesn't involve herself with them, either."

"I was just hoping to talk to her," I hedged. "I don't want to give her a hard time or anything."

"Why would you want to give her a hard time?" Ruby's eyes were full of curiosity. "I thought she knew your grandmother."

"She did." I was relatively certain that was true. "You just make it sound like she won't be welcoming if I knock on her door."

"Oh, that's the understatement of the year." Ruby loosed a low chuckle. "That woman has never been welcoming a day in her life. That shouldn't stop you from going over there, though. There's no harm in visiting ... even if Lisette thinks otherwise."

"What's the worst thing she can do?" I mused, more to myself than her.

"Oh, that's a totally different question." Ruby clucked her tongue. "Honestly, I'm looking forward to you finding out." She patted my knee. "You should head over. You don't want to be caught on this side of the city after dark on your own."

"Because it's not safe?" I glanced around. I had difficulty believing trouble ever touched that idyllic setting. I knew that was a naive thing to think, but with the sun shining and the music wafting down the street, it was the only thing I could believe.

"Because there's darkness in every city if you're not careful," she replied. "Just ... make sure you're on your way before it gets dark, okay?"

"Sure." I flashed a smile as I stood. "Thanks for your help."

"No problem." She waved off my gratitude. "I'm always happy to help a soul that needs peace."

That was an odd thing to say. I considered asking her why she said it, but when a shadow landed on her face, I couldn't stop myself from getting distracted and twirling to see if trouble had somehow found us. Instead of trouble, I found Jasper.

"Hey," I blurted, my awkwardness returning with a vengeance.

"That was going to be my opening line," he said drily, shaking his head. "I'm sorry I missed your call. You didn't have to ignore my return calls as payback, though."

"What?" Confused, I pulled my phone out of my pocket. I had five missed calls—and seven missed texts—all from Jasper. "I'm sorry," I said automatically. "I didn't hear it go off."

"Did you walk over here?" Jasper looked worried. "That was quite the hike if you did."

"Yeah. I didn't realize how far it was until I was already here."

"Well, I drove. There's no way you're walking home." He turned his attention to Ruby. "I know you, right?"

Ruby's smile was soft. "I'm not sure. You do look familiar."

"I'm Jasper Bentley." He extended his hand for her to shake.

"Oh." Recognition dawned on her features. "You're Jen Bentley's boy. I met you at a crawfish boil about six months back or so. There was a big ghost-story festival."

"That's right." Jasper snapped his fingers. "You were manning the boil, if I remember correctly." He pressed his fingers to his lips in a chef's kiss. "It was quite the boil."

"And I remember you," Ruby shot back. "You have a charm streak a mile wide, just like your daddy."

"That is my lot in life," Jasper agreed with a cheeky grin.

"Yeah, if I remember correctly, you left a few girls in tears that night because you didn't ask for their phone numbers."

"Oh, no way." Rather than appearing worried, Jasper wagged a chiding finger. "I'm not an idiot. I know how this goes. There's no way I'm romancing a Bywater girl. I've known too many Bywater daddies. Just because I'm handsome, that doesn't make me an idiot."

Ruby snorted in delight. "You're definitely not stupid." She flicked her eyes to me. "I don't think you were holding those girls at arm's length because you were afraid of their daddies, though."

"Oh, we're not together," I volunteered out of nowhere. I had no idea why I felt the need to explain my relationship with Jasper, yet I did. "He's helping me on a project." I looked at Jasper for confirmation. "Right?"

He didn't respond immediately. Instead, he studied my face for what felt like a really long time. An emotion I couldn't quite put a name to was lurking in the depths of his eyes. If I didn't know better, I would say it was longing. That was ridiculous, of course. Jasper was the love-them-and-leave-them type. He might've wanted a quick roll in the hay with me—maybe even three rolls in the hay—but nothing genuine was lurking between us. *Couldn't be.*

"Right?" I prodded again when he hadn't responded after a full ten seconds.

Ultimately, rather than agreeing, Jasper offered Ruby a sheepish smile. "We're still figuring out what we are to one another."

"What?" I was dumbfounded.

Jasper kept his gaze on Ruby. "I find her absolutely delightful. She doesn't seem to understand why. To me, that indicates a self-esteem issue. I haven't yet decided how I'm going to handle the situation. So for now, we're just adventuring."

I couldn't believe he'd said that with a straight face. For her part, Ruby appeared absolutely thrilled with his response. "People are destined to find one another at the right time," she said.

I had to nip the conversation in the bud—and quickly. "He's just trying to charm you," I argued. "He's not really interested in me. He likes messing with me, sure, but we're not looking for the same things in life."

"Oh, no?" Ruby flicked her eyes back to me. "What are you looking for?"

"Answers," I replied simply.

"What are you looking for, Romeo?" she asked Jasper.

"A good time," he answered, not missing a beat.

"Are you not looking for a good time?" she asked me.

"Oh, I'm always looking for a good time," I replied.

"The thing is not all good times are created equal. He's looking for the sort of good time that stops after a night or two so he can move on to have a good time with somebody else. I'm looking for the sort of good time that lasts forever ... just as soon as I can trust that forever is actually an option."

Ruby blinked several times as if absorbing my words, then she flashed that blinding smile again. "I don't suppose it ever occurred to you that the things you're looking for actually overlap, huh?"

I flicked a look toward Jasper, who was watching me with heavy-lidded interest. "Not so much," I said finally. "I think we're better as friends. That's been working for both of us."

"Oh, I'm not saying you shouldn't be friends. You misunderstand." Ruby was grave. "You should definitely be friends." She eyed Jasper with fresh interest. "I'm just saying, when it comes down to it, you shouldn't limit your expectations of this boy. Eventually, despite his best efforts, he will become a man."

"Oh, you wound me." Jasper mock clutched at his heart. "I happen to think I'm already a man."

"In some ways," Ruby agreed. "In the biggest, you're not there yet. It won't be long, though. You just need the right person to show you the way. Or maybe 'light the way' is the better way to put it." She shot me a knowing look.

"Let me guess," I said drily. "You think I'm the one who is going to light the way for him."

"Yup, just like he's going to light the way for you."

"Well, then." I flashed a bland smile for Jasper's benefit. "Doesn't that sound fun?"

"It sounds like more fun than a barrel of drunks making beignets," he replied, laughing when I made a face. "Don't think too hard on it. As for you, ma'am, you keep doing what you're doing." He swooped in and snagged Ruby's hand, pressing a kiss to her knuckles. "You're utterly delightful just as you are."

Ruby didn't move to pull her hand away. Instead, she shook her head. "You're not quite the empty vessel you pretend to be," she offered. "That's the armor you wear, but you're about to fight with a different weapon altogether."

"Please tell me it's a sword," Jasper shot back, not missing a beat. "I happen to love a good sword."

"Yeah, I think you're in for a rude awakening, just like this one." She jerked a thumb toward me as she stood. "Either way, I think this adventure is going to be exactly what you're looking for. You just don't realize it yet. Either of you."

"On the contrary," Jasper drawled. "I'm looking forward to the adventure."

"Yeah, you come and talk to me again when you're crying in a month or so," Ruby suggested. "You'll be more open to my brand of truth then."

"I'm open to whatever you want to give me now."

"Sure you are, Mr. Charm." Ruby shook her head, rolling her eyes until they landed on me. "You're going to have your hands full with this one. There's no getting around it."

I opened my mouth to remind her we weren't together, but she barreled forward without giving me a chance to respond.

"He's going to be worth the effort," she continued. "Just keep telling yourself that. A boy can't become a man without making a few waves." She leaned close. "And a girl can't become a woman without embracing the fun." She patted my cheek. "You don't need to be so serious. Embrace this one's baser urges and allow the fun in. Together, I think you're going to be spectacular."

My mouth was still gaping when she disappeared around the corner. Finally, I remembered I wasn't alone and turned to find Jasper staring at me. His eyes were clouded as though he was thinking hard, but when he saw me looking, he pasted that gregarious smile of his firmly in place.

"I take it you found out where Lisette lives," he prodded.

"Yeah." I nodded. *Really, what else am I supposed to say?* "I need to Google it, but I don't think it's far."

"Well, let's get to it." He swirled a finger around to get me moving. "I want my curse story."

I wondered if that was all he wanted. For the umpteenth time, I had to question myself as to what he was getting out of this partnership. Ultimately, I simply shook my head. "Yeah. Let's find Lisette. The sooner we talk to her, the sooner we'll be able to put this behind us."

"Won't that be fun?"

"I really hope it will be."

Eighteen

I was nervous as we made our way to Lisette Michel's front door. *Was this it? Were we finally going to get some answers? Was I about to find out that there was no curse, and I was losing my mind? Worse, was I going to find out my mother had likely sabotaged her entire life believing in something that wasn't real?*

"Take a breath," Jasper instructed, his gaze keen as it roamed over my face. "It's going to be fine."

I mustered a glare for him—my emotions were so frazzled that it was all I could manage—but didn't respond.

"Seriously," Jasper growled. "I'm uncomfortable just looking at you. Act natural, or she really is going to curse you."

That snapped me out of it at least enough to plaster a smile on my face.

"Oh, that's much better," Jasper drawled, rolling his eyes. "You don't look demented at all now."

I wanted to kill him, to really wrap my fingers around his neck and squeeze until he couldn't make fun of me. "Just knock," I growled.

"You look constipated."

"Maybe that's what I'm feeling."

A ridiculous smirk washed over his features. "Well, in that case, be careful if you use the bathroom. This woman is definitely going to think we're weird if you lock yourself inside for an hour and start growling."

"Why would I growl?"

"You know ... squeezing it out isn't always easy. It's okay. I get it. Maybe add some more roughage into your diet or something."

I held up my hand to obliterate his face. "I can't even talk to you right now."

"That's a bummer, and here I thought this conversation was going to be one for the record books." He rapped on the screen door three times in quick succession, so loudly that it jolted me. "Let me do the talking."

My mouth dropped open. I had a definite opinion about that suggestion. I never got to utter it, however, because the inside door swung open at that moment to reveal a pretty woman with a confused look on her face. Her skin was dark and flawless. I couldn't see her hair because it was tucked underneath some sort of purple turban, but she had a regal look about her. She also couldn't have been older than thirty, and I was guessing she might've been even younger. I was bad at guessing ages.

"Can I help you?" The woman didn't open the door, instead swinging her gaze between Jasper and me. "We don't need any Scentsy."

Since my mouth was hanging open, likely swinging like a shutter in the breeze, I didn't want to know what she was thinking of us. "Scentsy?"

"I smell just fine," the woman replied. "The house smells good too. We're making gumbo. We don't need any help making it smell better." She moved to shut the door.

"We're not selling Scentsy," Jasper offered hurriedly. Obviously, he also wasn't prepared for the face that had answered the door because his notorious charm wasn't on full display for a change.

"We don't need hair conditioner either."

"We're not selling anything," Jasper reassured her quickly.

"No?" The woman cocked her head, suggesting she didn't believe us—at all. "What do you want? If you're from that real estate company, we're not interested in selling either. Not everybody thinks that gentrification is a good thing."

"We're not buying." Jasper had managed to recover from his surprise, and the smile that I'd become all too familiar with had decided to make an appearance. "We're looking for Lisette Michel."

The woman's demeanor didn't change. "She's not interested in falling for any scam regarding her Social Security," she warned. "I'll beat you silly with a hammer if you even try. I mean ... preying on an old woman. What is the matter with you?"

This conversation was quickly slipping from my grasp, and I was terrified I wouldn't get a second chance. "We're not here to hurt her," I blurted, ignoring the warning look Jasper shot me. "It's nothing like that. We just want to talk to her."

Rather than ushering us inside, the woman crossed her arms over her chest. "Why?"

"Because... because..." I had no idea how to fix the situation and started to panic. "Because I think she cursed my grandmother—like a bad curse, not one of the ones where hair falls out or dicks get boils or anything—and I'm desperate to have the curse lifted."

"Oh geez." Jasper slapped a hand over his face. "I cannot believe you just said that. I mean... What in the hell? Are you trying to kill me?"

I kept my eyes on the woman. "Please. We're not selling or stealing. We mean no harm to her. I'm just desperate."

I figured she would laugh in our faces and slam the door shut. Instead, she unlatched the hook, leaving the screen in place, and threw open the door. "You should've just said so. Come on."

I remained rooted to my spot, dumbfounded. "Um..."

"Come on," she repeated, her eyes flashing. "You guys are going to let all the cool air out, and it won't be pretty if you do."

I shot an uncertain look toward Jasper, but all he did while opening the screen was raise an eyebrow. That was enough for me. I ducked under his arm, slapped at the free hand he used to pinch my flank as payback, and stepped into the house, which was like crossing into another world.

"Oh, wow." My breath escaped in a sigh as I took in the colorful art adorning the walls. I recognized the faces staring back at me, but only because I liked to read during downtime at work. "It's the loas."

The woman gave me an appraising look. "Are you local? You don't sound local."

"Salem," I replied. "Massachusetts," I added when she didn't immediately speak.

"That's supposed to be a cool town," she said as she gestured for us to follow her into another room. The rich scent emanating from it told me we were going into the kitchen even before I saw the stove. "I'm Sophie. Lisette is my grandmother."

"It's nice to meet you." I stuck out my hand like a dork. "I'm Rowan. This is Jasper." I inclined my head toward his immovable presence, which had appeared at my back.

"Boyfriend?" Sophie asked.

"No," we answered at the same time.

"I'm her guide," Jasper replied. "She's new to the area and needs someone to show her the ropes."

"Uh-huh." Sophie didn't look convinced. "You're local?"

"Yup." Jasper bobbed his head. "My last name is Bentley. We run tours around the city."

"I recognize the last name." Sophie stared at him a beat longer, then turned her gaze toward me. "Why do you think you're cursed?"

I didn't like how she phrased that, but I knew better than to correct her. It was the truth or bust at that point. "My mother told me on her deathbed."

"And she's dated about thirty losers—all of whom should be locked up—over the course of the last year," Jasper replied. "She's either got the worst taste in men ever, or she's definitely cursed."

"Maybe she simply has terrible taste in men," Sophie suggested.

"Yeah, but the odds of her picking five guys who all had the police chasing them? That doesn't seem feasible."

"No." Sophie stared hard at him, then shook her head as she crossed to the stove. "How is it you think that your grandmother crossed paths with my grandmother?"

I wanted to ask where her grandmother was—telling the story twice was a waste of time—but she'd invited us into her home when she didn't have to. Manners were necessary.

"I believe that my grandmother came to New Orleans for an annual conference," I started, swiping my forearm across my face to get rid of the sweat. Sophie had said the air conditioner was running, but I had my doubts. "We own a store in Salem. Back then, it wasn't as easy to get supplies. I think she came to New Orleans once a year to stock up on those supplies."

"Oh." Sophie nodded as though that made all the sense in

the world. "My grandmother used to run events over in the Quarter. She made a ton of money doing it too. She bought this house ... and one for Uncle Terrence. He never did like to work, so Grammy had to help him out or be stuck with him forever. I can see them meeting that way."

I waited for her to continue. When she didn't, I decided to prod her. "Is your grandmother here? I would really like to talk to her."

"She is, but you need to talk to me first." Sophie was matter-of-fact. "What sort of curse are we talking, here? It sounds like a love curse."

"I'm not sure." I clenched my hands together. *Why is it so hot in here?* "May I sit down?"

"Sure." Sophie gestured toward the table. "I'll get you some water."

"Are you okay?" Jasper looked genuinely concerned as he helped me sit, one hand on my back. "Are you feeling faint?"

"I'm fine," I reassured him even though I felt anything other than fine. Right then, I really could've used a bed and some ice and maybe a pedestal fan pointed straight at my face. I felt like I was overheating.

"You don't look fine." Jasper pressed the back of one hand to my forehead. "You're so hot you could melt plastic." That didn't sound like a compliment.

"It's just warm out."

"She's a northerner," Sophie noted as she appeared at the edge of the table with a glass of water. "She's not used to the heat."

"I guess." Jasper was grim.

"She's also worked up," Sophie added. "I can't help you if I don't know what you're dealing with." She was calm as she sat in the chair next to mine. "If you're worried I won't believe you, that's not going to be a thing. My grandmother has always had a certain ... reputation. She thrives on it. The thing is she's cast more than one type of curse in her life."

"Oh." I was taken aback as I pressed the glass of water to my forehead. That wasn't the response I was expecting. In hindsight, it should've been, but I felt like a bit of a dolt. "I guess you want the whole story."

"That would be best," she agreed, extending a finger toward the stove. "Go over there and stir."

For a moment, I thought she was talking to me. Then I realized her eyes were on Jasper.

"You want me to cook?" Jasper's lips curved. "How do you know I won't ruin it?"

"I don't. You seem like the sort of guy who expects women to do all the work in the kitchen. Even a guy such as yourself can stir, however."

Jasper's eyebrows moved toward one another. "I'm not that sort of guy. If anything, I'm a takeout guy. I don't expect anybody to cook for me. I'm willing to pay for the privilege, though."

"Lovely," Sophie drawled. "Now, go over there and stir. I'm going to be mad if it burns."

Jasper cast one more look at me before heading over, grumbling under his breath all the while. I couldn't make out the words, but they didn't sound flattering.

"Don't worry about your friend," Sophie tossed out. "I'll take care of her." A pleasant smile was firmly fixed on her face as she regarded me. "Tell me the story." Her knuckles brushed over my forehead. "And take a few deep breaths while you're doing it. I think you might be having a panic attack."

I wanted to laugh at the suggestion—I wasn't the type to panic—but I was feeling out of sorts enough that it struck me as a legitimate possibility. "It's been a busy few days," I said lamely. "Actually, it's been a busy few months."

"Tell me about it." Sophie was calm. "You can trust me."

Because I did—although I would have to think later on why trusting her was so easy—I launched into the tale. My voice was flat, emotionless, and devoid of recrimination when I talked about my mother. Telling the story was easier when I removed my emotions from the memory. When I got to the string of men and their dastardly deeds, Sophie cracked a smile. A few times, she looked genuinely concerned when I explained what certain men had done to get on the police's radar. When I was finished, she let loose a whoosh of air.

"Girl, that is the craziest story I've ever heard," she said when I was finished. "I mean... What in the hell?"

I could only laugh in response. "I know. It sounds unbelievable when you string it all together like that."

"It sounds way worse than unbelievable." She popped her lips. "Man alive. I've never heard a story like that." She darted her eyes to Jasper. "You don't have any outstanding warrants, do you?"

Jasper, a wooden spoon clutched in his hand, shot her a dark look. "No, and we're not together. I'm just helping her end the curse."

"Right. You're just helping ... out of the goodness of your heart."

"Actually, I'm looking for a story." Jasper turned prim now. "I told you I do tours. One is a voodoo tour. I would love a genuine story to go along with the tour. You know ... one I was a witness to."

Sophie blinked twice then loosed the most unladylike snort I'd ever heard. "That's not why you're with her. Good grief." She shook her head and turned back to me. "I'm sorry about your mother."

That was not the tack I'd expected her to take. "Thank you." My voice was shakier than I anticipated. "She got sick fast. She was in so much pain at the end that it was a blessing."

"For her, maybe," Sophie agreed. "It wasn't a blessing for you because you clearly weren't ready to say goodbye."

"I don't think anybody is ever ready to say goodbye to a parent."

"Probably not," she agreed readily, not missing a beat. "I lost my mother when I was five. I barely remember her. My grandmother raised me ... and two aunts. I used to think the worst thing in the world was not knowing her. I heard stories, of course, but it wasn't the same. I think it might be worse knowing what you've lost, though."

I nodded. "Yeah, it's been rough. Realizing the curse might be real has only added to it."

"Yeah, well, here's the thing." Sophie sighed, the sound long and dragged out, and drummed her fingers on the tabletop. "My grandmother is a unique soul who has done a lot of good for the community. She feeds the homeless, donates supplies when a house needs to be fixed up, and even volunteers as a babysitter from time to time when single mothers need to get to work and have childcare issues."

I immediately balked. "I wasn't saying she was a bad person."

Sophie continued as if I hadn't spoken. "She's also a vindictive pain in the ass who likes to curse people when bored. It's entirely possible your grandmother somehow stepped on her toes, and it might've been over something stupid ... like a bad gumbo recipe or the fact that my grandmother hates all northerners."

"So you believe me?" I couldn't find the words to express my relief.

"I believe you." Sophie's voice was soft. "There's a problem, though." She motioned for me to stand and led me to a window at the back of the kitchen. "Do you see out there?" She pointed at a hunched-over figure in the garden. "That's my grandmother."

My heart leaped in anticipation. I was finally going to meet the woman who could put an end to all of this.

"Six months ago, she started showing signs of dementia," Sophie continued, her voice cracking. "She doesn't have an official diagnosis. Those things take time. There are days when she still has a few coherent hours. She mostly wants to talk about old times when she's lucid. There are more days when she can't remember where she is, though. The only thing that helps is working in her garden."

My heart sank.

"Are you saying it's a bad day?" Jasper asked. He'd followed us to the window, the wooden spoon still clutched in his hand.

"I'm saying it's a bad day," Sophie confirmed. "Actually, it's been a bad week. She thinks I'm my mother sometimes."

I thought my heart might break for her. "I'm so sorry." I meant it. "That has to be awful."

"She loved my mother so much. You're not supposed to have favorite children, but my mother was hers. She raised me ... and loved me. She never got over losing my mother, though. Now, when I have to tell her my mother is gone, I have to break her heart all over again."

I swallowed what felt like glass in my throat. "I don't know what to say," I said finally.

"You don't have to say anything." Sophie's eyes were earnest. "You've been through it too. The thing is, I can't help you. My grandmother can't help you either. If she did curse your family, that memory is long gone. She lives in another world now."

My stomach constricted to the point that it sent pains shooting through my abdomen. "I'm sorry we bothered you."

"No, I'm sorry." She rested a hand on my forearm. "I honestly wish I could've helped you. I just... Well, there's nothing I can offer."

"It's not your fault. The world clearly likes to kick me when I'm down."

"I really am sorry."

I could read the truth in her eyes. "I'm sorry too. Life isn't fair."

"No. It definitely isn't."

Nineteen

Jasper insisted on taking me out to dinner. That was after he insisted on driving us back to the Quarter. He didn't come right out and say it, but he was clearly worried I was going to pass out or something if I tried to walk, and the idea of carrying me seemed to hold little appeal.

He picked a restaurant called Willa Jean, which I'd never heard of before, and I was charmed by the cozy atmosphere the minute we walked through the door.

"Oh, wow." The aromas practically hit me over the head, causing my nostrils to flare. "What is that?"

"It's everything good in the world," he replied as we settled at a corner table. "I'm buying," he said when I accepted a menu. "I don't want to hear a word of complaint."

I thought about arguing but didn't have the energy. "You just feel sorry for me," I groused as I perused the offerings.

"I don't feel sorry for you." He made a face. "I'm simply ... concerned."

"Because I'm a pathetic mess?"

"You're many things, but pathetic isn't one of them." He took me by surprise as he reached over and snagged my hand.

"It's okay to be upset. You don't always have to put on such a brave face."

Because he was so earnest, my heart skipped a beat. "I feel like I'm being pathetic. I can't help it. My mother didn't raise me to be this ... ridiculous."

He stared, and I thought he was going to say something—maybe about my mother.

Instead, he gave my hand another squeeze before releasing it and focusing on the menu. "Do you know what the best thing is when you're sad?"

"Cake?"

He cocked his head, considering. "Cake is actually a good answer. I was going for 'cocktails,' though. They have some good ones here."

"I don't think getting drunk is the solution to my problem."

"Nobody said anything about getting drunk. One or two cocktails can't possibly hurt, though. You need to relax."

Because I didn't disagree, I decided to play the game his way for a change. "Sure. What do they have?" I looked over the menu, my forehead creasing. "Party drinks? I like how they actually call them that."

"You need to get your party on, so pick one."

A lot were there to choose from. "A Painkiller sounds good," I said after a beat. "I'm in pain."

"A Painkiller is common. If you want that for your second drink, I won't argue. Try something fun, though, something different." He paused for dramatic effect. "Something decadent."

I laughed because I couldn't help myself. "Something decadent, huh?" I looked again. "I think bourbon and bananas sounds gross, not decadent."

"There's chocolate in that drink too."

"Yeah, that doesn't make it better." I pursed my lips. "I

think I'm going to try Willa's Fancy Brew. Rum, amaro, RumChata, cinnamon, and vanilla cream."

"That sounds good."

"What are you going to get?"

"I happen to love bourbon and bananas, so I'm getting the O'Keefe and Girod."

"Can I taste it when you get it?"

He grinned. "I think that can be arranged."

"You know, just for posterity, so I can say I tried it."

"That's a fine idea." He leaned back in his chair and stretched his long legs out in front of himself. "It's an eclectic menu. If you want something more substantial for dinner, we can go someplace else."

"Oh no." I shook my head. "I'm good. I can eat almost anywhere."

"Good. The hangover bowl is a particular favorite of mine. It's delicious whether you have a hangover or not."

I found it on the menu and read the ingredients. "Who gets brisket with cheesy grits?"

"People who have hangovers and needed them cured. It's good."

"I don't really like grits." I didn't say that too loudly in case the workers might overhear and spit in my food. I'd heard stories about that, and although I'd never worked in a restaurant, I could see that happening if the customer was too demanding.

"You don't like grits?" Jasper acted as if that was the craziest thing he'd ever heard. "They're going to deport you to the north if you're not careful. Those are fighting words in the South."

Laughter bubbled up, and I couldn't contain it. "Is that a fact?"

"It is ... and you should do that more often."

"What?"

"Laugh, Rowan," he replied, his voice soft. "Do you know you light up the entire room when you laugh? You don't do it nearly enough."

"I laugh." Suddenly I felt defensive. "I laugh all the time."

He didn't immediately respond, but a challenge glowed in his eyes.

"I'm a fun girl," I insisted.

That elicited a response, a gregarious belly chuckle. "Oh, you're definitely fun," he said when he was finished. "Like ... so fun I don't know what to do with you sometimes. You don't let yourself have fun a lot of the time, though. It's like... It's like you catch yourself when you're having fun and immediately stop yourself before you can enjoy the moment. I think it's because you feel like you shouldn't be having fun."

I carefully averted my gaze. "Why would I think something like that?"

"Don't," he chided softly, reaching over to tap my chin, getting me to raise my eyes. "Please don't be sad. This is exactly what I'm talking about."

"And I don't understand what you're talking about," I insisted. "I'm tons of fun."

"You miss your mother," he countered. "You miss her so much I think it's left a hole in your heart. Sometimes you forget she's gone—or maybe it's that you forget you shouldn't be having fun, at least in your head—and you light up yourself and everybody around you."

"She died a horrible death."

"I know, and it's okay to mourn her. Everything you've told me about her suggests she wouldn't want you to be unhappy, though. It's okay to love her, miss her, and move on. You know that, right?"

I was distinctly uncomfortable. "I'm going to get the tomato soup and a cheese biscuit," I blurted out of nowhere.

He blinked then nodded. "Comfort food. That sounds good, especially if you're going to be a grits snob."

That was enough to make me narrow my eyes. "I'm not a snob about grits. I'm just blunt enough to admit they taste like ass."

"Eat a lot of ass, do you?"

"It's not my fault that the South has become synonymous with grits and that they're gross. I didn't create this situation."

His lips curved. "What's your favorite meal in Salem?"

That felt like a trap, somehow. Thankfully, the server picked that moment to take our orders. When she was gone, I had every intention of "forgetting" the question. Jasper, ever persistent, refused to let me.

"What's your favorite meal in Salem?" he repeated.

I sighed heavily. "I'm a big seafood fan. Stuffed lobster is my favorite."

"So you have expensive taste. That's what you're telling me."

"Actually, because of the fishing community up there, lobster isn't that expensive. I can get a stuffed lobster with all the fixings for twenty bucks, depending on the season."

"Seriously?" Jasper seemed surprised. "I thought that was like a sixty-dollar meal on the low end."

"Not there."

"So stuffed lobster is your favorite." He seemed to be filing the information away.

"It's one of my favorites," I clarified. "In actuality, my favorite is the clam chowder at this little hole-in-the-wall diner on the outskirts of town. In the winter, I like to get all bundled up and walk along the water. It can't be during a snowstorm or anything because that would be absolutely brutal, but the day after a snowstorm, that's one of the things I love to do.

"I stop at my favorite coffee shop, splurge on a full-fat

latte, and then walk around the bay," I continued. "I'm usually wearing so much clothing that it's a full workout. It takes me twenty minutes to get there, and when I do, I sit in my favorite window seat, order the clam chowder with a grilled cheese, and then I dream."

He was so still that I thought he might've fallen asleep.

"What?" I straightened when I realized he was staring at me. "You asked."

"And I'm glad you told me." His voice was suddenly husky. "I like the picture you're painting."

"Have you even seen snow?"

"No. It's on my bucket list, though."

That cracked me up. "Wow. You'll have to come up to Salem one winter. I'll show you all the good spots, take you on a tour and everything. You'll love it."

"Maybe I'll do that." His expression was impossible to read. "What do you dream about?"

I couldn't figure out why he was asking until I remembered I'd thrown in that admission at the end. I liked to sit at a window and dream. Of course he would glom onto that. "I don't know. What do all people dream about? I guess I dream about tropical beaches and fruity drinks."

"That sounds nice. I don't think it's what you truly dream about, though."

"I think I just dream about being happy."

"Are you not happy?"

"I'm working on it." I forced a smile for his benefit. "That's why I came here to end the curse."

"Oh, so you need a man to be happy." His tone was teasing but there was a serious glint in his eyes.

"I don't think you need a man to be happy," I countered. "Look at Toni. A man wouldn't make her happy."

"See, that's an evasive response. I know a man wouldn't

make Toni happy. I'm not being sexist. I was talking about you specifically."

"So was I. My mother didn't have a man. After my father left, it was always just her and my aunt. They raised me."

"And they were always happy?"

I hesitated before I answered although I didn't mean to. "Of course."

He stared hard, almost as if trying to see inside my soul. "I don't think you believe that," he said finally. "You didn't just come here because of the curse. Maybe trying to find a solution helped you land on this place, but you're really searching for something else."

"And what's that?"

"Peace."

"Peace?" I barked out a humorless laugh. "I'm not one of those hippy-dippy northerners looking for the answer to world peace. I'm much too cynical for that. I know it will never truly exist."

"Not peace for the world. You want peace for yourself."

"Oh yeah? What makes you think that?"

"Because I have never in my entire life met someone who is so desperately trying to soothe herself."

"You make me sound like a basket case."

"No, Rowan, you're not a basket case. You're just searching for the one thing you need to take a breath. Before you get worked up, I recognize that trait in you because I'm searching for the same thing."

"You want to take a breath?" I was honestly curious.

"More than anything," he confirmed. "I want to take a breath, and I want to be able to sleep through the night without wondering where I'm going to end up. I love my family—don't get me wrong—but I don't necessarily want to live the same life they do. It's expected of me, and I haven't found anything else that I want to do, but I don't believe I've found my one thing yet."

"So you can't take your breath," I mused.

"No, and I don't think you can either."

"When will we be able to take our breaths?"

"I don't know. For both our sakes, I hope it's soon, though."

WE DIDN'T GET DRUNK. TWO COCKTAILS WERE not enough to make either of us tipsy. Still, my inhibitions had been lowered some, and by the time Jasper and I arrived in front of my building, I was feeling much better than I had been when we left Bywater.

"Maybe I can turn being cursed into a moneymaking endeavor," I suggested as I hopped over a crack. Jasper and I had started playing the "miss the crack" game not long after we left Willa Jean. "Like ... maybe I can become a circus attraction."

Jasper snorted as he contorted. His feet were much bigger than mine, and some of the NOLA sidewalks were old. That meant the spaces without cracks were often few and far between. "What would your shtick be? Like ... you don't have to shave a beard every morning, do you?"

I glared at him. "No, and don't be a douche. I meant that people could come watch me live out my life in a cage. I'll be the girl who was cursed ... and lived."

"What? Are you saying you would become Harriet Potter?"

Only then did I realize what he was getting at. "Maybe I need to rethink this, so I don't step on anybody's trademark." I almost tripped as I tried to avoid a crack, but Jasper's arm jerked out and grabbed me around the waist, keeping me on my feet. Momentum landed me against his chest.

All the oxygen that had been expanding in my lungs immediately started contracting when I realized his face was directly in front of mine.

"Careful," he admonished in a gruff voice. "You're going to fall and hurt yourself." He didn't release me.

"I'm graceful as a cat," I countered. "I don't fall. I fly."

"I think you're destined to soar," he agreed in a soft voice. The way he looked at me set my skin on fire, like he wanted to devour me. I'd seen that expression on his face a time or two before, in close proximity. It had always been fleeting—not that time, however.

"I'm not grits," I blurted.

"Hmm?"

"I'm not grits. You can't throw me in a hangover bowl and eat me as comfort food."

His lips split into a huge grin, but he didn't adjust his grip on me. "What makes you think I want to do that?"

"Because you're holding me in a very romantic way."

"I am indeed." He almost seemed surprised at the realization. "Does it bother you?"

"I haven't decided yet. I feel a bit dazed."

"That's because you fly." He leaned closer, his lips a hair's breadth from mine. "I want to kiss you."

"You're kidding." A nervous giggle escaped. "I never would've guessed, what with your lips kind of hovering over mine. My breath doesn't stink, does it?"

"You smell like bourbon and bananas."

"That drink was surprisingly good. I was shocked."

"Yeah." The fingers of his free hand came up to stroke my cheek, but his eyes never left mine. He seemed almost in a trance. "Did I mention I want to kiss you?"

I thought my heart was going to pound out of my chest, reminding me of a time my mother's car wouldn't start one winter. The engine turned over—and over and over and over—but it wouldn't catch. That's what my heart was doing.

"I don't do one-night stands," I said. "I just ... don't."

"Maybe it doesn't have to be a one-night stand. It can be more."

"You don't do relationships," I reminded him.

"Maybe it doesn't have to be a relationship. It can be less."

I huffed out a laugh. "What does that leave us with?"

"Fun. We can have fun ... and go out together ... and do things."

"Like sexy things?"

"See, you read my mind." He licked his lips, giving me the distinct impression he was about to go in for that kiss.

"I'm cursed," I reminded him.

"Yeah, but I have no outstanding warrants. Also, this isn't a relationship. We're just going to have fun together. Maybe the curse only works if you have serious intentions."

That was an interesting notion. "You can't get attached to me." I was deadly serious.

"I'm the one who doesn't do relationships, remember?"

That was impossible to forget.

"Oh, screw it." I grabbed both sides of his face. "We won't get attached to each other. I still have a curse to break, and you ... will have moved on to someone else in less than a week. There's no reason we can't have fun." Even as I said it, my heart pinched. *What if you're wrong?*

"There's no reason we can't fly," he agreed.

"So, let's fly." I sucked in a breath, ignoring my persistent inner voice as his lips descended toward mine. "You'd better not be a bad kisser after all this buildup."

He didn't laugh. Instead, the gleam in his eyes told me he didn't find the situation particularly funny. "I promise I'm not a bad kisser."

"We have that in common."

"Prove it."

"Gladly."

I was done waiting for him to finish making his move. I understood he was trying to be respectful, but I needed a distraction. The day had gone poorly. Truth be told, it was more than that, though. Whenever I was near him, I felt a pull in my gut directing me toward him. My hormones didn't care that I was on a man fast. They didn't care that he was a player.

For once in my life, I was going to be casual. That was something my mother would've frowned upon. For the time, however, I figured that was the safest course.

The second our lips touched, fireworks went off in my head. There was no awkward posturing, no readjusting to get a better angle. There was just need, and we both went for it with the sort of gusto I hadn't believed existed outside of soap operas and romance novels.

I lost myself in him, in the stroke of his tongue and the pressure he kept on my back as he gripped me more tightly. At some point, I realized I was practically climbing him and wondered how long we'd been making out like teenagers. I completely lost track of time. I was breathless when I finally pulled back, my face burning and my chest heaving.

"That was ... interesting," I said.

He laughed, then moaned when he leaned in to kiss me again. "I'm not ready to be done."

I wasn't either. Perhaps being reckless—just this once—wasn't the worst thing ever. "Do you want to come upstairs?" The invitation was out before I could think better of it.

He looked taken aback by the suggestion. "Are you sure you're okay with that?"

I nodded without hesitation. "You're not a boyfriend. You're not wanted by the police. I think it's fine."

He laughed, then his eyes filled with intensity. "I would love to come upstairs ... as long as you're sure."

"I'm sure." I gripped the front of his shirt. "I think I'll explode if I don't take you up there with me."

"Good answer."

"I hope so."

"Come on." He gave me another kiss, that one almost chaste it was so soft. "I'm ready to see that smile in full bloom."

That was a nice sentiment. I was ready to give it to him. Heck, I was ready to give it to him more than once. The time had come to take a break from life, and I couldn't think of a better distraction than Jasper.

Twenty

It was unbelievably warm when I woke the next morning, to the point that I thought I might've been kicked into early menopause somehow.

"What...?" I dragged a hand through my hair, which felt as if birds could be nesting in it, and realized the warmth was coming from the body draped around mine.

Jasper.

I flopped backward out of instinct and took a moment to study his features. Morning stubble dotted his chin and cheeks, and his face looked serene in sleep. His dark hair was mussed like mine, but somehow that made him more attractive, which should've been impossible.

Dammit! That wasn't what I'd signed on for. *Why did he spend the night? Why did he have to look so good after a vigorous—and I do mean vigorous—night of moaning and groaning? And, for the love of all that was holy, why did he have to be a cuddler?*

All those complaints flew through my mind. Despite them, however, I found myself reaching out to touch his cheek. His skin was rough thanks to the stubble, yet he looked vulnerable somehow. That made him more appealing, which was not what I was looking for at the moment.

You're on a man fast, I reminded myself. *This isn't real. He doesn't do relationships.*

A second voice, a deeper one, popped inside my head: *You're fine with that. He doesn't do serious, and you can't. It's okay to have fun. He's hot. He's fun. Climb him like a tree as long as it lasts, then live off the memories for decades when you get home and decide to settle down.*

I involuntarily shuddered when the words "settle down" flowed through my head. *Settle down? What would that even look like?* My mother had never settled down. She'd tried, of course, but my father had taken off and blown her dreams out of the water. He left her with a tiny child and a business. She made the best of it, turned the shop into something magnificent, and carved out a life for me in an expensive town with good schools and a fun atmosphere. Along with Aunt Mindy, they joined in various community events. They celebrated Halloween with the best of them. They laughed and had fun, yet I always knew something was missing. Did I ever have dreams about how my life would turn out? Did I know how I wanted to live? I was starting to question everything, which made me feel unbelievably guilty.

"It's way too early to be having serious thoughts," Jasper murmured out of nowhere, jolting me out of my reverie. "Go back to sleep." The arm he had draped over my waist tightened as he pulled me toward him.

The warmth he exuded was almost overwhelming. I knew I shouldn't allow myself to get comfortable with him, yet nothing could've dragged me from that spot right then. "I didn't mean to wake you." I subconsciously tried to finger comb my hair. "I was just ... thinking."

"I noticed." He snagged my hand and tucked it under the covers. Apparently, he didn't care about bedhead. "If the gears in your mind were working any harder, you would wake up the whole building. Now ... shh."

I made a face but didn't immediately respond, instead marveling at the way his cheek felt against mine. Why did he have to be so cuddly? That wasn't what I'd expected. Three bouts of sex the previous night? That was different. He was popular in the Quarter for a reason. I'd figured he would be adept in the bedroom, and he was. The first round was gritty and demanding. The second was playful. The third was soft, though, and I was still haunted by the way he sighed as he picked a lazy pace and dragged me along for the ride. I couldn't wrap my head around the many faces of Jasper Bentley, which was making me squirmy.

"You're still thinking," Jasper complained after a few seconds.

"How can you possibly know that?" I was cranky and curious.

"Because when you actually allowed yourself to sleep, you were soft and pliable. You just kind of melted against me. And you made little sighing sounds in your sleep. When you're awake, you're thinking. I guess that's not necessarily a bad thing—I like a smart woman—but you're going to give yourself an ulcer by forty if you don't give it a rest."

I narrowed my eyes. "When did you become such a student of the human condition? I mean ... just out of curiosity, how much time did you spend watching me sleep?"

He chuckled. "Not a lot. I woke up when your freaking ice-cold feet slid between my legs and made me think I'd wandered onto a frozen tundra. It was so bad I dreamed I was in a plane crash and cannibalism was the only option."

I arched an eyebrow. "You ate me?" I asked, horrified.

His face flushed with flirty intent. "Not that way."

"Knock it off." I slapped his chest, but he caught my hand

and pulled me tight against him. "I'm being serious," I warned. "I don't think cannibalism is sexy."

"Oh, it's not," he agreed. "I do have a question about your ridiculous feet, though. Why do you keep them out in the open instead of under the covers when you sleep?"

That was absolutely not the question I was expecting. "I don't know. I've never really thought about it."

"No?" He didn't look convinced. "No offense, my little witch, but that's not safe. What do you do when the creature that lives under your bed wants a nibble? Don't you know you have to keep your feet covered to prevent that?"

The question made me laugh. "The monster that lives under the bed?"

"Don't tell me you didn't have one of those. Everybody did."

"If you say so." I rolled my neck until it cracked. Then I frowned. "I honestly never thought about the covers thing. My mother used to complain about having to come into my room and cover my feet when I was a kid. It drove her nuts."

Something occurred to me, and I angled my face to study him. "That was in Salem, though, where we have brutal winters. It's always hot here. What are you worried about?"

"It's New Orleans. We have zombies. They hide under beds."

He said it with such conviction that I could do nothing but sputter out a laugh. "Is that a fact?"

"Totally." He was grave, solemn, almost earnest. "That's what we're famous for. Chicory, gumbo, beignets, and zombies."

"Well, at least you have your branding slogan." I lightly patted his chest. I was determined to pull away and put some distance between us, maybe to suggest breakfast as a way to get us out of bed, but he pulled me back until I was pressed against him.

"I'm being serious about the foot thing. It freaks me out."

I gave up pulling away and let myself lean. That was nice although it wasn't something I would admit to anybody who didn't live inside my head. "Let me guess—you were one of those kids who used to brush his teeth and then take a running jump to land on the bed at night because you wanted to make sure nothing grabbed you from below."

"I believe that's what I just acknowledged," Jasper said with a chuckle. "My brother and I shared a room. We both did that."

"And your sister?"

He took a moment to think back. "She didn't do it," he said finally. "At least, I don't think she did. Obviously, she wasn't in a room with us. She had her own room ... and man, was that a source of bitterness in our house. My brother and I hated sharing, and she lorded it over us that she had not only her own bedroom but her own bathroom too. She was a real snot."

A giggle escaped me. "See, I was an only child. I had my own everything. I always wanted a sibling."

"Because you wanted someone to play with?" His fingers were light as they combed through my hair. He'd apparently given up on the idea of going back to sleep.

I shrugged. "I just didn't like the idea of being alone one day. Being an only child is a lot of pressure. Like ... had my mother survived, I would've been the one who had to take care of her once time caught up. There would've been nobody else. Aunt Mindy didn't have children, so it will still be my responsibility later with her, but my mother was a real stickler for details.

"She always told me which assisted living homes were acceptable and which ones weren't," I continued. "She always explained what age she wanted to retire at, which meant I would have to take over day-to-day operations of the store. She wanted two grandchildren—a boy and a girl—and she didn't talk about *if* I would meet the right man but *when* I would meet the wrong one."

Incredulous, Jasper pulled back far enough to study my face. "What, now?"

His reaction surprised me. "It was the curse," I said automatically.

He didn't look convinced. "You know that's not normal, right?" he said after a beat. "Parents don't do that sort of thing unless they want to raise a basket case."

I didn't like his tone. "My mother loved me."

"Of course she did." His tone was soothing. "I think she might've warped you a bit, though. You're right that having siblings would've made things better in that respect. The burden wouldn't have solely been on you. Most of that stuff you just mentioned shouldn't have been foisted on any kid, though."

"Your parents haven't told you what assisted living center they'd prefer?" I teased.

"No. In fact, it's been decided by my brother and me that they're going to live with my sister when it's time. She had her own room and was spoiled. It's a fair trade-off. The assisted living place is weird, but I kind of get it. She was sending you a message that she didn't want to be a burden. You strike me as the sort of person who would take everything on your shoulders whether you could handle it or not."

"I don't think handling it was a consideration." I opted for the truth. "She was my mother. It was my job to take care of her. I always knew it would be up to me. Now, she's gone, though." I chewed on my bottom lip. "I don't know what I'm supposed to do now, Jasper." I didn't realize I was going to admit that until the words were already out of my mouth.

"I know." He surprised me by pressing a kiss to my forehead. "I figured that out pretty quickly after meeting you. The thing is, Rowan, you're not supposed to know how your whole life is going to play out. It's supposed to be an adventure."

"Yeah... I'm a planner. I like planning."

"Do you? Because it seems to me you've had the most fun since you got here when not planning things out."

"How do you figure?"

"Henri's bar? My tours? Drinks at the Bombay Club?" He swallowed hard. "Last night?" He suddenly looked nervous.

"You don't have to worry, Jasper. I'm not going to get weird on you. I know that this isn't a relationship. It's just a ... distraction."

"A distraction?"

I shrugged. "Maybe that wasn't the right word. It's a dalliance or a temporary thing. It's fun. I'm only here to end a curse, and then I'm going home. It's not as if I'm going to suddenly get clingy and want to spend the rest of my life with you. This is just a ... fling."

"And you're okay with that?" Dubiousness lurked in the depths of his eyes as he searched my face. "I thought you weren't a fling girl."

"I'm not, but this is a weird situation." I took a breath. "Everything about my life is temporary right now. I can't have a relationship. That doesn't mean I don't like hanging out with you. Why not enjoy it for what it is instead of asking a bunch of questions that have ugly answers?"

"That's generally my philosophy." He said the words, yet for a moment, his doubt reflected back at me. "I don't want to make life harder for you. I think you're carrying enough weight on those diminutive shoulders that one extra ounce is going to be too much.

"I also don't want to lie to you," he continued. "I'm not a relationship guy. I think there will come a time when I am—I want kids and a family down the road—but I'm enjoying life too much right now to change things up. The thing is I like spending time with you. I'd like to keep doing it ... as long as it's not going to hurt you in the process."

"Do I look hurt?" I challenged.

"No, but I really do like you." Sincerity reverberated off every word. "I know you're going to go back to Salem in a few weeks ... or whenever you wrap things up here. When that happens, I picture us texting and calling each other on the phone occasionally because we both enjoy giving people a hard time.

"I picture taking a trip to Salem in five years so I can finally see what all the fuss is about," he continued, a smile curving his lips and a far-off look in his eyes. "I really do want to see the town, and I want you to be the one to show me around when I get a chance to go up there." He was serious when he turned back to me. "That's not going to happen if I hurt you. I need you to know, really understand, that's the last thing I want."

Irritation bubbled up and grabbed me by the throat, followed by a quick wash of angst that seemed to have appeared out of nowhere. I brutally pushed that aside. "I'm not weak," I said when I was reasonably assured I could speak without snapping at him. "You don't always have to look at me like I'm fragile."

"That's not how I look at you," he argued.

"It is. I see it all the time. You feel sorry for me."

"No, Rowan." Sadness flashed hot across his face, then disappeared. "Am I sorry you lost your mother? Yes. Do I think you're searching for your place in this world? Yes. I don't feel sorry for you because of that, though. I'm looking for my place too. That's not it."

"Then what do you think when you see me?"

"That you're incredibly strong," he replied, not missing a beat. "How many people do you know who could pack up and temporarily move to a place without a single friend? You found a job. You've bonded with Toni. You even opened yourself to those party rats on the roof. Most people would've shied away from all of that, but not you.

"You left the only home you've ever known, a place where you own a business, and you came down here," he continued. "You're searching for answers every single day, and even when you have a disappointment—like yesterday with Lisette—you somehow manage to stay on your feet. That's not something to be pitied. It's something to marvel at."

"Then why are you so worried about me?" I demanded. "If I'm so good at taking care of myself, why are you convinced I'm going to fall apart because of you?"

He made an amused sound in his throat. "Well, when you put it like that." He tickled my side. "I just don't want to hurt you." He was momentarily earnest. "I really do like you. I'm just limited in what I have to offer. You've already been through so much."

"It's just fun, right?" I pressed.

"Just fun."

"So let's keep having fun." Since I'd had a taste of what he could offer, I wasn't quite ready to give him up. We had time. I wasn't leaving New Orleans right away. I still had answers to find and a curse to end. I could keep him until then, and when the time came to go home, we would part with laughter and friendship. Heck, he might even come up to Salem and visit one day. He'd said it himself. It was a good plan.

"I just want you to be sure." He put his hand on top of my head. "Just out of curiosity, do rats live in your hair and you didn't tell me?"

That elicited a genuine laugh. "I am sure, and it's not rats. It's invisible elves who like to play games in my hair overnight. They live under the bed although they never grab my ankles."

"Well, that's good to know." Jasper brightened considerably. "As long as you're sure, I'm good. If you ever become unsure ... then I need you to tell me. That's the only rule."

"I think I can survive a fling." I meant it. At least, I thought I did. "I'm sick of talking about it, though. I have work today. I could use some breakfast before then, though. You sexed all my strength out of me. I need nourishment."

He cracked a wide smile. "I think I can manage that. How do grits sound?"

I glared at him. "Do you want me to hurt you?"

"Hash browns it is." He pressed a kiss to my forehead that wasn't tentative or light. "I'm glad things are still good between us. I would hate to have things turn uncomfortable."

"They're fine." I meant it. "I might not be an expert on flings, but something tells me I'm going to be good at this one."

"Probably. You're good at everything else, right?"

"Oh, you have no idea. Wait until you see me eat my weight in eggs and hash browns."

"Oddly, I'm looking forward to it."

Twenty-One

"You don't have to eat it all in one bite," Jasper teased as I shoveled a huge forkful of eggs and potatoes into my mouth. He'd picked a diner around the corner from the magic store. His hair was still damp from a quick jaunt in my shower—with me to give him a tour—but he was in the same clothes he'd worn the previous day.

"I'm hungry." I wasn't going to apologize for loving food. "One thing you guys don't lack for down here is good food."

"Definitely not." He narrowed his eyes as he studied my plate. "You're very particular about how you eat your food, I've noticed."

"Meaning what?"

He shrugged. "Nothing. It's just ... you dunked the toast in the egg yolks and ate that first. Then you mashed the hash browns and leftover eggs together. You haven't touched your sausage yet. It's like you have a schedule you stick to when you eat."

"Maybe I just like sausage," I suggested. "Perhaps I want to keep it until the end because it's my favorite."

He gave me a hot look. "Don't start something you can't finish," he warned as he sipped his coffee.

"Oh, we've already finished that for now." I was firm on that. "I won't be able to walk if we go again. Besides, Toni will be at the store when I get there." I checked the clock on the wall. "I would prefer not having to answer questions regarding ... any of this."

Jasper nodded as he took a bite of his biscuits and gravy. Despite his bold talk, he'd avoided the grits on the menu. "She won't be happy when she finds out about us." He scowled as he mulled that over. "I guess I'm glad she never went to the dairy farm on that one trip we had in school because if she had, she would've learned about the marvel of castration. Something tells me that's exactly what she's going to want to do to me."

That was a lot to take in. "We don't have to tell her," I said finally.

"You want to keep it a secret?"

I paused, considering. I couldn't tell how he felt about the possibility. "I'm not sure. Maybe." I lifted one shoulder. "The thing is, she was adamant when she warned me about you and your intentions. I told her it wasn't going to be an issue—I am on a man fast, after all—but if I admit that I broke my fast for a fling with you, I'm probably going to get an earful."

"That's better than the assful of foot I'm going to get when she finds out," he mused. "I don't know, though," he hedged after a beat. "I don't like the idea of keeping it secret. I'm too old to be sneaking around."

"I don't think we need to sneak around." I mostly meant that. "I just don't think we need to volunteer the information. It's nobody's business. Besides, it's a temporary thing. Why borrow trouble when there's nothing to be gained from an argument?"

He nodded and continued chewing. Once he swallowed,

he took a different tack. "How about we play it by ear? If she asks me, I'm not going to lie. We're friends, and I don't want to risk that."

"She won't ask you." I was certain that was true. Or maybe I simply hoped that was true. "I'm not going to volunteer the information. I don't think she's going to ask. She's much more interested in the curse ever since she found out it's real and not just a figment of my imagination."

"Are you going to tell her about Lisette?"

I nodded. "Yeah. I want to get her take on it."

"I know you're upset about how that played out," he hedged. "Toni's mother is a powerful bruja, though. Maybe she can come up with a counterspell, and you won't even have to worry about Lisette."

"It's a possibility." I bobbed my head. "I'm honestly not sure what the answer is here, but it's definitely something I need to think on."

"To be fair, we don't know for sure that Lisette is the Michel that we're looking for. Charlie is still tracking names for us. I'll check in with him. It can't hurt to follow that track to the natural conclusion ... just in case."

I didn't disagree. "Just in case." I finished off my juice, realizing that we'd talked about nothing but me and my problems since we'd woken up wrapped around each other. It was probably time to focus on him. "What are your plans for the day?"

Jasper checked his watch. "Well, I have three tours. The first one is in an hour. I have time to run home and change clothes."

"When is your last tour today?" I had no idea why I was so interested. Part of me wanted to know what he would be doing when I was dodging questions from Toni, however.

"It's early. It's at three." His eyes were unreadable when they locked with mine. "How do you feel about dinner ... and hanging out ... when I'm done? I can meet you somewhere when your shift is over."

My lips curved. "You want to hang out, do you?"

He turned sheepish. "I thought it was better to refer to it that way. I can be cruder if you want."

A raspy chuckle escaped my throat. "I think I'm good with the 'hanging out' terminology. As for dinner and 'hanging out,' I'm all for it." I used the appropriate air quotes.

He grinned. "Awesome. I'll text you when I'm done."

"Sure. I—"

Before I could finish, he swooped in and gave me a kiss. It was something more than friendly, yet it wasn't all about lust either. It didn't speak to a fling. It was more comfortable than that. My eyes widened.

Jasper continued as if he hadn't noticed my reaction. "Have fun at work. I'll check with Charlie between tours and see if he's come up with anything on other potential Michels ... or Michelles. If something happens with Toni and you feel you need to tell her, don't hesitate on my account. She'll be mad, but I'm used to it. She wants to rip my head off my shoulders at least three times a year. We always make up."

For some reason, I found that amusing. "She's like a sister to you."

"A really hot sister who I would totally sleep with if she wasn't a lesbian."

I made a face. "Oh, did you have to take it there? That's so gross."

"Hey, that's what I do." To my utter surprise, he gave me another kiss, such a coupley thing to do that I didn't know what to make of it. "Have fun at work, *dear*." His tone was teasing. "We'll talk later about your weird refusal to cover your feet when sleeping. I'm still not ready to let that go."

"I think you're the only one who has a problem with that."

"Oh no." He shook his head firmly. "On this one, I'm not the weirdo. That's you. We're definitely going to talk about it later."

"In a weird way, or perhaps a weirdo way, I'm looking forward to it."

"You won't feel that way when I'm done with you."

"Bring it on."

TONI WAS IN A FUNK WHEN I ARRIVED for my shift, and she was pouty as she watched me unload a box of books badly needed to restock the shelves.

"You're lucky your mother is dead," she announced out of nowhere.

My back went rigid at her words. "What?"

"I'm sorry if you think that's a horrible thing to say—and I mostly don't mean it—but my mother drives me crazy," she lamented. "Do you know what she did?"

I forced myself to remain calm. Toni didn't mean anything by her words. I was the one with the problem, not her. She was just being herself.

"I'm almost afraid to ask," I said.

Toni barreled forward as though I hadn't spoken. "We were supposed to have dinner at Irene's last night. It's an Italian place over on the east side. She was late—something I'm used to—but do you know who showed up? I'll give you a hint. It wasn't my mother."

I was well and truly lost. "Your mother set up a dinner with you and didn't show?"

"Exactly." Toni emphatically bobbed her head. "Who does that?"

"I can't believe your mother stood you up." I tried to picture my mother standing me up for dinner and came up empty. "That's kind of mean."

"Oh, it's worse than that." Toni lodged one elbow against the counter and leaned in as though imparting some great secret to me and only me. "She sent someone in her stead. Care to place a wager on who that someone was?"

"You have aunts, right?" That was my first guess.

"I do, but none of them want to have dinner with me. They're afraid lesbianism is catching."

My stomach heaved for her. "I'm sorry."

"I haven't even gotten to the worst part yet. You're going to want to shower me with cocktails when I'm finished."

My lips twitched. She was dramatic to the point of being ridiculous sometimes, but I couldn't help but like her. "Lay it on me."

"His name was Gerardo, and he told me that my mother saw him in Jackson Square earlier in the day—he sells paintings there—and she approached him because she thought his skin and my skin would make for a perfect baby." Toni's smile was sharp enough to cut glass. "She told him I had breeding hips and was ready for marriage. Come to find out, she also told him she was going to shrink his penis until it was nothing more than a pimple if he didn't show up and wow me, but that's not even important to the story."

My mouth dropped open. "Are you kidding me?"

"No." She folded her arms across her chest. "Can you believe that?"

I honestly couldn't. "I'm sorry." I meant it. "I thought maybe you were joking when you said she didn't accept the fact that you're a lesbian, but obviously that's not the case."

"Oh, no." Toni was emphatic as she gripped her hands into fists. "Not only does she refuse to acknowledge that I'm a lesbian, but she also pretends that it's not a real thing. She insists it's something I'm trying on for size because I want to irritate her. I just want to..." She mimed strangling an invisible person.

"I really am sorry," I said as I finished emptying the box. "It seems disrespectful that she won't acknowledge that you're allowed to make decisions for yourself. I don't know what to say."

"You don't have to say anything. I was thinking maybe we could get dressed in all black and murder her under the cover of darkness this evening. She has her prayer circle with the other voodoo queens tonight. They always get drunk enough that she wouldn't even hear me enter her bedroom."

"I see you've given this some thought," I said, my laugh strangled.

"So much thought," she agreed, her eyes drifting to the door as it opened. Though I couldn't see who was entering, given the angle from where I was located, her expression told me she wasn't happy. "Just give it some thought." She straightened and pasted a tight smile on her face as she welcomed the customer. "Well, you're the last person I would've expected here."

I reminded myself it wasn't my business who Toni was talking to. This was her shop, her town, her people. None of that was my concern. Then I heard the responding voice.

"I was hoping you could help me with a curse," a female voice said primly. "I have a pimple on my ass I want to pop."

"I would try a needle," Toni replied, not missing a beat. "We don't have curses that tackle pimples."

"What if the pimple is actually a person out to steal my man?"

I cringed internally and pressed my eyes shut before straightening. I didn't want to deal with that situation but didn't see a way around it. "Hey, Savannah," I offered by way of greeting. The two words felt as if they were being tugged out of my mouth by an unseen force.

"Ah, there's the pimple now," Savannah drawled.

Toni's eyes darted between Savannah and me before ultimately landing on the other woman. "What's your problem?"

"I want her gone." Savannah extended her index finger in my direction. "That's my problem. Since she's working for you, and you claim to be magical, I figured it was best to come right to the source."

Toni folded her arms across her chest and went silent for a really long time. Then she turned her eyes toward me. "Do you know what she's talking about?"

That was not a conversation I'd seen myself getting into when I told Jasper I could handle Toni and keep our newfound fling status under wraps. Still, all was not lost, I told myself. I could handle this. I was an adult, for crying out loud.

"I believe she's talking about Jasper," I explained in measured tones.

"Oh, right." Toni's eye roll was pronounced. "You always did have a thing for him, didn't you?" She tsked and shook her head. "When are you going to get that he's never going to look at you the way you want him to look at you, Savannah?"

I was caught off guard by Toni's aggressive response to the librarian. "I think there's been a misunderstanding," I hedged, suddenly nervous. "Jasper has been helping me with my little problem. I think she's mistaken regarding my intentions toward him."

Toni blinked twice and wrinkled her nose. "She's not mistaken. She's always been like this, ever since we were kids. She was two years younger than us and used to chase Jasper around like a lost puppy dog. It was pathetic."

"We're working things out," Savannah insisted. "I have a plan."

"Oh, please." Toni looked irritated rather than sympathetic. "Your plan is to somehow trap that boy into thinking he loves you. The problem is he doesn't. Jasper doesn't love anybody. He's incapable of loving anybody right now. He won't be able to open himself up to something like that until he matures ... a lot."

My stomach constricted, and I chewed on my bottom lip.

"Jasper and Rowan aren't involved the way you think they're involved," she continued, not missing a beat. "Jasper likes flirting with her, don't get me wrong, but that's what he does. He's just helping her with a project she's working on." Toni waved disdainfully. "That doesn't change the fact that Jasper is never going to see you the way you want to be seen. You need to let him go."

"Jasper and I have a connection," Savannah insisted. "He always comes back to me. Yeah, he's not ready to settle down yet ... but that's *yet*. He's going to get there. I'm not going to sit back and watch that one steal my happy ending. I'm here to make sure she understands that Jasper is not available for ... well ... whatever she thinks he's available for."

Toni decided that was the time to put me on the spot. "Is Jasper not giving you something you think he should be giving you?"

My mouth went dry. "No, and ... that's a really weird question."

"That's because this is a really weird predicament. Savannah always makes things weird." Toni's glare was withering when it landed on the librarian. "There are times I feel sorry for you. No, it's totally true. This is not one of those times, though. You have to let Jasper go, for your own sake as well as his. He's never going to become an adult for you."

"That shows what you know," Savannah spat. "He is an adult, and we're figuring things out. He came to the library the other day to take me on a date and everything. You were there." She shot an accusatory finger toward me. "You saw."

Toni didn't look convinced. "Did you see Jasper pick Savannah up for a date?"

I felt put on the spot, which I really didn't like. It did

bring up an uncomfortable conundrum, however. In my haste to get Jasper naked the night before, I'd forgotten to ask him who else he was flinging with. That was something we would have to discuss. It was one thing to have casual sex with a guy. It was quite another to open myself up to the fact that he might be having casual sex with other people at the same time.

"I was at the library, researching the name Michel," I explained lamely. "Savannah was there, working. Jasper did come in to talk to her."

"He came in to take me to lunch," Savannah spat. "You were there. Don't bother denying it."

At that point, days removed from the situation—and following a night of sexual bliss—I wasn't certain what I'd seen. I was determined to find out, though. "I really think you should take this up with Jasper," I insisted. "This is between you and him, not us."

"And it's stupid," Toni added. "You need to get your head out of your ass, girl. Jasper has never been interested in you. When he finally does get his act together for a woman—we're talking a decade down the road at this point because he's a man child—you're not the one who is going to benefit. It's going to be someone else, someone special. You need to move on."

"It's going to be me." Savannah was adamant. "As for you, stay away from him. I didn't put this much work in to have you waltz off with him. Just ... stay away. You're not even his type."

I kept quiet until she was gone, then fixed Toni with a curious look. "What did she mean when she said I wasn't his type?" That really wasn't the question I should've been asking, but I couldn't seem to stop myself.

"Just that Jasper is all flash and no substance," Toni replied. "He's always been that way. When he finally does decide he's ready to be an adult—years and years from now—

it's going to be because the substance is better than the flash. Jasper needs a woman who is going to knock him on his ass to make him grow up. That's not Savannah."

It's not you either, I told myself. *It's a fling. Get it together.*

As much as I knew my inner voice was right, I couldn't ignore the pang in my chest. What if I wanted it to be me? I recovered quickly. That was ridiculous. We were having a fling, nothing more. I wasn't going to be the woman to knock Jasper on his ass. That wasn't who I was, and I needed to accept that. Otherwise, I might lose myself, which would make everything much worse.

Twenty-Two

I was still thinking about Savannah's insistence on staking her claim to Jasper when I left work after my shift. Toni had invited me to an art gallery opening—one of her friends was taking the plunge—but I politely declined. I liked art as much as the next person, but Toni would have more fun without me. Nothing was worse than being forced to entertain the one person who doesn't know anybody else. I didn't want that for her.

Besides, I had other things on my mind.

I was lost in thought when I rounded the corner onto Bourbon Street. As much as I hated the revelers—and I well and truly did—that was the safest route home. The police took up stations every half block or so to keep things under control, and nobody tried to run off with a purse because escape was difficult when surrounded by that many people. I'd made it only two steps when a muscular arm shot out from an alcove and jerked me inside.

My first instinct was to fight, and I lashed out viciously, landing a punch on a solid jaw.

"Hey!" A disgruntled male voice became apparent. "It's me!"

I stopped myself before landing a second punch. "Jasper?" I was caught off guard. "What are you doing?"

"I was trying to be romantic." He ruefully rubbed his jaw where I'd landed the punch and gave me a saucy wink. "Apparently, you're not into that though, huh?"

He has to be joking. "First off, who told you that grabbing a woman when she's walking alone and dragging her into a dark corner was considered romantic?"

"Every romantic comedy I've ever seen," he replied, not missing a beat.

"That's crap. I thought I was about to get mugged ... or worse."

Legitimate contrition flooded his features. "I'm sorry. I didn't mean to frighten you. I just thought we could play a little game."

My heart was still pounding although I couldn't decide if that was from the momentary flash of fear or his proximity. "And what game is that?"

"This one." He stopped rubbing his jaw and leaned close, his lips meeting mine with little preamble.

My mind exploded, a variety of colors flashing behind my eyes, and before I realized what I was doing, I had the front of his shirt gripped in a fist and was greedily dragging him toward me. I wanted to bathe in the feelings he was eliciting, something I didn't dwell on too long. Flings were about living in the moment, so that's what I decided to do.

When he finally pulled back—*Was it minutes? Hours? Years?*—his eyes were heavy lidded and his smile smug.

"See, *that* was the plan," he said.

I recovered my wits quickly enough to glower at him. "You don't grab women and drag them into dirty little corners as a general rule. I really did think something bad was about to happen."

"I'm sorry." He held up his hands in supplication. "I thought you saw me. I waved when I was cutting through the crowd."

"I didn't. I was ... thinking."

"About what?"

That was a conversation I wasn't certain I wanted to have. To buy myself time, I shrugged. "About curses and stuff."

He chuckled. "Well, you're in luck." He slid an arm around my shoulders. "Charlie came through with a list for me. We have a few more potential hits on the Michel list."

"Really?" I perked up considerably. "Like what?"

"How about I tell you over cocktails?"

"How about you tell me, and then I'll decide on cocktails?"

He shook his head, his eyes gleaming. "I know a place. It's right over there."

He gestured toward a bar with a purple front and gray storm shutters. I'd seen it before and marveled at how cool it looked.

"It's more low-key than the other Bourbon Street places," he said.

I hesitated. "Is this you trying to get me drunk so you can take advantage of me?" I asked finally.

"I'm pretty sure I don't have to get you drunk for that." His smile was so wide it eclipsed his entire face. "I mean ... you did just try to climb me when we were kissing."

I glared at him. "I think you're remembering wrong." Why I felt so defensive was beyond me. He wasn't wrong about the climbing. I didn't want to acknowledge it, however, even to myself.

"Uh-huh." He gripped me more tightly to his side. "Come on. Moxie's Cantina has these really creative drinks where they use dry ice to make cocktails. So their Witch's Brew drink? Yeah, it actually smokes. It's amazing. The owners are awesome too."

"Fine."

I saw no point in not saying yes. He wasn't going to just let it go, and truth be told, I'd liked all the places he'd taken me so far. I wanted to soak up as many memories as possible of New Orleans before the end came. I needed to live in the moment because my past was going to chase me straight through to my future before it was all said and done.

MOXIE'S CANTINA WAS INDEED THE SORT OF bar I could imagine myself falling in love with. The ambiance was calm, with no live music that evening, and the twinkle lights overhead were purple, pink, and teal, creating a relaxing environment.

"How come we never came to this place before?" I complained as I got comfortable at one of the tables.

Jasper held out his hands as he leaned back in his chair, a softness to his eyes that I couldn't quite identify. "I don't know. The bar has only been open a couple months, but the owners launched two other bars down the way last year, so I know them from those locations. Cher and Flambeaux."

I pictured the bars in my mind. "Those are both on Bourbon but across a cross street from each other, correct?"

He nodded. "Very good. They fell in love, competing with one another to see who had the better bar."

I was caught off guard. "Is that a thing?"

"It was for them." Jasper pointed at the bar, where a blonde was wrapped around a handsome man. The man poured drinks as she plastered herself against him, clearly whispering sweet nothings in his ear.

"That doesn't look like a pragmatic approach to pouring

drinks," I noted after a beat, frowning when the woman pulled back far enough that I could see her face. She looked completely gone for the man. And when he looked at her, the cocktail shaker in his hands ceased to exist. All he saw was her.

Witnessing it made my heart hurt. I also recognized the woman from days before. She'd been the one to provide directions to the library.

"I don't think they care," Jasper replied, chuckling at my dubious stare. "I've known Gus for ... well ... a really long time." He scratched his chin. "His parents are essentially New Orleans real estate royalty. They own, like, fifty bars all across the region. Gus wanted to make a name for himself separate from his parents, and that's how he found Moxie."

"I'm not sure Moxie is a name," I mused.

"No, Moxie is a state of mind," a woman announced from my right.

Her voice was so close that I almost jumped out of my skin, and when I swiveled, I found the blonde had abandoned the bartender and was prepared to wait on us. Also, her protruding belly told me something I hadn't noticed from my previous angle. She was even more pregnant than I'd assumed during our brief first meeting.

"Hey, Mox," Jasper said by way of greeting, his eyes on her midriff rather than her face. "I heard a rumor ... and I'm guessing it's true. Congratulations."

Moxie's smile was blissful. "Thank you. We would've told you ourselves, but we haven't seen you in a month. We were keeping it under wraps before then ... just in case. The doctor says it's safe for people to know now, though."

"That's good. I'm sorry about not being around. I've been busy."

"So I've heard." Moxie's eyes drifted to me. She almost looked sorry for me. "Where have you been shopping for dates these days? This one looks way smarter than your normal companions. I gave her directions to the library the other day and everything."

I was caught off guard by her bluntness. Jasper, however, laughed so hard that I thought he might fall out of his chair.

"This is Rowan," Jasper said when he could speak again without gasping for breath. "She works for my friend Toni. You know the one who owns the voodoo store, right? I met her there. We've been hanging out."

Nothing he said was untrue. I felt a zing to my heart when he said it, though. *Hanging out?* I felt like we were doing more, yet I'd agreed to the arrangement. I was starting to wonder if that had been a mistake.

"It's nice to meet you." I extended a hand to be polite. "I love your place. The ambiance is really cool."

"Thank you." Moxie's smile appeared genuine. Then she surprised me by plopping down in one of the open chairs at our table. "Do you want to know what sucks the most about being pregnant?"

"I'm guessing it's that none of your clothes fit," Jasper replied, not missing a beat. "I think it's time to hit the maternity store, Mox. That shirt is too small for you." He inclined his head toward the two inches of stomach visible thanks to her shirt riding up.

Moxie narrowed her eyes to dangerous slits. "Do you want me to hurt you?"

"Definitely not." Jasper flicked his eyes to an approaching Gus. "Your wife-to-be wants to kill me. I think she's serious."

"That's probably because you're an idiot," Gus replied, his hands landing on the blonde's shoulders so he could rub. With the sort of affection I couldn't remember ever having seen up close and personal, he dropped a kiss on the top of her head. "Also, she's not going to be my wife-to-be for long. We're getting married next weekend."

Genuine surprise registered on Jasper's face. "I guess I'm

not invited, huh? I didn't get a 'save the date' card in the mail or anything."

"This is your invitation." Gus moved his fingers to the spot between Moxie's shoulder blades and grinned at the groaning noise she made. "We want to get married before we're parents. That's important to both of us. The thing is we still want to have a big party to celebrate the wedding. Moxie refuses to get into an expensive white dress while pregnant, though. She says that it freaks her out to think about it." He shot his fiancée an adoring look despite the way he was telling the story.

"So, that means we're having a very small ceremony a week from Sunday," Gus continued. "Like ... very small. Moxie might wear shorts with an elastic waist because she's just that disgruntled with her wardrobe right now."

Moxie bobbed her head. "Maternity clothes are stupid. I hate them."

"We're going to have a party here when we're done," Gus added. "The only people who are going to be at the actual ceremony—which is going to be at the courthouse—are my parents and brothers and her former roommates. Once the baby is born and we're not so tired we're zombies, we're going to have another ceremony. This one is going to be bigger, and there will be a white dress."

"Maybe," Moxie hedged. "*Maybe* there will be a white dress. I can't help but think I'll feel like a poser if I wear a white dress after I push your kid's huge head out of my loins."

Gus snorted. "How do you know the kid is going to have my big head?" he demanded. "Your head is huge too."

"Please." Moxie was having none of that. "We both know that your head is twice as big as mine." Her eyes were on me, with an emotion bubbling there I couldn't identify. "So, how did you meet Jasper?"

As far as transitions went, it wasn't a stellar offering.

"At Toni's store," I replied. "I work there. Jasper came in for hex bags for his tours."

"And you hit it off just like that, huh?" Moxie's gaze was suspicious when it landed on Jasper. "You're not going to break this poor girl's heart, are you?"

Jasper balked. "Why do you always assume I'm the one who is going to be breaking hearts? How do you know she isn't going to break my heart?"

"Because I'm familiar with your work," Moxie replied, unruffled. "Do you remember lana. She didn't capitalize her name. That's how I always remember her. She said that Lana with a capitalized L was a common name but lana with a little l meant she was special."

Suddenly, Jasper was the picture of innocence. "I don't know if I remember who you're referring to. Also, you of all people shouldn't be making fun of people's names, *Moxie*."

Moxie pretended she hadn't heard the dig. "If I remember correctly, you brought lana here for drinks one night. She squealed and gushed over your muscles. There was some tongue action." She didn't look impressed by any of that. "I didn't see her again for a week after that." The bar owner took on a far-off expression. "When I did see her again, she showed up with greasy hair and red, puffy eyes, and she had a chocolate stain on her cheek. She was looking to stalk you, but you were nowhere to be found. Apparently, you decided three sexcapades was enough and then walked away, leaving her a shell of her former self." Moxie leaned closer to me. "The girl —lana without a capital L—is the one who told me the shell stuff. I never would use that phrase myself, for fear of looking like an idiot."

"Oh, you don't have to worry," Jasper said drily. "You don't need help looking like an idiot."

"Hey!" Gus extended a warning finger in Jasper's direction. "Don't talk about the woman I love that way. I'll be forced to kick your ass."

Jasper's snort was full of disdain. "Right. Like you could kick my ass."

"Hey, I have two brothers." Gus was having none of it. "Plus, I'm responsible for producing the first grandchild in my family. That means I'm suddenly the favored child. My father will hire someone to kick your ass if it means making Moxie happy."

Jasper's laugh was gregarious. "Well, I see you've given it some thought." Still smiling, he darted his eyes to me. "Just FYI, Rowan isn't staying in town. She's here for some business, and then she's heading back to Salem. We've both agreed that a fling works for both of us."

Moxie didn't look convinced. "Yeah, you should shut up." She pointed a palm at Jasper's face and focused on me. "You realize that he's a horn dog, right? I mean ... he's a nice guy. He's fun and very loyal to his friends. He can tell a story with the best of them, which is good because he's a tour guide. He really is a dirty dog, though."

"Hey!" Jasper looked wounded. "I can't believe you would say that about me, given the number of tours I've conveniently ended at your establishment."

Moxie didn't look moved in the least. "I love you, Jasper. No, I really do. This poor girl, though." She made a clucking sound with her tongue. "I can tell just by looking at her that she's a good girl. If you want to run around with bad girls and dip your wick, knock yourself out. This poor good girl deserves better than that, though."

Jasper's eye roll was pronounced. "We've got it under control, Moxie. We like each other but are both aware that it can't work out as an actual relationship. I believe that's a pretty adult decision, don't you?"

"I haven't decided yet." Moxie's hand rubbed her stomach, which only looked big because she was relatively small. "Don't fall for him." She was deadly serious. "He's the best friend you could have in the world—I'm not exaggerating even a little—but he's a complete tool as a love interest. He's the bad boy that women always think they can change on all of those nighttime soaps.

"Television has taught us it's possible to change those guys, but it isn't," she continued. "There is no changing a dirty dog. I don't want to tell you your business if you really do want a fling, but you'll never get anything else out of this guy."

She was so sincere I didn't know how to respond. Finally, I found my voice. "I'm cursed with men." Why I blurted that out, I couldn't say. It was the truth, though. "I've literally already had the worst luck with men that it's possible to have."

"She's not lying," Jasper offered.

"I don't want anything serious," I continued. "I need a fling because ... well ... it's like a palate cleanser. I just want some space to breathe. I like hanging out with Jasper, and there's no pressure. I don't have a problem with his dirty-dog reputation."

Jasper shot Moxie a triumphant look. "Now what do you have to say, big mouth?"

Moxie was silent for a long beat, her eyes drifting between us. When she sighed, I thought she was going to concede defeat. Instead, she shook her head and stood. "You're both blind morons."

"What is that supposed to mean?" Jasper demanded.

"Exactly what I said." Moxie shifted her finger back and forth. "Two Witch's Brews? You always bring the women here for the smoke show, so I'm assuming that's what you want."

Jasper glowered at her. "I want to know what you meant when you said we were blind."

"I meant exactly what I said." Moxie was firm. "I'm not

going to explain it to you. You guys are going to have to figure it out on your own. Witch's Brews, right?"

Jasper's morose pout was on full display as he nodded. "Yes, and a little less attitude, if you don't mind."

"Yeah, that's not going to happen." Moxie swung her hips as she headed toward the bar. "I'm the boss here. What I say goes."

Gus watched her with the sort of affection that churned my stomach. "She's the love of my life," he said out of nowhere. "I didn't even know it was possible to love somebody as much as I love her."

The emotion on his face touched me. "It's nice you guys found each other," I offered.

"Yeah. I wasn't expecting her, didn't see her coming, but I wouldn't change her for anything." His gaze was pointed when it landed on Jasper. "It's going to happen to you one day, no matter what you think."

Jasper's laugh was nervous. "If you say so."

Gus's gaze was heavy when it landed on me, causing a tsunami of discomfort that would've knocked me down if I'd been standing. "I know so."

Twenty-Three

Three cocktails later, we left. I was feeling good, but I was still worried about one thing. I opted not to bring it up while Moxie was flitting around because I figured it would just give her ammunition against Jasper, something that didn't seem fair, given the circumstances. It was fair game once we were outside.

"So, I didn't mention it before, but Savannah stopped in the store today," I hedged as we slid closer to a building on one of the side streets, making room for drunk revelers who were clearly on their way to Bourbon Street.

"Savannah?" Jasper made a face as he slowed his pace. "What did she want?" He looked genuinely confused.

"To warn me away from her man."

"Are you kidding me?"

"Nope." I shook my head. "She seemed pretty intense. I played it off for Toni—she didn't even act suspicious—but Savannah clearly thinks something is going on between us."

Jasper glanced down at our linked fingers. I hadn't even realized we were holding hands.

"Well, she's not wrong." His grin was light. "Don't worry about her. She's always had a thing for me."

"That's what Toni said." I truly didn't want to cause a ruckus, but I also didn't want to insert myself into a situation that would cause the sort of drama I was desperately trying to avoid. "Are you guys together?"

"No." His response was almost instantaneous.

"She seems to think you are."

"No, she thinks that if she waits it out long enough, we will somehow magically become a couple. That's never going to happen."

"Have you been together before?"

Jasper hesitated, then offered a stiff nod. "Once. I was twenty-two, and we went to a party as a group. That was years ago, and I had way too much to drink. I made a grievous error in judgement."

His phrasing was enough to make me smile. "A grievous error, huh?"

"Yeah." He almost looked pained as he recounted the tale. "I was always honest with her, that I didn't see her as more than a friend. It was impossible not to recognize that she had a crush on me, but I assumed she would outgrow it and move on."

"I don't think that's happening." I was rueful. "She was pretty forceful when she staked her claim today."

"Yes, well, that's on her."

"Except you had sex with her."

"Once. Forever ago. I told her the next morning it was a mistake. She was making all these grand plans for us to go to tea with her mother, and there was some party she wanted to go to that night. I told her it wasn't happening and apologized for losing my head. I was drunk, though. She should've realized."

I understood where he was coming from. I also understood why Savannah might've been confused in the moment. "How did she take it when you told her it was a mistake?" I tried to picture how I would feel under the same circumstances, and my stomach lodged a complaint at the visuals bouncing through my head.

"She was mad. She said I used her. The thing is, she wasn't wrong. I was drunk, and sex sounded great in the moment. That was a very important learning experience for me, though. After that, I always made sure my intentions were spelled out from the start."

"She obviously got over it," I noted. "You guys are friends again."

"I don't know about that," he said while we paused at the intersection in front of my building to wait for traffic to clear. "She burned my name in effigy for several weeks. Then I didn't hear anything from her for several months. When she started sniffing around again, her attitude was different."

"Meaning?"

"Meaning that she said she was fine with the fact that I didn't want a relationship. She missed hanging out with the group. I made a promise in her absence that I would never sleep with anybody in our friend group again—and that's a rule I live by now—but there are times I'm convinced she's playing a game."

"You mean she wants to stick close to you for when you finally are ready for a relationship."

"Pretty much," he agreed as we started across the street. "My parents have been desperately in love with one another for the entirety of my life. They look at each other as if nobody else in the world exists. They were good role models to grow up with."

"Unlike me." I managed a half snort. "My mother was the exact opposite, and my father is such a nonentity he might as well be invisible."

"I definitely prefer the situation I grew up in," he said. "Someday, I do want what they have. I'm just not there yet. I have time."

"Sure you do. I don't think it's that you're not ready yet, though. I think it's that you're afraid you'll somehow not live up to the lofty standards they've set. They have that once-in-a-lifetime love that everybody dreams about. If you fail and pick the wrong person, I think, you're worried you'll somehow tarnish the family legacy."

"Wow." Jasper's eyes sparkled with amusement as we arrived at the front entrance. "Those are some pretty deep thoughts to be having after three of Moxie's signature cocktails. How drunk are you?"

I laughed drily. "I'm not drunk at all." I was a little tipsy at most. "That's just what I see. When you talk about your parents, it's in reverent tones. I get it. You don't have to explain yourself to me. I don't expect anything from you."

"Are you sure?" He used his free hand to brush my dark hair away from my face. "I do like you. I don't want to hurt you. If you've changed your mind..."

A sharp pang of panic licked at my heart. Was he already making his exit? "I haven't changed my mind. Why do you think that?"

"Moxie can be very convincing. She's clearly running high on hormones right now, on top of her usual attitude, which wasn't all that great to begin with."

"I thought you liked her."

"Oh, I love her." Jasper's tone took on a soft edge. "I'm just glad I'm not the one who is going to be shackled to her for the rest of my life. Gus seems to get off on that bossy nature of hers although I have no idea why. Me? She's way too much work. I like my women simple."

"I'm not simple."

"You're not permanent, either. You're tons of fun for now

and then a friendship forever. I think that's the best combination."

His words made me smile. "I'm fine," I assured him. "I'm not looking for forever. Quite frankly, I just need some fun with a guy who I don't have to worry about the cops taking into custody."

"Then I think I'm your man." He wrinkled his nose and leaned in to kiss me. "I mean ... if you want to invite me up that is."

That was the only thing I was interested in right then. "I think something can be arranged. We still have that list Charlie sent you to go through anyway."

"How about we worry about the list tomorrow morning over breakfast? I expect we'll both have appetites by the time we're done."

"See, now that's an offer I can't refuse."

"I was hoping you would say that."

THE SUN WAS UP, AND THE ROOM was warm when I woke the next morning. Jasper's eyes were already open, and he was glaring at my bare feet, poking out from beneath the blanket yet again.

"Oh, don't make this a thing," I complained as I rolled onto my back and shielded my eyes.

He had that look on his face, and I knew I was about to get an earful.

"This is a serious situation," he insisted as he tucked me in at his side. "You cannot sleep with your feet poking out from under the blanket. It's against the law."

"Against the law?" I choked on a laugh. "Are you telling me that if the wrong people find out about this, I could wake up to a police raid one morning and never see the light of day again?"

Jasper was solemn as he nodded. "That's exactly what I'm telling you. Do you want to live out the rest of your days in prison? I guarantee that things won't go well if you don't cover your feet when you sleep in the joint."

"What is your deal with my feet?" I demanded. "It's a very weird thing to get hung up on."

"I have no idea. It just freaks me out."

"Well, it's weird." I rolled so that I could rest my head on his bare chest. It was well defined, hard, and muscled, and he clearly liked to manscape. "How often do you shave your chest?"

Jasper arched a surprised eyebrow. "Who says I shave my chest?"

"Um ... hello." I gestured toward the smooth expanse.

"For all you know, I could be follicly challenged."

"You have a full head of hair."

"So? Maybe my head didn't get the memo the rest of my body sent."

"You have hair other places too."

He smirked. "I shave it once a week. How often do you shave your legs?"

"Every three days except when it's winter in Salem. Then I sometimes go longer than that."

"I can see that." He looked to be considering that a bit too closely. "It's cold there in winter, right?"

"It gets below zero sometimes, and if a nor'easter is coming in? Look out. We could be trapped in our homes for days under those circumstances."

"So there's really no need to shave your legs then."

"No, plus it's like an added layer of warmth, and I'm all about staying warm."

He barked out a laugh. "Except for your feet in the middle of the night."

"Leave my feet alone."

He tickled my side, causing me to gasp, then rolled me onto my back. He was careful as he rested his weight on top of mine. His eyes were still sleepy, yet a gleam appeared in them. "Tell me something about Salem that most people don't know."

"You're really interested in Salem," I noted.

"I am. I think the whole thing is fascinating. I've never understood wanting to live somewhere where you could be snowed in for days, but I like the idea of snow ... as long as I don't have to deal with it."

I could see that. "Snow is romantic and dreamy for people who only see it in movies. Right after a storm, it's fresh ... and white ... and looks powdery and beautiful. Movies don't include the part where it turns filthy and dirty five minutes after a car drives down the road."

"That's a little too real."

I laughed. "Um... I don't know what you want me to tell you." I was legitimately stumped. "Can you give me a hint?"

"Sure." He nuzzled his nose against my cheek. "What's your favorite memory of Salem? I want one that doesn't include your mother."

The stipulation threw me. "Why can't my mother be involved?"

"Because it makes you sad, and I have no interest in making you sad. We're naked and warm, and I have plans for you before breakfast. I want a happy memory for inspiration."

For some reason, his words formed a lump in my throat, and I had to blink back tears. Since his face was buried in the crook of my neck, he didn't notice, thankfully.

I managed to gain control of my emotions within a few seconds. "So ... a happy memory that doesn't involve my mother." I was at a loss, then something popped into my head. "We have a wax museum in Salem. Did you know that?"

"No, but I love a good wax museum. We used to have one

on Conti. It was weird but very NOLA. It closed in 2016, which was a real bummer because I loved using it for my tours. People said it was haunted, so it fit right in."

"I'm sorry I missed it. I love a good wax museum too." I played with his soft hair. "Our wax museum in Salem is different. It's over in Salem Witch Village, which is basically a tourist trap although it's one of my favorites."

His lips were warm against my collarbone. "Why is it one of your favorites?"

"They have food trucks, and they sell the sort of stuff I absolutely love, like apple-cinnamon fried dough and warm doughnuts."

"Who doesn't love warm doughnuts?"

"Nobody I ever want to spend time with—that's for sure."

I rested my cheek against his forehead. I couldn't remember ever having been that comfortable. That was a dangerous thought. I wondered what having mornings like that for the rest of my life would be like. As much as I wanted that to be a possibility, I knew it wasn't, with Jasper. That meant I had to enjoy our time while I could, then let him go.

"Tell me about the museum." He sounded sleepy and happy. "I want to hear the memory."

"It's not a big deal," I warned him.

"Tell me." He was demanding when he wanted to be, which had never been more apparent.

"Our wax museum is literally like sixteen bays. It's in a relatively small room, and there are sheets set up so people have to follow a certain trail."

"That sounds classy."

"Oh, it's unbelievable. Some of the body parts don't match. Like ... sometimes, the bottom half of a body will clearly not have been designed for the top half, so the bodies will be contorted in ways that humans couldn't possibly contort."

He was silent a beat. "Well, that's freaky."

"Definitely. My aunt took me there when I was five or so for the first time, and I had nightmares. My mother forbade me to ever return."

"Okay, I told you I wanted a happy memory," he stressed.

"It is a happy memory." My lips curved as I thought back. "When I was sixteen, I had a crush on a guy named Dakota Ludington. My mother hated his parents, so she forbade me from dating him. To be fair, I hadn't dated much up until that point anyway. My mother was so weird about it that it was just easier to give in to her demands."

"When are we getting to the happy part?"

"I'm almost there." I pinched his well-muscled rear end, causing him to squirm. "Anyway, Dakota asked me out. I hadn't even kissed a boy at that point. I told my mother I was going out with a group of friends. We liked to haunt Essex Street during Halloween periods because messing with tourists was something we absolutely loved."

"Yeah, we did that as teens during Mardi Gras here."

"Dakota and I snuck away from the group and headed over to Salem Witch Village. My love for apple-cinnamon dough was infamous. We got some, and I mentioned I hadn't been inside the wax museum since I was five. He thought that was so funny he bought tickets ... and we proceeded to head inside."

"Is this going to turn into a sexy story?" He almost sounded forlorn at the prospect.

"You wanted a happy memory," I reminded him. "This memory always makes me smile."

"Fine. Lay it on me."

"We held hands going through. Dakota was a history buff, so he liked to talk about the scenes that were being depicted. I found it boring, but since he was captivating to me, the stories didn't bother me for a change. Then it happened."

"What happened?" Jasper lifted his head, curious.

"In front of the third bay, he kissed me."

Jasper waited. When I didn't continue, he shot me an exasperated look. "And?"

I shrugged. "And nothing. He kissed me. It was sweet. He had no idea what to do with his tongue although I didn't realize that at the time. Imagine my surprise when I kissed my second guy, and he actually moved his tongue."

"Oh, geez." Jasper squeezed his eyes shut. "This is not a happy story."

"But it is." I was insistent. "In that moment, when he kissed me in front of the third bay, I knew that anything was possible. I knew I wouldn't have to live my mother's life if I didn't want to. I figured out I could go on adventures ... and break the rules ... and eat sugar-coated dough more than once a week without risking my teeth falling out of my head from rot."

"Your mother was a real stickler for the rules, wasn't she?"

I nodded. "Yeah. She wanted to protect me. I get it. You asked for a happy memory, though. That's mine. I like thinking anything is possible ... even if you are plagued by a curse."

He blew out a sigh. "Wow."

"Good memory, huh?"

"No. That was terrible." He shifted to sit cross-legged on the bed and drew me onto his lap. "I clearly need to start making some good memories with you. I'm not sending you back to Salem with that memory in your top ten. I need to get on the stick."

I shifted on his lap. "Yeah, I feel the stick."

He laughed as he kissed my cheek. "How about we make a memory here and then I take you for breakfast, huh? I need to put some real thought into making memories. I'm still half asleep. I need caffeine to do it properly."

"I guess I would be up for that," I said, shifting on his lap again. "All I can think about is the stick now that you brought it up."

"That was a good answer."

"Somehow, I knew you would like it."

His mouth was on mine as we rolled back onto the bed. "Prepare to be amazed ... and I don't ever want to hear that stupid wax museum story again. I'm going to give you way better memories."

He was so earnest when he said it that my heart heaved. That was exactly what I was afraid of.

Twenty-Four

We settled into a routine over the next week although it wasn't without worry. We spent every night together, laughing and hanging out at various bars. Every morning, we cuddled in bed—very nonflingy—then went out for breakfast. We grew more and more comfortable, something I saw as bad and Jasper seemed indifferent to. Still, our routine was comfortably acceptable, and that was why I was so surprised when things took a turn the following Thursday.

We were on our way to the elevator when trouble bubbled up. Jasper did something so unexpected I almost jumped out of my panties.

"What are you doing?" I demanded.

Calmly, Jasper slid his eyes to me as he poked the button next to the elevator bank with his right hand. His left-hand fingers were twined with mine. "What are you talking about?" He looked genuinely confused.

"That." I gestured toward our clasped hands with my free hand.

Holding hands when cutting through a crowd on

Bourbon Street was one thing. That was survival. This was something else entirely.

"What about it?" His voice remained even.

"We're not together," I reminded him.

He made a big show of looking behind us and then down the hallway. "It looks like we're together. Am I missing something?"

I glared at him. "We're not a couple," I insisted. "That's what I meant. This is just ... you know."

"Just what?" His lips twitched.

"It's just a fling."

"Ah." He bobbed his head sagely. "Is that what we're calling it? I wondered. I was thinking about calling it a dalliance. It's a fancier word, and it confuses people, but if you want to go with 'fling,' I guess I can deal with that." His eyes twinkled, and he didn't release my hand.

"I'm being serious." Despite my determination to argue with him, I didn't pull my hand away. Later, when I was alone, I would think about my reasoning. For the time being, I put my best stern-teacher expression on display. "This isn't a relationship, right?"

When he shrugged, my heart stuttered.

"I don't like labels," he replied. "Does everything need a label?"

I was taken aback. "You don't do relationships," I reminded him. "You're the one who cautioned me right at the start that this wasn't a relationship. You felt strongly about it then."

"I know, but ... we're having fun. Why does that have to change?"

"Nobody said it had to change. Holding hands is something couples do, however, and we're not a couple." I was trying to be reasonable. Why wasn't he getting it?

"Rowan, you're high-strung," he started.

I glared at him. "I most definitely am not high-strung. I'm easygoing."

That made him laugh, which only served to infuriate me more. "You're high-strung," he continued, not missing a beat. "You can't seem to help yourself. I think your mother did this to you."

Anger bubbled up. "She was a wonderful mother."

He held up his free hand to placate me as the elevator dinged and the doors slid open. Thankfully, nobody was on it. The last thing I needed was a witness to our uncomfortable conversation.

"I'm not saying she wasn't a wonderful mother," he insisted as he led me onto the elevator. "You're a pretty great person, and she raised you mostly alone, other than the aunt I kind of want to meet because she sounds fun. If she wasn't a good mother, then you would be even more of a neurotic mess than you already are."

Apparently, he wasn't interested in burying his insults.

"You're starting to piss me off," I said.

"That's not my intention." He hit the button for the lobby. "I'm just saying that you seem to be struggling with your place in this world now that she's gone. Life doesn't have to be this hard, though. Why not just let things happen as they're supposed to happen?" That wasn't what I'd been expecting.

"You don't do relationships." I was stuck on that.

The elevator doors closed, and we started down.

"I don't like labels," he repeated, avoiding the crux of the argument. "Hand-holding is harmless."

"But we're not in a relationship."

"Geez." He pinched the bridge of his nose with his free hand, all the while keeping a firm grasp on mine. "You are going to take some work, aren't you?"

"What is that supposed to mean?"

"Nothing." He didn't bother smiling when the elevator came to a stop. "It's just something I'm coming to understand."

"And that is?"

"You're a pain in the ass."

"Oh, coming from you, that's rich."

"I didn't say I wasn't a pain in the ass," he argued just as the door opened. "I'm simply saying that you're just as much of a pain in the ass as me, and it's not something I'm used to. What's even more frustrating is that for some reason, it turns me on."

I was floored by his response and didn't even look up when he drew me out into the lobby. Instead, I was staring at him with the sort of wonder I normally reserved for people who found the Kardashians interesting. That turned out to be a mistake because I was so focused on him that I accidentally ran into someone getting on the elevator.

"I'm sorry," I murmured absently.

"That's okay." The female voice was familiar, causing me to snap my head up. It was Posh, with Hal at her side, and she looked amused.

"Oh, hey." If I thought I'd felt awkward before, that was nothing compared to what I was feeling right then. "How is it going?" I shifted from one foot to the other like an idiot.

"It's going well." Posh's expression was impossible to read as she glanced at us both.

If I had to peg her current mood, I would've said "amused."

"I've been meaning to head back up to the pool," I offered. "I've just been busy."

"I can see that." Her lips curved at the corners as she studied Jasper. "You look familiar. Do I know you?"

My heart plummeted. Of course they knew each other.

Jasper had slept his way across three parishes, as far as I could tell. Well, wasn't that just a kick in the pants?

"Yes, we met when I was hanging out at the pool lounge about a week and a half ago," Jasper replied smoothly. "You were with that randy blonde who wouldn't stop grabbing my ass."

"Portia," Posh confirmed. "She has a certain type. You look the type."

I didn't realize I was frowning until Posh flicked her eyes back to me.

"I didn't realize he was your type," she said to me, delight evident. "For some reason, I pictured you with a banker ... or an attorney."

I was appalled. "An attorney?"

"No offense," she added hurriedly.

Oh, why would I find offense at that? "I think she's saying I'm boring," I muttered to Jasper.

"Not boring," she argued hurriedly. "Just ... set in your ways. You're the sort of person who knows exactly how her life is going to turn out. That's a good thing."

"Right." I could feel Jasper's gaze on me but refused to meet it. "Well, we're going out to breakfast. I guess I'll see you later."

"Rowan, I didn't mean anything bad by it," Posh insisted as she trailed behind me. "I like you. You're fun. I loved getting to know you the other night. It's just ... he's a different kind of fun."

"He is," I readily agreed, seeing no point in denying the obvious. "We should probably get going. I have a shift in two hours, and I don't want to be late." The smile I forced was flat. "I'm the type of person who is never late for work, which is probably something else we don't have in common, huh?"

Jasper was calm as he followed me toward the front door, our hands still clasped together. My first instinct had been to pull away from him upon seeing Posh. That hadn't happened, though, which I found interesting.

"I'm never late for work," he countered, flashing a smile over his shoulder for Posh's benefit before pushing open the glass doors so that we could head outside. "I know I come across as lazy, but I'm actually good at my job."

"I never said you were lazy." My mind was elsewhere, but I couldn't ignore his words. "You actually strike me as a hard worker. You're just lackadaisical about certain things. If you're late to a tour, you probably don't freak out about it."

"I'm never late." He was calm as we walked down the sidewalk. "I mean ... never. My parents might own the company, but they instilled a solid work ethic in us. I think it would be akin to being in a restaurant family. You always fight with family, but when there's work to be done, you get it done."

"Huh." I dragged my eyes onto him. "You're never late?" I asked, finding my view of him shaken.

"Never." He was solemn. "I believe in doing the work. That being said, when I'm done with the work, I believe in having fun." He leaned close, staring directly into my eyes. "You can be both a diligent worker and a wild party woman." He grinned. "This is New Orleans. You're expected to be both."

"Yeah." For some reason, I felt an unidentifiable ache in my chest. "I'm starting to wonder if I've ever truly had fun." I hadn't meant to say that out loud. Once I had, though, I couldn't haul it back.

Instead of telling me I had it wrong, he offered a bemused grin. "Why would you think that?"

"Because I always did what was expected of me. I didn't want to make things harder for my mother. She was raising me alone—well, with Aunt Mindy, but still—and she worked so hard. I didn't want to be an extra burden."

"Did she suggest you were a burden?" Jasper looked annoyed at the possibility.

"No." I shook my head. "Not even a little. She always said I was a gift. Heck, she encouraged me to have fun. I just ... always played by the rules."

He touched the tip of his tongue to his top lip, considering, then smiled. "I think that you're a good girl at heart. You might yearn to be a bad girl occasionally. That's probably the Salem thing. You're a witch, right?"

I nodded. "Everybody in Salem is a witch. That's part of the game."

"Well, give in and embrace your inner witch. There's nothing wrong with being both a good girl and a bad witch. You can be a good worker, responsible, and cut loose occasionally at the same time. It's allowed."

I worked my jaw for a beat. "I think I want to try grits again for breakfast." As far as transitions went, that was a weak one. I wanted to break out of my shell, though. In New Orleans, I saw no reason to be so rigid.

"I thought you didn't like grits."

"They taste like ass. I always get the same thing, though. Maybe it's time to try something different."

"I think that sounds like a good idea." He lifted our clasped hands. "Does that include this?"

Although still hesitant, I nodded. I couldn't figure out why he was so adamant about holding my hand. "I'm fine with it."

He snorted.

"I am," I insisted. "I'm totally fine with it. I don't think it's weird at all."

"Right." He sighed. "Well, let's take it one step at a time. We'll get some breakfast and make plans for the day—nothing too crazy—and then we'll go from there."

"I have to work today."

"Yes, but there are twenty-four hours in a day. You only work eight of them. That means we can cut loose tonight."

I hesitated and then stated the obvious. "I didn't realize we were doing anything tonight."

"It's New Orleans. There's always something to do."

"Yeah, but..." I trailed off, deciding on the spot that it was time to embrace the fun. "That sounds like a plan."

"I thought you would like it."

JASPER TOOK ME TO OCEANA, A RESTAURANT I associated with hangovers, given its proximity to Bourbon Street. I'd eaten there once when I first arrived in town—the restaurant was hard to miss—and had enjoyed my meal. I was determined to branch out.

"What are you getting?" I leaned closer to him and studied the menu in his hand.

Jasper arched an eyebrow. "Is your order contingent on my order?"

"No."

"Then don't worry about it. For once, don't order what you think you should. Order what you want."

"I told you I'm going to try grits again." I meant it. "Maybe I'm missing something."

"If you think they taste like ass—I'm dying to know how much ass you've sampled, by the way—then why is that suddenly going to change?"

"Because it's possible I had preconceived notions regarding grits," I admitted. "My mother always said they tasted like ass."

"Ah." He nodded in understanding. "You're trying to figure out if you really hate them or if you convinced yourself that you hated them because of your mother."

"Pretty much."

"Well, I think it's a fine idea. Just make sure to get something you know you're going to like to go with the grits. I don't want you going to work on an empty stomach because you decided to become a wild woman on a whim."

"I can be a wild woman." Even as I said that, I wasn't certain it was true. "I'll get an omelet with hash browns—I'm thinking the crawfish one—and the grits on the side. You know, just in case."

"Good plan."

We placed our orders and then talked about mundane stuff. He had three tours to give throughout the day, all of them different.

"So, the murder and mayhem tour is your favorite?" I asked as I sipped my coffee. "I'm trying to understand why."

"Because the people on the tour are always horrified by the stories," he replied as he leaned back in his chair. "They think they like the gruesome, the macabre." His eyes gleamed as he leaned forward and pressed his forehead toward mine, surprising me. "Most of them get the heebie-jeebies by the end, though. New Orleans has a dark history if you're willing to dig. There are a random few who don't get squeamish, though, and they're my favorites."

"And why is that?"

"Because I always imagine them being described on a similar tour in a different town twenty years from now ... after they've killed someone."

My heart skipped a beat. "What, now?"

He laughed, pressing a surprise kiss to my forehead before pulling back. "I think you should go on a tour with me one day when you're not working. You don't have to pay or anything. It's hard to explain what I do to someone who hasn't experienced the joy of a Jasper tour."

I rolled my eyes. "Your ego is huge."

"It's not the only thing about me that's huge." He winked,

and his eyes slid toward the door. Momentary surprise registered, then he broke out into a wide grin. "Hey, man. I was going to call you later to see if you'd made any headway on the Michel thing."

I swiveled in my seat, confused, and let out a breath when I recognized Charlie. He was alone, seeming freshly showered because his hair was damp, and I was relieved when he moved to join us. For some reason, I was having trouble interacting with Jasper normally. That wasn't something I'd considered possible until the elevator incident—everything had been so comfortable before—but I was all discombobulated and had no idea what to make of it.

"I was actually looking for you," Charlie noted as he sat in the chair to my left. "I've got a list I managed to work up. It's not much." He flashed me a smile. "Was Lisette not who you were looking for? I figured she was the one."

"Lisette is apparently suffering from dementia," Jasper replied. "She could very well be the person we're looking for, but if she is, she likely doesn't remember what she did. We talked to her granddaughter Sophie. She said it sounded like something her grandmother would've done back in the day, but there's no way to be certain."

Rather than cluck his tongue and offer sympathy, Charlie made a face. "Are you sure?"

"I'm sure that her granddaughter told us that," Jasper replied. "Why?"

"Did you get the feeling the granddaughter was messing with you?" Charlie was intense. "I mean ... just out of curiosity."

"Not really." Jasper slid his eyes to me. "I thought she was sincere."

I nodded. "I thought she was sincere too. She said her grandmother was notorious for curses and hexes in her prime but that her mind had begun to slip. She seemed genuinely upset about it. Is there a reason we shouldn't believe her?"

"Well, it's just that I saw Lisette in Jackson Square about a week and a half ago," Charlie hedged. "She didn't look lost."

"Did she have a caregiver with her?" Jasper asked.

"No. She was talking to the vendors and buying fudge. She seemed perfectly fine."

Jasper focused on me. "That's weird, huh?"

I nodded. "Are you certain it was her? I mean ... you didn't act like you knew her when we were talking about her the other night."

"I don't know her well," Charlie replied. "I've crossed paths with her at events before, though. I've definitely seen her around. I'm positive it was her ... and she seemed fine."

Well, that was something new to consider. "Huh. Sophie was adamant her grandmother was losing her faculties. I guess it's possible she was lying to me. I didn't feel as though that was the case, though."

"Well, it's worth checking out, I guess," Jasper said. "Perhaps we should tailor this evening's activities around Lisette."

I hesitated then nodded. "I liked Bywater. Maybe we can head over there."

"Now, that right there sounds like a grand idea." His smile was charming. "A wild woman would totally want to go to Bywater."

I glared at him. "Keep it up, and I'll show you just how wild I can be."

"You say that like it's a threat."

"It's a promise."

"Be still, my beating heart."

Twenty-Five

"Well?" Jasper's gaze was expectant as he watched me slide a heaping spoonful of grits into my mouth. He didn't smile outwardly although he was clearly grinning from ear to ear inside that busy brain of his.

"They still taste like ass," I said once I swallowed, frowning as I stared at the offending plate. "How can this have actually become a thing?"

"I think it's an acquired taste." Amusement ran roughshod over his features. "You don't have to eat them."

"But people like them." I shoved the plate away, making a face. "I thought maybe if I tried them again, this time with an open mind, that I might like them."

"You were convinced that you disliked them because your mother disliked them. I get it. It's okay not to like something, though. I'm not a big fan of pizza. It is what it is."

My frown grew in scope. "How can you not like pizza? That's, like, America's food."

"Technically, I think that's a hamburger."

"Whatever. I'm being serious. How can you not like pizza?"

"How can you not like grits?" he shot back.

I folded my arms over my chest. "It's not the same thing, and you know it. Grits have the consistency of something that's already been eaten and thrown up. Pizza is... Well, it's the gift that keeps on giving."

"It does keep giving," he readily agreed. "It keeps giving me heartburn."

"Oh." I pursed my lips. "I guess I can see why you don't like it."

"It's tomato-based stuff. It does funny things to my stomach. If you listen to my mother, I've always had a sensitive stomach. She swears I once threw up on a clown at a festival after eating ketchup. She even tried to fool me with green ketchup back when that was a thing—remember when they tried to make ketchup different colors when we were kids?—but I still got sick."

"That's kind of a bummer. I happen to love tomato-based stuff. In winter, I make these deconstructed stuffed cabbage rolls in the Crock-Pot. They're awesome."

"I'll take your word for it. You just said something that fills me with fear."

"Crock-Pot?"

He smirked. "Winter. Our version of winter down here is vastly different from what you guys get up there, at least if television has taught me anything."

"Yeah, I never considered that." I took a bite of my omelet, thinking. "People who don't live with snow think it's beautiful—and it is—but after a few hours, it turns filthy, and it's not fun to live in a cold-weather climate if you don't like winter sports."

"I can see that. Do you like winter sports?"

"Does reading in front of the fireplace count?"

He grinned. "I think that's the best sport." After a few seconds of eating, he turned serious. "What did you think about what Charlie said?"

"The stuff about Lisette?"

He nodded.

"I find it interesting." That was the best word I could come up with to describe what I was feeling, and it felt woefully inadequate. "Why would Lisette's granddaughter lie about her being sick?"

"Maybe because Lisette has made a name for herself casting curses all over the Quarter. She might not have been all that worried about us, but if there's a blanket rule on what to tell anybody who comes to track down Lisette, we might've fallen victim to the standard story."

I thought hard about what he suggested. "I don't know. I thought Sophie came across as the real deal. Maybe I just don't want to believe that she was lying to us."

"I think it will be easy enough to figure out," he said. "Instead of going to the granddaughter this time, we'll go to the people in the neighborhood. We'll have a good time, grab a few drinks, and make sure it appears we don't have an agenda."

"And what? How are we going to turn the conversation to Lisette without making them suspicious?"

"You leave that to me."

I waited for him to expand. When he didn't, I shot him a there-has-to-be-more look.

"I've got it," he said. "Just ... trust me."

I wanted to, I realized—to trust him. I hadn't considered that when we first met. He was just a handsome guy who liked to schmooze women. He'd somehow become something more. How much more, though? I wasn't sure I was ready to give that the amount of thought required to come up with an answer, so I decided to change the subject.

"So, three tours today, right? Do you have your speeches planned out?"

"They're not speeches. I know the general stories, and then I kind of go with the flow. Speeches are boring. I'm not boring."

"Huh. Somehow, I knew you were going to say that."

JASPER WALKED ME TO HEX APPEAL BEFORE heading off to work. He caught me in front of the window before I could separate.

"Text me when you think you're going to get off work." He slid an arm around my waist in a subtle move that wouldn't have felt out of the ordinary if he was somebody else. When he did it, my heart stuttered, and my mind started firing on all cylinders ... but not in a good way.

"Um ... what?" I was too distracted by his close proximity, and in public no less, to focus on his words.

"You're hilarious," he said with a chuckle, shaking his head before leaning in. "I have some stuff I want to talk to you about later."

I'd thought I was bad at transitions until I witnessed his attempt. "That sounds ominous."

"I'm not sure it is." His expression was hard to read. "I've just been ... thinking."

"About what?"

"Nothing we have time to deal with now." He gave me a quick kiss that stole my breath before going in for something deeper. Just when I was convinced I was about to die of asphyxiation, he finally stopped kissing me and straightened. "It struck me last night."

"What did?" My mind refused to work, and my lips were numb. Had he just done that in public?

"Just ... things." He flashed his trademark smile. "We'll talk about it later."

"Is it something big?"

His face flushed red. "I guess it could lead to something big." He pressed himself close to me, frizzing my brain with sexual chemistry I didn't even know was possible. I was close to combusting. "Don't worry about it, though. It's not something that's going to end the world. It's just a discussion I want to have with you."

"Just a discussion." The kiss had somehow rendered me stupid, and I had no idea why ... or how, for that matter.

"Just a discussion." He gave me another kiss, that one light. "I need to get to work, and so do you." He inclined his head toward the store. "Have fun with Toni today."

"I will." I was slow as I started toward the door. "Are you sure you don't want to have this conversation now?" What I really meant to say was "I will drive myself—and those around me—crazy if you don't tell me what's going on," but I kept my mouth shut.

"Later is better. I have a few things I need to work out." He cracked another grin. "Don't look at me that way. I just ... think I want to try something different."

"With Lisette?"

"That too." His grin was back, impish and delightful. "Just keep it together, Rowan. This is the sort of conversation we need hours to get through. It's going to be fine."

He sounded so sure of himself that I wanted to believe him, yet ... something felt off.

I just couldn't let it go. "We were together for hours this morning."

"Yes, but I was working through it myself this morning. Now, I think I'm ready to work through it with you. Well, at least mostly. We'll talk. There's a lot to deal with."

He sounded blasé, yet I was bothered. Despite that, I had

to get to work. I only had five minutes until my shift, and I hadn't been lying when I said I was always on time. "I guess ... um ... have fun doing your tours."

"I will. You have fun with Toni."

"I always have fun with Toni."

"That's good, because she's watching us from the other side of the window." Jasper pointed for emphasis and waved at his former schoolmate, who didn't even bother to hide the fact that she was watching us.

My heart skipped a beat as I met Toni's dark gaze. I'd told her nothing would happen between Jasper and me. I'd meant it at the time. Things were different.

"You did that on purpose," I muttered, shooting Jasper a dark look though he'd already moved down the sidewalk.

"We'll talk later," he called out, offering me a haphazard wave. "Have fun with Toni. When she burns my name in effigy, remind her that I'm the one who took her to the winter formal that one time and saved the day when her mother was on her about being embarrassed because she didn't have a date."

Was I supposed to know what that meant? "I'm mad at you," I barked at his back.

"We'll talk about that later too." With that, he was gone.

I couldn't keep yelling at him when he crossed the road—although I really wanted to—and the last glimpse I got of him was as he paused on the street corner one block down and blew a kiss in my direction.

I ignored the way that kiss stirred my loins—*ugh, did I just think that?*—and squared my shoulders to walk into Hex Appeal. Jasper was out of my reach, which meant I had to deal with Toni.

"Hey." I pasted a bright smile on my face and greeted Toni with what I hoped would come across as casual indifference. "How are things? Sorry I was almost late."

Toni stood next to the hex bags and planted her hands on her hips. Nervous, I kept chattering as though it was the most normal thing in the world. "I tried grits again this morning. I was convinced that maybe I'd been mistaken, that somehow I'd convinced myself I disliked them because my mother disliked them. Turns out they still taste like ass." Something occurred to me, and I slowed my pace as I reached to retrieve my name tag. "You probably like grits, don't you?"

"I like shrimp and grits," she replied. There was nothing friendly about her tone. "They have to be made the right way, though. I don't like grits just to like grits. They're gross on their own. They need to be a conduit for another food."

Hmm. I cocked my head. "I guess I never considered that before. Maybe I should've tried them with something instead of on the side of something."

"That would probably be smart," she agreed.

"Next time." I grabbed a rag from behind the counter. "I'll dust over by the masks." I was hoping my nervous chatter would either distract her or make her think better about asking the obvious question. I wasn't that lucky—like, as a general rule. I had bad luck, and it was on full display.

"Was that Jasper I just saw you with?" she demanded as she followed me around the store.

"Who?"

"Oh, don't even."

I blew out a sigh. "Maybe." I refused to make eye contact. "Do you have a problem with Jasper? I thought he was your friend."

"He is my friend. He wasn't supposed to be your friend."

I straightened. "Wait ... are you one of those people who doesn't want to share friends?"

I didn't know what to make of that. It was so not what I was expecting.

"Don't be ridiculous." She lightly cuffed the back of my

head, not hard enough to do damage but insistent enough to show she meant business. "What did I tell you about him?"

Apparently, we were having this conversation whether I wanted to or not. "That he was a tool."

"Not just a tool."

"That he was a womanizer," I corrected.

"That would be what I told you." Incredulous, she bumped me with her hip hard enough to spin me, forcing me to look at her. "What were you thinking?"

I didn't know how I was supposed to explain to her when I didn't understand it myself. "It's nothing," I said finally, grasping for a response that wouldn't make me sound sad and pathetic. "We're just having a fling."

"A fling?" She arched a dubious eyebrow. "No offense, girl, but you're not the type who has flings."

I balked. "I can have flings."

"No, you can't." She vehemently shook her head. "I'm sorry, but you're not a fling girl. You came to New Orleans because you're not a fling girl. You want the dream—you know the dream, right? Handsome husband, two-point-five kids, house-trained dog—and Jasper can't give you the dream."

I took a moment to absorb that statement. "I'm not sure I want the dream." I didn't realize that was true until it escaped from my mouth.

"You told me you did," Toni insisted. "You said you came to New Orleans to end the family curse because you kept getting saddled with frogs. You didn't want your mother's life because she had to go through it without the prince. You want the prince. Wasn't that the reason you came here in the first place?"

"Yes." I felt exposed, like a raw nerve waiting to react. "I'm starting to think that the life I didn't want was the Salem life."

When I said that, things clicked into place in my mind, and not in an obvious way.

"Meaning what?" Toni's voice softened, all traces of accusation gone.

"Meaning that I've been doing some thinking since I got here, and not all the thinking has been my choice." I was rueful as I regarded her. "My mother was a good woman. Like ... the best woman. She raised me with no help other than from my aunt, and in a very expensive city."

"Okay." Toni looked as if she was waiting for a bomb to go off.

"I was expected to act a certain way, want certain things, and live a specific life. There was never any question I was going to do those things because it's what she wanted, and I know she wanted it because she brought it up all the time. Except ... well ... looking back, I'm starting to wonder if I saw things that weren't there."

"Like what?"

"Like all of it. I think she just wanted me to be happy. When I was a kid, I thought I had to be perfect to make things better for her. Now, though, I don't think I need to be perfect. I think I just need to be me."

"I don't disagree," Toni said. "I think being you sounds like a fantastic way to be. That still doesn't explain Jasper."

"He was helping me with the curse."

"How did helping you with the curse turn into making out on the street?"

"It just sort of happened."

"What happened? Wait!" Toni held up her hand. "Are you going to tell me the story of Jasper and his aggressive peen? If so, I'm going to need a drink."

For some reason, that struck me as funny, and I choked on a laugh. "I had every intention of listening to what you said," I offered when I could speak again. "I knew he wasn't a relationship guy. That was okay with me because I wasn't looking for a relationship here. I thought I could do a fling."

"Well, Jasper is definitely good for a fling." She almost looked sad as she studied my features. "He's a good guy. When he's finally ready to settle down, he's going to make some woman very happy. He won't stray. He'll be a tremendous father. He's a great worker."

Her description made me smile.

"He's not ready yet, though," Toni insisted. " That guy has seen more tail than a judge at a dog show."

"He wasn't supposed to be a boyfriend." I sounded more forlorn than I expected. "Like ... at all. He was just supposed to be a distraction, a few orgasms and a solved curse. That was the plan."

"Honey, I saw you guys in front of the window," Toni said. "That didn't look like a fling to me. That looked like the real deal ... except Jasper doesn't do real."

"I know." My chest suddenly ached, and I rubbed it absently. "Somehow, things spiraled. It's only been a week and a half. I don't understand how it happened."

"Jasper happened," she said darkly. "He's always been this way. He's too charming for his own good. He's going to break your heart."

"I know." The words barely escaped on a whisper. That was the conclusion I'd slowly been coming to over the course of the morning. The reason I was so hypersensitive to Jasper wanting to cuddle in bed and holding my hand on the elevator and kissing in front of my place of business was because those things triggered reactions in me. I was falling for him despite what I'd told him. "How did this happen?" I asked nobody in particular.

"I'll tell you how it happened," Toni growled. "Jasper decided you were hot, and he couldn't keep Little Jasper in check. In typical fashion, he let Little Jasper do his thinking. I'm totally going to smack him around."

"Little Jasper isn't all that little," I offered automatically.

"Oh, don't give me nightmares." She looked disgusted. "What are you going to do?"

That was a very good question. I didn't have an answer. "I don't know. I'm afraid it's too late, though."

"Girl, I can see your face right now, and you can't. It's definitely too late."

That was so not what I wanted to hear.

Twenty-Six

Toni was in surprisingly sunny spirits throughout our shift. I thought admitting I'd fallen off the wagon—explaining I'd accidentally ended my man fast without realizing it—would put her in a sour mood. Instead, once we finished the discussion, she dropped it and started asking probing questions about my quest to end the curse.

"So, wait ... Charlie saw Lisette in Jackson Square, but her granddaughter told you she has dementia and couldn't possibly do anything to help you?"

I nodded as I dusted a naked fertility statue. It was garish to the point of no return, yet I loved it anyway. If I had a house in New Orleans, the piece would've been one of the first things I purchased as a decoration. I couldn't explain it. "That's it in a nutshell."

"Is it possible Charlie was mistaken, and he saw someone who looked like Lisette instead?"

That was something I hadn't considered. "I don't know. I guess anything is possible. He seemed like he was on the up-and-up when I met him, though."

"Oh, Charlie is a good guy. I've always liked him." Toni was thoughtful. "My mother knows Lisette. I can call her, ask if she can do a little digging. It's possible the granddaughter was simply protecting her grandmother. I'm sure Lisette has cursed more than a few people over the years. It could be a security measure."

"That's true." I pursed my lips. "If you can ask your mother, I would appreciate the help. I just don't want to be a burden."

Toni's eyes narrowed. "Why would you think that asking for a favor makes you a burden?"

I shrugged, noncommittal. "I don't know. I've only met your mother twice, and now I'm asking for a favor. That seems wrong somehow."

"Yeah, that's not how it works." Toni looked annoyed. "First off, my mother is a complete and total busybody. If there's gossip to be gleaned, she'll want to be in the middle of things. That's simply who she is. Secondly, it's hardly a big favor. I mean ... it's, like, two calls."

"Well, I appreciate her helping."

"I'll tell her that." Toni's expression told me she wanted to say more. Since she wasn't known for keeping her opinion to herself, I braced myself for something I wouldn't like. It came fast. "Did your mother refer to you as a burden when she was still alive?"

Whatever question I'd been expecting, it wasn't that. "No," I sputtered. "Why would you think that?"

"Because you have a tendency to try to shrink yourself to make others more comfortable, and it's not the sort of thing that pops up out of nowhere. It's something that's ingrained in somebody's psyche."

"My mother was great. She always bolstered me."

"My mother is great, too, but she doesn't always bolster me. Some mothers—maybe it's all mothers—don't always understand the effect they have on their children, especially daughters."

"I..." I had no idea what she was getting at or what I was supposed to say.

"I'm probably out of line," Toni continued, barreling forward. "I'm just going to say it, though. I think your mother overprotected you as a kid. I'm guessing that your father taking off the way he did left her wounded, and in response, she built a wall around you. The problem is she was the dominant figure inside that wall, and she kind of ran roughshod over you in the process."

"All my mother ever said to me was that I should be a good person," I argued. "She wanted me to be responsible."

"There it is." Toni bobbed her head. "Responsible? Maybe because your father wasn't responsible, and she was forced into that position against her will?"

I balked. "No. She was a good mother." The statement came out much shriller than I intended.

"Okay." She held up her hands in supplication. "It was just a question."

I had more I wanted to say—I was sure of it—but the sound of my phone going off in my pocket distracted me. When I pulled it out, my aunt's name scrolled across the screen, and my stomach did an uneasy somersault. "I should probably take this."

"Go ahead," Toni encouraged. "It's not like we're overrun with customers right now."

"It's my aunt. I haven't talked to her in almost two weeks."

That realization hit me hard. That wasn't what a responsible niece did. She didn't ignore her only remaining relative for two weeks and wonder why she'd done that. I answered quickly.

"Aunt Mindy, it's so good to hear from you. I was going to call you tonight. I've just been so busy getting settled."

And running around with a randy tour guide, I added silently.

"Oh, it's fine." Aunt Mindy's tone was breezy. "I wasn't expecting you to call me every night. You're an adult, for crying out loud." Her laugh was gregarious. "I'm not your mother. I don't need constant updates."

The words were like a blow to my heart although I couldn't say exactly why. "I didn't expect you to take over for my mother," I said dumbly.

"Of course not." She sounded entirely too reasonable. "That's not what I meant. It's just ... your mother always expected you to check in, even when you were an adult and could take care of yourself. I told her she was being unreasonable, but she wouldn't listen. She just kept saying that somebody had to protect you."

"I don't necessarily think I need protection."

"Oh, I knew that. You've always been a smart girl, pragmatic, and capable of running your own life. That's why I was so happy for you when you decided to travel. You need to see the world. There's no reason for you to be trapped in our little corner of it any longer. That's actually the reason I'm calling."

My mouth went dry. Something was about to happen—I could feel it. "Do you need me to come home?"

"No. Actually, it's the opposite. The thing is ... um ... there's a thing." She sounded distinctly uncomfortable, which only ratcheted up my anxiety. "I've been approached by a man named David Dunbar. He and his wife just moved to Salem about six months ago, and her dream has always been to own a store in Salem. She's big on the witch stuff."

I had no idea where she was going with this, so I just listened.

"He heard about your mother dying and waited before approaching me," she continued. "He would like to buy into the store, a straight fifty-fifty split. He wants his wife to learn from me, and eventually, they would like to buy out my half too when it's time for me to retire. At that point, his daughter would be old enough to join the family business with his wife."

If I weren't on the phone with my aunt at that exact moment, I would've looked up the signs of a stroke, because I was fairly certain I was having one. "You want to sell the store?" I had to force out the words.

"Well, right now, I want to sell your mother's half of the store," Aunt Mindy hedged. "All that money would go to you, which would allow you to travel and decide what you want to do with your life. It would also bring in extra help for me so I wouldn't have to work so many hours. It's a great situation because when I'm ready to retire in five years or so, everything will already be set in motion. We're going to have a retirement clause built into the contract and everything."

Contract? How long had she been considering this? "You have a contract? When have you had time to have a contract drafted?"

"Well, we started talking before you left for New Orleans," she explained. "Running the store is a lot of work. He approached me. I thought about mentioning it to you, but I figured if I did that, you wouldn't go ... and I think you needed to go. You've spent your whole life in Salem. You need to see the world."

How is this happening? I couldn't wrap my head around it. "That's Mom's legacy, though."

"Her legacy? No, Rowan. The store is what she did for a living. She loved it—although if you want to know the truth, I think the thing she loved most was being her own boss—but it wasn't the great love of her life."

"You're talking about my father."

"No, I'm talking about you. She wanted to give you a stable life. She was a bit manic about it, really, and I think that was to your detriment. That's neither here nor there, though. This is a way for both of us to plan our futures. You'll get a lot of money from the sale. You'll be able to do almost anything you want, including settle in New Orleans if that's your goal."

Settle in New Orleans? Had I stepped into an alternate universe and not realized it? "This was only supposed to be a temporary trip."

"So you said, yet I've never seen you as excited as you were before you left. You had a sparkle, Rowan. You were going on an adventure. It was your first real adventure, and I want you to keep that sparkle. You won't if you're tethered to this store for the rest of your life."

"But what about Mom?" I was fighting to hold back tears, which wasn't lost on Toni as she watched me from behind the counter. "Wouldn't this be the exact opposite of what she wanted?"

"No, Rowan. She wanted you to be happy. Yes, she was a bit overprotective. She made big jokes and tried to be as flamboyant as possible, but she regretted not having more adventures. She wanted you to be happy above all else, and I think she would be proud of you for realizing that the store wasn't going to make you happy."

"But..." I was floundering.

"Just think about it," Aunt Mindy said. "You don't have to make your decision right this second. I told David that you were ultimately the one who would have the final say. He understands that. I didn't tell you about the offer before you left because I knew you wouldn't leave under those circumstances. I'm telling you now because I want you to think about it ... and have fun there when you're thinking about it. You're a young woman. You should have some fun, not be saddled to a store your mother started because she wanted to provide a good life for you."

I was lost, well and truly lost. "I'll think about it," I said out of the blue. "I'm going to need some time. This is all such a surprise."

"I know. If you take the time to think about it, though, I think you'll realize it's not all that surprising after all."

"I guess." I licked my lips and ordered my heart to stop pounding. "Is everything else okay with you?"

"Oh, it's really great. I even met a man at bingo, and we're going out this weekend."

I couldn't remember my aunt ever having gone out on a date. I knew she had—she and my mother joked about their bad dates constantly when I was younger—but that was a foreign concept. "You're dating? What about the curse?"

"I've decided the curse is a state of mind that I'm not going to embrace."

"But..."

"You should follow my example," she continued, barely taking a breath. "Go on a date. Have some fun. Do something reckless ... although not too reckless. Don't get one of those diseases you can't knock out with a dose of penicillin, or anything."

The conversation had taken a turn I wasn't comfortable with. "I'll think about what you said and give you a call in a few days. Um ... have fun with your date."

"That's the plan. You have fun in New Orleans. I hear it's a magical city."

"It's pretty cool." *But is it what I want?*

I WAS ON AUTOPILOT FOR THE rest of my shift, and I left Hex Appeal later with a heavy heart. I shuffled along the sidewalk, my gaze focused down instead of at the people sliding by. My life had suddenly turned topsy-turvy, and I had no idea how to fix it.

I was so lost in thought that I made it halfway home before remembering Jasper was supposed to meet me at work at the end of my shift. He'd never come, which made my heart twist in a new direction, on top of everything else. *Why didn't he come?*

On a whim, I dug in my pocket to check my phone. I hadn't as much as looked at it after disconnecting with my aunt. That conversation had thrown me, and I was scrambling to keep up all day. I couldn't take another distraction.

Sure enough, I'd missed a text message from Jasper: *Something came up. I can meet you later than I expected. I have to do something first.*

That was it—no explanation of what had forced him to change his plans, no firm plan for a meeting, nothing other than his vague message. That irritated me to distraction.

"Whatever," I muttered to the phone before shoving it in my pocket. All I wanted at that point was to crawl into bed, pull the covers over my head, and shut out the world.

To say my aunt's bombshell hadn't rocked my world would be a lie. Of all the things I'd expected her to say to me, that wasn't even in contention. *She wanted to sell the store? She wanted me to sell my mother's half of the store? Could I even consider it?*

The problem was she wasn't wrong. Even though I'd been traveling to New Orleans to kill the curse, I'd been excited about the trip. I'd never been farther away than Maine in my entire life. New Orleans was a completely different world, and it was one I wanted to explore. It was only supposed to be temporary, though. It wasn't supposed to be the beginning of a lifelong adventure.

I scuffed my feet on the sidewalk, unease rolling over me like waves of a tsunami. My feet had always been planted firmly on the ground when I was growing up. I always knew what the day would hold, thanks to my mother. But now, I was actually contemplating embarking on a life without roots. *How did things shift so fast?*

Before my mind could continue rolling, I was forced to one side by a group of partiers taking up the entire sidewalk. They were drunk and having a good time, and I was careful not to make eye contact. That meant looking to my left, inside one of the bars I'd passed before but never entered, and when my gaze landed on the bar area, the feeling of crushing uncertainty I'd been grappling with for hours doubled in scope.

Jasper. He was inside, and he wasn't alone.

He was on one of the stools with a drink in front of him, and he was with a group of people. One of those people was Savannah. Sitting on the stool to his left, she laughed at whatever he was saying and leaned close to whisper.

Jasper inclined his head as he listened and broke out in a huge smile. His hand landed on her back which he rubbed lightly as he announced something that clearly made the rest of his group fall into fits of laughter.

I couldn't look anywhere but at his hand. It was continuously rubbing Savannah's back in a manner that was more than friendly.

You're not a couple, I reminded myself. *This is just a fling.*

Knowing that and ignoring the emotions bubbling up inside me were entirely different things. My heart hurt as I watched Jasper having fun with somebody else, and that's when I knew I'd made the mistake to end all mistakes. I'd allowed myself to start feeling something real for Jasper. I didn't even know how I'd let that happen. I'd gone in recognizing I couldn't allow that, yet there I was, my heart threatening to break into a million pieces as I stood on the sidewalk, separated from him.

It wasn't just Savannah—although I wasn't happy to see her—but it was the fact that he belonged there. It was his home, and he fit in. Everybody knew him. Everybody loved him. I, on the other hand, was anchorless and without roots.

Slowly, I turned away from the window, doing my best to ignore the nausea rolling through my stomach. I'd gone from being the woman with a plan, someone who always knew the way her life would go, to someone who had nothing.

Perhaps I was always destined to end up this way, I mused. Maybe that's what my mother was trying to protect me from.

Rather than remaining an outsider looking in on Jasper's life, I pointed myself toward home. My bed and covers were calling me, and the interference was so loud in my head that my only hope was to shut out the noise.

I needed peace, and I wasn't going to get it there.

Twenty-Seven

Jasper started texting twenty minutes after I got home.
Where are you?
I'll come to you.
There's something I want to talk to you about.

I didn't respond. Instead, I put my phone on silent and crawled into bed. Someone knocked on my door thirty minutes later, but I didn't get up to check. I knew it was him, and the last thing I wanted was to see his stupid face. Finally, after what felt like forever, I fell asleep.

I woke at five o'clock, which was slightly better than what I'd been managing when it came to sleep before I started hooking up with Jasper, but I felt draggy. When I checked my phone, which felt like a chore, I found I'd missed three calls from Jasper. All of them went to voice mail, which I didn't listen to. There were texts too, which got increasingly frustrated as they progressed:

I know I said I would pick you up after work and we could go on a Lisette hunt, but something came up. It was something I had to do. I'm sorry.

You could at least text back, so I know you're okay. I'm getting worried.

Seriously, Rowan, where are you? I don't like this.

They went on and on until the last one.

I'll find you tomorrow. I don't know what happened, but we'll talk it through. It will be fine.

The last line bothered me the most. *It will be fine.* No, it most certainly wasn't going to be fine. My aunt was selling my mother's legacy. She was essentially rendering me homeless. I would have no reason to return to Salem if she followed through.

I understood wanting to have a plan in place for retirement. When I took off, I'd left her with all the work. That was unfair, and it was something that would have to be remedied. I already knew what I was going to do. I would find a solution for the curse—that was why I was in New Orleans—then go home. I would take over the store completely and let her rest. She would be okay with that.

No, she would *have* to be okay with that. It was the only solution I could come up with. For a split second, when she mentioned her plan on the phone, my heart had soared at the prospect of being set free. That was before I saw Jasper with Savannah, however, before that strange pressure began in my chest, which I'd yet to get rid of.

I wondered why I was so agitated by that scene. I was the one who'd put the ground rules for the fling in place, and I'd meant it when I said it couldn't be anything serious. *So why, for the love of all that is holy, is my nose so far out of joint?* It made zero sense. He'd done nothing wrong.

"He made you hope."

That niggling voice inside my head said the one thing I would never admit out loud. Despite my protestations to the contrary, I'd enjoyed spending time with him. I'd even started developing feelings for him. That was my mistake, not his ... yet I still wanted to punish him. His date with Savannah—sure, other people had been there with them, but she was the one hanging on his every word—felt like a betrayal.

So I made up my mind. I needed to solve the curse situation sooner rather than later. That had to be my focus. With that in mind, I pulled out my phone and shot off a text to Toni.

I'm not feeling well. I can't work my shift today.

I felt guilty even writing it. I never called off work. I was always the person who showed up, no matter how horrible I felt. Toni had given me a shot even though she didn't know me, and I was essentially rewarding her generosity with a slap in the face. That's when I added something to the message, something that made me feel sick.

You were right about Jasper.

With that, I placed the phone on the nightstand and headed to the shower. My curse conundrum wasn't going to solve itself. I had to push Jasper out of my mind—he was never going to be a viable option for me anyway—and get to the heart of matters. That meant finding Lisette and questioning her. She was the only one with answers.

I DIDN'T BOTHER GOING ALL OUT when getting ready. I wouldn't be seeing anybody I knew, and I was too tired to bother with makeup and straightened hair. Instead, I pulled my wet hair back in a loose bun, tugged on a pair of capris and a simple white T-shirt, and headed toward Jackson Square.

Charlie had said he saw Lisette hanging out there, and I thought she might return. Tables were always set up there for palm readers and voodoo people who didn't own their own stores, and I hoped to find her hanging out with them. I wasn't opposed to returning to Bywater—it had an amazing vibe—but solving my problems without leaving the French Quarter would've been more convenient.

The day was still early when I arrived, although people were milling about and setting up. The artists had started putting their works on a fence. The tarot card readers had their tables out and were decorating them with knickknacks. The food vendors who normally set up along Decatur Street hadn't arrived yet, but I knew that was only a matter of time.

My first order of business was questioning the fortune tellers. It wasn't that I didn't trust Charlie. I figured if anybody knew the truth about Lisette, however, they would be the people who ran in the same circles with her.

"Do you need something, hon?" A blonde in an ankle-length skirt with small bells attached to the drawstrings fixed me with an odd look as I glanced in her direction.

I probably looked like a crazy person, I realized. The way I'd been scanning them was definitely suspicious.

"Actually, I was looking for someone." My palms were suddenly sweaty, and I wiped them on my capris. I could do this. I *needed* to do this. It was my way out of New Orleans and back to my old life. "Do you know Lisette Michel?"

The woman's expression was neutral, but I didn't miss the momentary flash in her eyes. She shuttered quickly and offered an easy smile. "Of course. Everybody in these parts knows Lisette. She's a legend."

"I was kind of hoping to talk to her."

"I don't see her around right now." The way the woman averted her eyes told me she was lying.

My heart skipped a beat. Could Lisette be close? I'd seen her through the window of her Bywater home. I knew what she looked like. I would be able to recognize her. Carefully, I sucked in a breath to steady myself. "I just want to talk to her." I kept my voice low. "I'm not trying to cause trouble."

"Lisette is important to us." The woman's gaze was probing. "May I ask why you want to talk to her?"

I wondered how I should answer. Before I gave it enough thought, I just blurted it out. "Because I think she cursed my family a million years ago, and I want to ask her to lift the curse."

The woman blinked several times, surprise registering fast and hard, then smirked. "Well, why didn't you just say so?" She relaxed visibly. "Lisette has her morning coffee over on the steps that lead up to the riverwalk. We're not supposed to rat on her because her granddaughter is always trying to track her down. I thought maybe you were friends with Sophie."

"I've met Sophie," I replied. "We're not friends, though. I just want to talk to Lisette."

"Head that way." The woman inclined her head toward the far side of Jackson Square. "She's over there."

"And she's ... cognizant?" I felt strange asking the question, but the last thing I wanted to do was verbally accost a woman with dementia.

"Cognizant? Yeah. Why wouldn't she be?" The woman appeared baffled.

"Just checking." I sent her a sunny smile I didn't feel and started in the direction she'd indicated.

The park was still closed and locked, so I had to skirt around it to reach my destination. When I arrived at the corner of the park, sure enough, I found a lone woman sitting on the steps. She had a to-go coffee cup sitting in the shade next to her, along with a container of beignets from Cafe du Monde on her lap. I hesitated only long enough to gather my courage, then I set off to cross the street. It was still early enough that the traffic was almost nonexistent.

"Stop right there," Lisette barked when I was almost directly in front of her. "If you're planning to rob me, be forewarned—I'll curse you into the next century."

That was an effective threat, given what I knew about her, so I immediately stopped moving. "Why would I rob you?"

"Because that happens a lot around here." She looked me up and down. "You look familiar. Where do I know you from?"

"I was at your house a little more than a week ago."

"My house?" Her forehead wrinkled in concentration. "Doing what?"

"I stopped to see you with a friend. Your granddaughter met us at the door. She explained that we couldn't see you because you were sick. I looked through the window and got a glance, but we never talked."

"Oh, right." Lisette bobbed her head, her lips curving in amusement. "You think you're cursed. I asked Sophie about you after you left, and she told me the whole story."

"I don't *think* I'm cursed. I *know* I am." I angled my head toward the stairs. "May I sit?"

"Sure." She didn't seem bothered that I was infringing on her private time. "I'm pretty sure I could take you if it came down to it."

"I'm pretty sure you're right." I licked my lips and focused on Jackson Square, rubbing my palms over my knees as I gathered my courage. "So, um, I believe you cursed my grandmother a long time ago. Her name was Henrietta Bancroft, and she lived in Salem. That's Massachusetts, not Oregon."

"Okay." Her expression didn't change.

Since she was giving me nothing, I had no choice but to press forward. "My mother died a little over a year ago."

"I'm sorry to hear that."

"I was too." My voice caught, and I had to battle back

tears. "Anyway, my mother told me on her deathbed that our family was cursed. I didn't believe her—I mean, it sounded ludicrous on the face of it—but then stuff started happening."

"What sort of stuff?" Lisette bit into a beignet, leaving powdered sugar on her cheeks, and chewed methodically as she looked at me.

"The sort of stuff that can't be explained when looking at it through a specific lens." I gave her a rundown, refusing to embellish in an attempt to make her laugh, and when I was finished, I sat straighter on the steps. "That's a curse, right? I'm cursed. My mother was right. She was never happy. I'm not going to be happy unless I end the curse."

"Uh-huh." Lisette used the back of one hand to wipe her mouth. "Have you considered that you don't want to be happy and that's why you pick idiots to date?"

That was not the reaction I was expecting. "What, now?" I slowly slid my eyes to her. "Are you saying you didn't curse my grandmother?"

Lisette offered a one-shoulder shrug. "I've cursed a lot of people over the course of my life. I don't specifically remember your grandmother, but it's entirely possible we had words back in the day. I remember hating some of those women who came down from the north when I was running those events. They were entitled, looking down their noses at the way we lived our lives here, and I wasn't a fan of the attitude I saw."

"I'm sorry if my grandmother did something to hurt you. I really am. I didn't know her. I don't remember her. I've heard stories, though, and supposedly, she was a bit of a bitch."

Lisette barked out a laugh. "Was that hard for you to say, girl?"

"What?"

"That your grandmother might've been a bitch. Just for the record, you should hear the things my grandchildren say about me. It doesn't mean they don't love me. It just means they find me difficult to deal with and need to vent occasionally. It's okay to vent. It's normal, even."

"I met your granddaughter," I argued. "Sophie. She's lovely, and she seems genuinely worried about you. She said..." I trailed off, briefly wondering if it was okay to tell a person with dementia that they had dementia. Could that trigger a meltdown? I didn't want to risk that.

Lisette's eyes danced with delight. "She said I'm losing my mind, right?"

"I don't believe she phrased it that way," I replied woodenly.

"She didn't phrase it that way. I did. Also, I'm not losing my mind. I just let my grandkids think that because, otherwise, they spend all their time following me around. They think I'm old, that as soon as I hit seventy I turned decrepit. They mean well, but they're smothering. So I started pretending I was losing it, and they left me to work in my garden for hours on end. They stopped following me constantly because they figured I was pruning roses or some other shit. It's better for all concerned this way. I'm not crazy, and yet they think they're helping."

My mouth dropped open. "You're pretending to have dementia?"

"Only three days a week. That baffles them. It entertains me."

"But ... don't you think that's cruel?"

"I think dementia is cruel," she replied. "I'm hopeful it never really happens to me. Do I think I'm being cruel to them? Hell no. They're busybodies. I happen to like our current situation."

"Huh." I rubbed a cheek, uncertain what to say. "What about the curse?" I asked finally. "Do you think you can get rid of it for me? You would've cast it a long time ago. My grandmother is gone. I can pay you if it comes to it. I might need to save up for a little bit, depending on how much you want, but I'll do whatever is necessary."

Lisette was quiet, too quiet. When I turned back to her, I almost expected to find the spot she'd been occupying empty. Instead, I found pity waiting for me as she shoved the beignet container to the side and inched closer.

"You're not going to curse me again, are you?" My stomach was so tight that I thought I might throw up.

"No, girl, I'm going to tell you the truth." Lisette stood, drawing herself up to her full height. Since she was barely over five feet tall, that wasn't saying much. Her smile was soft when she pointed it at me. "There is no curse."

My heart skipped ten beats. "What, now?" I had to have heard her wrong.

"There is no curse," she repeated. "Oh, don't get me wrong, I threatened to curse people left and right back then. I liked it when people were afraid of me." She smiled at the memory. "It's entirely possible your grandmother rubbed me the wrong way, and I told her she was cursed. I never really cursed anybody, though."

"You didn't?" I hadn't been expecting that answer. "How can you be sure?"

"Because curses aren't real."

I blinked. "But..."

"They're not real, girl." She tsked. "We might sell people on the idea of curses, but the truth is, they're often a self-fulfilling prophecy. We don't actually curse people, although I do love throwing that threat around in the neighborhood. I have a certain reputation, and the youngsters running around there these days crap their pants when they see me."

I didn't understand. I couldn't. "Did you not hear the stories I told you about my dating mishaps over the past year?" I demanded.

"I did hear them, and it sounds to me as if you created your own problems. You picked guys who were destined to fail from the start. If you ask me, your mother did you a disservice saying you were cursed with her dying breath. That skewed your thinking. You were already mourning her. This curse became something to focus on other than your grief."

"But..." This wasn't right. "She was never happy. She was cursed too. My father left her when I was a kid."

"That's because your father was an asshole." Lisette was matter-of-fact. "He's the one who made that decision. A curse didn't turn him into an asshole. He did it to himself. If your mother blamed the curse for his actions, that was her being deluded because she didn't want to admit the truth."

"And what's the truth?" I asked in a barely audible voice.

"Life is what we make of it. If you go into it afraid, believing that bad things are going to happen, then they're going to happen. You're going to make it happen."

"What if you go into it believing things are going to work out? What happens then?"

"Then they usually work out. Having faith in yourself is half the battle." She cocked her head. "Where's your friend? The man who came with you to my house. How come he isn't out here, tracking me down with you? You guys seemed pretty tight when I saw you leaving that day."

"He's ... otherwise engaged," I replied, averting my gaze. "He has other places he would rather be."

To my utter surprise, she let out the most disdainful snort I'd ever heard. "No, he doesn't." She unfurled a craggy finger toward the park corner across from Café du Monde. "Isn't that him?"

I thought my heart was going to pound right out of my chest as I followed her finger to Jasper, who looked as if he'd been through some sort of war yet somehow survived as he clutched his hands into fists at his sides and stared.

"What is he doing here?" I was beside myself.

"He's here to end your curse," Lisette replied calmly. "The question is, are you going to let him?"

"You act like it's my choice."

"Oh, girl, it was always your choice."

Twenty-Eight

My heart was pounding, a relentless thunderstorm in my ears. Still, I managed to put one foot in front of the other. Jasper was the one who crossed the road, and when he met me in front of the steps, his expression was a mixture of fear and annoyance. I didn't know what to make of either emotion.

"What are you doing?" I blurted.

"I've been trying to get in touch with you," he said at the same time. His tone was accusatory.

I swallowed hard. "Why?" I asked finally.

"What do you mean, 'Why'? We were supposed to meet up last night."

"Well ... um ... I didn't want to bother you." That was a copout, but it was the best I could come up with.

"Why would it be a bother?" He was intense as he looked me up and down, then he shifted his eyes to Lisette on the steps. "Is that who I think it is?"

I nodded. "She doesn't have dementia. She just lets her family think that, so they don't police her activities."

Despite the heavy undercurrent of tension flowing

between us, his lips twitched. "That's actually pretty genius when you think about it."

"Or diabolical."

"I guess. Did she solve your problem?"

"In a manner of speaking." I was unbelievably uncomfortable. "She says I was never cursed, that she just told people she was cursing them back in the day."

"Oh yeah?" His emotions were impossible to assess. "How do you feel about that?"

"I don't know." I opted for the truth. If this was going to be the last time we talked—and why wouldn't it?—being honest was best. "If I was never cursed, that means I did it all to myself. *All* of it. I picked those men, and I have to believe that I was at least partially aware of how things would turn out when I did it."

His tongue slid through the seam of his lips, and I could practically hear the gears in his mind working. "Are you telling me you never considered that yourself?" he asked finally.

"No, because that would mean I was self-sabotaging, and why would I want to do that?"

"Maybe 'want' is the wrong word. Maybe it wasn't an active choice but a defense mechanism."

"And what was I protecting myself from?"

"Living a life without your mother? Growing up? I don't know. I think it might've been a combination of things."

His words grated.

"I have no problem being an adult," I said. "I think it's rich that you, of all people, are suggesting I don't want to be an adult. I mean ... you're a grown man who makes a game of bedding women and sets his own expiration date with every interaction. How can you stand there and pretend you're the adult here?"

"I'm not pretending to be an adult. You're right. I'm an

idiot. I created my own set of problems. We're not talking about me right now, though. We're talking about you."

"Maybe we should be talking about you," I shot back, hating how defensive I sounded, but I couldn't seem to stop myself. "Maybe I'm not the problem at all."

"Okay." His tone was utterly reasonable. "If you want to talk about me, we can talk about me. Why didn't you return my calls and texts last night?"

"That's back to talking about me," I grumbled, folding my arms across my chest.

"Fine, we'll talk about you *and* me." He lowered his voice. "I was looking forward to spending time with you."

That just tore it. "I saw you on my way back home. You were in the bar ... with Savannah. Don't bother denying it. I know what you both look like."

He was taken aback. "You saw us?"

"I did, and you don't have to let me down easy or make excuses. I get it. You're you, and you don't owe me anything. Not a single thing. I shouldn't even be this upset about you seeing another woman. I mean... I knew what I was getting into when I hooked up with you." My hands were incredibly flaily, and no matter how hard I tried to control them, they refused to quit fluttering around like rabid butterflies.

"Maybe I don't see it that way," Jasper argued. "Maybe ... I want to owe you something." He almost seemed confused as his words escaped.

"I don't even know what that means," I groused.

"It means I met with my regular crew last night because I hadn't seen them in more than a week." He was calm as he stared into my eyes. "I didn't even realize that was true until Savannah texted to accuse me of forgetting about my friends. It made me realize I had forgotten about them ... and that's because I was completely focused on you."

"Well, I guess you don't have to worry about that any

longer." I was working overtime to keep my voice from cracking. "There is no curse, so you're free to return to your old life."

"You misunderstand, and that's probably because I'm crappy when it comes to explaining myself. You should probably get used to that if we're going to make a genuine go of being together, by the way. I'm going to make a million mistakes."

My heart skipped a beat. "What?" My voice was a breathy whisper when it escaped. "What are you even saying?"

"I'm saying that two nights ago, I realized I'd gone more than three weeks—almost four weeks, really, when you break it down, even though we didn't meet right away—without a random hookup. I didn't even want to go out and play the games I've always prided myself on playing. That's because of you."

"I thought I was your random hookup."

His eyebrows hopped in amusement. "Did you really think that?"

"Yes. You don't do relationships."

"And you're supposed to be temporary," he said. "That's why it was so easy to allow myself to get close to you. In the back of my head, I always had an escape hatch. You were the one who was going to be leaving. You were the one who had another life elsewhere. It was fine for me to spend time with you because there was no chance you would stay. What if that's not what I want, though?"

I couldn't wrap my head around what he was saying. "I don't understand." I was suddenly miserable. "You were with Savannah last night."

"I was with my entire party group last night," he countered. "She happened to be there. I didn't mean to stay out with them as long as I did, but it felt like the end of something, and I was dragging it out."

"Dragging what out?"

"I told them I would probably be around less because I was going to try something completely new."

"What? We're not talking about grits again, are we?"

He snorted. "No, and you're the one deflecting right now. I'm the one being serious, for a change, and it's a weird place for me to be. I need you to meet me halfway."

"Maybe I would if I knew what you were even talking about."

"I want to date you."

I waited for him to expand. When he didn't, I held my palms up to prod him. "I'm going to need more than that."

"Of course you do." Frustration practically oozed out of his pores as he dragged a hand through his hair. It didn't look washed, which I found interesting.

Had he bounced out of bed first thing this morning and come looking for me? If so, why?

"I want to try a relationship," Jasper said, vulnerability evident as he met my gaze shakily. "I always thought I didn't want a relationship, that I was better bouncing from woman to woman and focusing on fun instead of responsibility. The thing is, I believe I might've been selling myself short with that thinking."

"Of course you were," I said with a laugh. "You have the potential to be a great boyfriend and even a great husband and father one day. You're the one standing in your own way. It's like you're on the precipice of adulthood but you won't take the final leap to actually embrace your destiny ... or maybe a less cheesy word.

"If you could hear how your friends talk about you behind your back, you would understand," I continued. "Toni loves you like a brother. She warned me away from you for my benefit, but she also said you were going to be an amazing partner when you finally got your head out of your ass. She just had serious questions about when that was going to happen.

"People are drawn to you for a reason. You're charming ... and fun ... and loyal. You simply don't know how to put yourself first and make your own life better. You'll get there one day, though. I have faith."

His eyes were glassy. "What if I want to get there with you?" He seemed to realize what he'd said after the fact and regrouped quickly. "Or what if I really want to try to get there with you?"

"Do you?" As a foreign emotion crammed into my chest, I could barely breathe.

"Yeah. It struck me the night before last ... or maybe even before that. The highlight of my day—that's every day—for the past two weeks was the time I spent with you. For the first time ever, I wasn't thinking about how I was going to be able to get rid of you. I wasn't wondering what the next chick I hooked up with would look like. All I thought about was you.

"Now, I'm not going to pretend we're ready to drop *I love yous* and live happily ever after," he continued. "I'm not ready yet, and I'm going to be terrified when the time comes. You're not ready yet, either. I want us to get ready together. I want us to work toward becoming adults together because, believe it or not, you're straddling the same line I am."

Was I? That was a hard pill to swallow.

"You lived your life for your mother," he said as he grabbed my hand and flipped it over, tracing a finger over my palm as though he needed the contact to anchor himself. "Part of me thinks that's admirable. The other part, though, is mad at her on your behalf. She kind of held you hostage."

I made a sound of protestation, but he cut me off before I could complain about his word choice.

"Don't," he insisted. "You're not being disloyal to acknowledge that you did your living for her and your aunt.

You've paid your dues, though. Don't you think it's time to live for yourself? You're alive here. We can be alive together and figure out this adulting stuff as a team.

"I'm not going to pretend I'm going to be good at it right out of the gate," he continued. "I'm going to make a million mistakes. I like you, though. Right now, I can't imagine anybody I would rather make my mistakes with. It's you and only you. Just... I need you to give me a chance. That's what I need to make my final step. Whatever you need to make your final step, I'm willing to give it to you."

Slowly, I drew my hand back from him and heaved a sigh. I didn't pull away, though. Instead, I shifted my gaze to the top of the steps. I was suddenly reminded of a mountain, and it was one I didn't know if I had the strength to climb.

A man was directly in front of me, baring his soul and asking me to bare mine in return. He'd seemed a safe choice when I was looking to burn off some steam, but in hindsight, I had to wonder if I had an inkling of how this would turn out. Maybe I was only telling myself he was temporary because I didn't want to risk getting a broken heart out of the deal. Why else would I have reacted the way I had the previous evening?

"My aunt called yesterday," I said out of the blue. "She has a plan for the store up in Salem."

Confusion etched his features, but he remained silent, waiting me out.

"She wants me to sell my stake to a family, a husband who wants to give his wife the store of her dreams," I explained. "For the next few years, the wife would own fifty percent of the store and work with my aunt. Then Aunt Mindy would retire and sell her stake to the family when the daughter is old enough to become a full partner."

"And how do you feel about that?" Jasper almost looked afraid to hear the answer.

"I was upset when she first told me, but I'm starting to

think I wasn't upset at the thought of selling the store. I was really upset at myself because the first emotion I felt was relief."

He pressed his lips together and nodded. "I get it. It's your last piece of your mother."

"If I let it go, what does that say about me?"

"That you'll always love her but you're ready to live for yourself. I want you to live with me."

I frowned.

"Okay, not live *with* me," he corrected quickly. "It's too soon for that. I just want you to live your life with me. The moving-in stuff is a discussion for later."

"Much later," I stressed.

"At least two weeks," he agreed with a wicked grin. "Wait. Does that mean you're considering this?"

Am I? No. I'd already made my decision. Part of me wondered if I'd made it before he showed up in front of Jackson Square. "I love New Orleans." I was rueful as I regarded him. "I felt a kinship with this city as soon as I got here. It's like home but different."

"And what did you feel when you met me? Because when I met you, I felt as if I'd been hit by a truck. I was still breathing, my heart was still working, but everything was different. I'd never felt that way before, and it threw me."

"Basically, you're saying you really had no interest in helping me cure the curse so that you would have a story for your tour," I mused.

He smirked. "I started showing up long before I knew about the curse. Haven't you wondered why that is?"

"Yes, but I figured you probably wanted to tap the resources at The Annex before moving on to the female offerings at another location."

"I only wanted to tap one resource at The Annex ... and I don't want you phrasing it that way." He looked genuinely tortured. "I need you to know that I'm in this now, which means it's just you. I would never cheat on you."

I wasn't surprised that his head had gone there. "The thought never crossed my mind. I don't know how this is going to work though. I mean ... I'm going to have to go back to Salem at some point. My stuff is there. I have to sign some paperwork. I ... need to say goodbye to my mother."

Understanding washed across his features. "Maybe I could go with you, huh? I've always wanted to see Salem, and I would love to meet your aunt."

"She's dating somebody ... and is really happy."

"That's good, right?"

"It's different."

"Different is good, for both of us." He gently reached over and brushed my hair away from my face. "I've lost track of where this conversation is going. Have you agreed to be my girlfriend yet, or do I need to beg?"

For some reason, that struck me as funny, and I burst out laughing.

He caught my chin and lowered his mouth to mine, swallowing the sound with his own laugh as he kissed me. His arms were big and warm as they wrapped around me, and nothing had ever felt so right.

For the first time I could remember, I heard no bothersome voice whispering in the background that it should feel wrong. I sensed only encouragement, and it came in my mother's voice:

"Way to go."

I was breathless when I pulled back. "How are you going to explain this to all of your high school friends? You know they're going to mess with you for finally referring to yourself as a boyfriend, right?"

He grinned. "I'm prepared to take the ribbing. Believe it or not, we mess with each other all the time."

"I've noticed." I hesitated. "Toni is going to have questions."

"Oh, Toni is going to grill me like a steak on a barbecue. I'm ready for her. More importantly, I'm ready for you." He pressed his forehead against mine and wrapped me tightly. "It couldn't have been anyone else, to prod me to get my head out of my ass, I mean. It was always meant to be you."

For me too, I realized. It was always meant to be him. "We're totally going to make a mess of this."

"We are, but the adventure is half the fun, right? I can't wait for the adventure."

He wasn't the only one.

Epilogue
THREE MONTHS LATER

"Is this it?" With a bit of trepidation, Jasper looked at the stack of boxes in what used to be my bedroom. "This isn't a lot of stuff, Ro."

I arched an eyebrow and held out my hands. "Most of the stuff in the house belonged to my mother and aunt. I guess I was just ... keeping a room in their house." It was weird to think about all the things that had changed over the past few months. My life in Salem felt like someone else's life when I came back to sign papers and pack up to move to New Orleans permanently.

"Well, it's weird." Jasper flashed that impish smile of his.

He'd taken to being in a relationship more easily than I'd expected. I thought he would've experienced some growing pains. Sure, a few mistakes popped up here or there—we both made them—but the transition had been mostly seamless. In fact, he was the one who suggested we drive up together to sign the final paperwork divesting my half of the store and to pick up my stuff. He wanted to see my home, meet my aunt, and make sure I was comfortable with the big changes in my life.

I was, for the record. I was looking forward to calling New Orleans home. Even better than that, with my lease at The Annex running out in two months, we were starting to consider renting a house so that we could live together. We spent every night wrapped around one another already. It wouldn't be that big of a change. It would simply be the next step, and we were both keen to take any and all steps together.

"I'm sorry you think it's weird," I replied. "You know I go out of my way to make sure things aren't weird for you. That's my goal in life."

"So much snark," he growled as he grabbed me around the waist and dragged me to him, burying his face in my hair and inhaling deeply.

He was clearly in a playful mood. He'd been worried when the time came to sign the final papers to sell the store, but I hadn't balked. I hadn't even hesitated. This felt right, and I couldn't remember the last time things had felt right for me.

Well, before him.

"I'll have no problem fitting this stuff in the back of the truck," he said as he kissed my neck and released me. "Do you want to keep it at my place instead of moving it into your place, though? I still have four months on my lease, so you're going to be living with me two months before we can move to a house. This way, we'll only have to move the boxes one extra time."

"We can do that." I nodded.

We split time between his apartment and mine already, mostly because he was a big fan of the rooftop parties and refused to entirely abandon my place. I'd become a fan of them too.

"I'm going to want to check the house one more time before we go," I said. "With Aunt Mindy moving her boyfriend in, I want to make sure it's her space so they can ... well..."

"Have sex?" Jasper cocked a roguish eyebrow.

"I was going to say, 'start fresh together,' you big perv." I punched his arm lightly, causing him to chuckle. "I thought it would take us longer to pack. We still have two days in Salem before we go."

"Yes, but I want to actually see Salem," he reminded me. "This place always held some fascination for me, even before I met you. Now that I know my favorite person in the world grew up here, I want to see everything."

"You're favorite person, huh?" I was understandably dubious—and maybe a little charmed. "That's laying it on a bit thick."

"Doesn't mean it's not true." He brushed my hair away from my face and offered a soft smile. "You are my favorite person." He hesitated only a beat before saying the next part. "I love you."

I thought my heart might somehow explode from my chest. "W-what?" I was officially bewildered.

"I love you," he repeated calmly. "I've loved you for a long time now. I just wasn't sure how to say it because I've never said it to anybody before."

I was breathless. "I love you too."

"I know." He grinned. "You've been wanting to tell me for weeks now. You've caught yourself a few times. Don't think I haven't noticed."

"Not the most observant man in the world," I drawled in amusement, giggling when he pulled me flush against his chest. "I did catch myself," I admitted, sobering. "I've wanted to say it for weeks. I've felt it even longer. It's just ... well..." I wasn't certain if I should say the rest.

"You thought you would scare me away." He tapped the tip of my nose, amusement evident in his eyes. "I get it. I would've been afraid of that if I were you too. I don't want you to hold back, though. I want it all."

"All?"

"All." He pressed a palm against my back, making sure I was plastered against his front. He was earnest as he stared into my eyes. "I've loved you for a long time too. I didn't say anything because I felt you were dealing with enough. It's a lot. You're the one completely changing your life, and I didn't want to overwhelm you. I mean, according to Toni, I can be a lot to deal with."

I grinned. "You're just enough." I gave him a soft kiss and then rested my head against his chest.

His fingers gently massaged the back of my head. "I'm looking forward to this," he said in a low voice. "All of it. I want to do everything together. I'm just afraid that if I push too hard, you're going to finally realize it's happening too fast and put on the brakes."

"That's not going to happen."

"How can you be sure?"

"Because when something feels right, you want to keep doing it. This feels right."

He pulled back far enough to study my face. "So ... you're not worried I'm going to go to jail for some unspoken crime or anything?"

"Nope. I happen to think the curse has been lifted." I grinned then pinched his flank. "Maybe I lifted my own curse, huh?"

"I think that's exactly what you did." He gave me another kiss and then huffed out a breath. "Okay, we have two days in Salem and then a road trip back home. I'm going to want a witch tour, stuffed lobster, and a walk around that bay you told me about."

I was caught off guard. "The bay? Why?"

"Because that's the moment I knew I wanted to kiss you." His smile slid from earnest to roguish in an instant. "You were telling me how you liked walking around the bay, drinking your coffee, and watching the snow. There's no snow, but I want to see the rest of it. I want to see all of it, everything that made you, you."

My heart threatened to implode, but I held it together. "I think that can be arranged."

"I figured as much." He dropped a kiss on the crown of my head. "I also want a tarot reading, those pickle martinis you told me about, to go to the world's worst wax museum so I can fix that bad kiss memory, and to stuff my face with all the fried dough you can find. I want to sample it all."

I lifted an eyebrow. "We've only got two days. That's a lot to jam in."

"Oh, baby, we've got forever. I just want to start it out with a bang."

If I were a swooner, that would've been the moment I succumbed. Instead, I squared my shoulders. "Let's start with coffee and warm donuts and go from there."

"Oh, you do know the way to my heart." He beamed. "Actually, I've come to the realization that you are my heart."

"I feel the same way."

"I know. I'm a catch."

That made me laugh, and I held out a hand. "Come on. Adventure awaits."

"Now and forever," he agreed, taking my hand in his.

"Now and forever," I echoed, and when I exhaled, I could finally breathe without the walls closing in.

This was right. It had always been right. Now it was time to enjoy it.

Made in the USA
Middletown, DE
26 November 2023